EVA IS WAITING

Romola Farr

Inniscliffe School for Girls

Copyright © 2025 Romola Farr / Wildmoor Press

All rights reserved

The moral right of the author has been asserted.

Romola Farr has asserted the right under the Copyright, Designs and Patents Act 1988 to be identified as the author of this work.

This book is a work of fiction and any resemblance to actual persons, living or dead, or to businesses, organisations or institutions, is entirely coincidental or is used purely fictitiously.

No part of this book may be reproduced, or stored in a retrieval system, or transmitted in any form or by any means, electronic, mechanical, photocopying, recording, or otherwise, without express written permission of the publisher.

WILDMOOR
PRESS

For my loved ones

CHAPTER ONE

Late Autumn, 1963

Sylvia Cooper relished the strong northeasterly as it whipped her auburn hair, styled by Leonard of Mayfair and kept in shape by Giuseppe in the village of Hawksmead, her only extravagance since inheriting Inniscliffe School for Girls from her late Godmother.

Ten months on, she still couldn't quite believe that the neo-gothic building, situated in a vast estate that encompassed woodland, playing fields, white cliffs rising above a rocky shore, and the thirty-nine steps, as they were colloquially called, was all hers. Unfortunately, so were all the problems. She had attended the school as a pupil and was dismayed to discover, nine years later, that all the good mistresses had left and the one she had loathed the most, even as Head Girl, was still firmly entrenched.

Where was her husband when she needed him? Most likely in the arms of his latest floozy. His last great marital act was to try and persuade her to go for a quick sale, no doubt to get his hands on as much of her cash as possible. She had suggested they try and make a go of running the school as a couple, but he scoffed at the idea and immediately booked a bed and breakfast in the seaside town of Brighton, hired the services of a local photographer and, with evidence in hand, initiated divorce proceedings. Thank God she had never taken his surname.

Loveless, childless, and with parents residing in Rhodesia, Sylvia felt truly alone until Bella came into her life. A farmer with sheep on the fells asked if she would be interested in a border-collie puppy. Selecting Bella was an easy choice. As soon as Sylvia lifted her up and looked into her sweet black and white face she swooned. When Bella licked Sylvia's nose, the high price was suddenly no object. Six months on, Bella had become her constant companion; boisterous, inquisitive, and utterly loyal. Sylvia had always slightly despised people who loved animals almost above humans, but she understood the feeling, now.

The grass on the sward that led to the sheer cliffs was kept reasonably short by the school's handyman who had recommended putting in a fence near the top to avoid the risk of an accident. When presented with an estimate of the cost, Sylvia decided it was cheaper to make the sward out of bounds to her pupils. There were plenty of playing fields and spaces to run around within the grounds although when Sylvia was a girl at the school, she did lie on her front and drag herself to the edge of the cliff to look down at the beach a hundred and forty feet below. When the tide was in, there was no beach, just grey waves pounding the cliffs.

The wind had picked up as she looked around for her dog. In the distance she could see the twinkling lights from the school windows before the sweeping beam of a lighthouse caught a section of the formidable building.

'Bella!'

The biting wind slapped the name back in her face. She shone her heavy torch but could see nothing in the darkness.

'Bella,' she called again. The beam from the lighthouse was too high to be any good and her torch was not powerful enough to penetrate the black that cloaked the remote coastline.

Where was her dog? Bella knew not to go near the cliff edge and as the wind was onshore, she was unlikely to have been blown over. Panic rising, Sylvia swung her torch in a circle and called in desperation. Clouds parted and the bright, full moon lit a path. Pushing against the wind she walked carefully towards the sheer drop.

'Bella!' she called again, the wind barely allowing her words to leave her lips. Soon, it would be blowing a gale. She got down on her hands and knees and crawled towards certain death. For the last few feet, she lay flat on the grass and pulled herself forward until she could see over the edge. A thick cloud momentarily hid the moon, but she could just discern a shape tossed back and forth in the white surf far below.

Tears flooded her eyes and she sobbed as shock and grief overwhelmed her. It hurt so much she wanted to drag her whole self into the enticing void.

A yellow life raft rose high on the crest of a breaking wave and was hurled onto the rocky shore, spitting out its occupant. Another wave crashed onto the jagged rocks and swept up to the base of the vertical cliff. A young man, wearing a faded yellow life vest, tried to stand but was knocked over by a huge roller. He hauled himself to his feet and in the patchy moonlight looked to his left and right, searching for escape. A mighty curler smashed into him, and he was propelled to the base of the chalk cliff. Icy tentacles hauled him back into the embrace of another mountainous wave. This time it carried him higher up the cliff and he was able to grab hold of the rockface. In the merciless grip of the rising tide he knew if he didn't find a way out, the North Sea would claim him.

Through a gap in the clouds, the moon shone almost as brightly as the lighthouse beam, rotating high above his head. A sign fixed to a rock glowed white. He chose his moment and waded as fast as the foamy water would allow. Another wave enveloped him, and he was tossed to the base of the cliff. His fingers gripped rough, conical limpet shells that tore at his sea-softened flesh. He hung on until he could take a breath, then scrambled to his feet. Through the swirling water and deep rockpools, he fought to reach the dim white glow.

A mouth opened, and he was standing by the narrow entrance to a tunnel. He looked at the rusting metal sign and was able to discern the words, *Ministry of Defence*, before a giant wave crashed over him and washed him to the far end of the brick-lined passage. His fingers gripped the rusted bars of an iron gate, and he hung on as long talons of surging water tugged at his clothes. Pale phosphorescence clung to worn steps carved in the rock and adrenaline pumped through his veins. With all his diminishing strength, he pulled and pushed the iron gate, but it was locked fast. His numb fingertips searched for a catch and found a key on the far side, but his joy was subsumed by another wave roaring into the manmade cave. He hung onto the bars as the water retreated. In the few seconds of respite, he tried to turn the key, giving it every ounce of his remaining resolve, but it was as unyielding as the gate's rust-pocked bars.

Roff! Roff

A warm tongue licked his hand.

'Get help, boy. Get help.'

The dog barked until a wave roared up the cave and immersed them both. As it pulled back, the dog vigorously shook off the water.

'Master!' the man shouted. 'Go get master.' Seawater swirled mockingly around his ankles.

The dog barked again.

'Bitte Mein Freund. Holen Sie sich Hilfe.'

Another wave came, flooded the passage, and he was completely immersed.

Was she imagining it? Could Bella have survived such a fall?

Roff! Roff!

The barking was barely discernible and not coming from the shore below. She pushed back from the edge and stood.

Roff! Roff!

It had to be Bella but where was she? Guided by her torch, Sylvia approached the cliff steps. At the top, Bella's bark was more distinct, even above the sound of pounding waves.

Roff! Roff!

She called down the steps. 'Bella! Come to mummy.' She paused a moment, then called again. 'Bella! Come here, girl.'

She waited.

'Please. Help me.' The feeble cry was consumed by the echoing roar of the incoming tide.

Not quite believing her ears, Sylvia shone the torch onto the steps. Overgrown with vegetation, the prospect of venturing down several short flights of enclosed, slippery steps required her to summon up more courage than she felt she had.

'Help!' came the plea again, followed by a mighty crash. A few seconds later, Bella came bounding up the steps, wide-eyed and soaked.

'Hello girl.' Sylvia squatted and hugged her best friend. 'You're such a clever girl. Well done.' She wished she'd brought Bella's lead but normally, at this hour, the walk was brief and to the point, although Bella quickly learned that as soon as Sylvia saw her take a pee, she called the dog to come in, so Bella often delayed the process.

'Wait here.' Sylvia gripped the old iron handrail with one hand and pointed the torch down the stone steps with the other. The cacophony bouncing off the hewn chalk scared her, but she kept on going until she reached the first dogleg turn. Now it was really dark. She pressed on, feeling slime beneath her shoes. She turned again and again, fearing what she would see. Part of her hoped that the cry for help was in her imagination and she could run up the steps, away from the grasping sea, as she had done as a child when visiting her Godmother. She came to the final turn and fingers of icy water gripped and pulled her calves. The torch beam began to fade, and she banged it against the palm of her left hand. It went out.

'Oh no...' She felt Bella press against her, then jumped when the dog barked.

'Please. Gate. Key.'

Another wave roared through the bars and swirled around her grass-stained slacks. Without any light, she felt for the oval end of the key and tried to turn it. The man's shivering hand encased hers.

The key wouldn't budge.

'Wait!' she said. 'We're turning it the wrong way.' Using both hands she used all her strength to turn the key and felt the lock mechanism give. The cave filled with rushing water and the man landed on top of her. Air was crushed from her lungs, and she thought she was going to drown. The surge receded and she coughed and spluttered as the man lifted himself off her.

'Vielen dank.' He helped Sylvia back onto her feet and, soaked and shaking, the two felt their way up the steps. They emerged above ground and the wind whipped their soaking clothes.

'Du rettest mein Leben,' he said through chattering teeth, as his arms hugged his thin frame.

Sylvia pulled away. The bright moon found another gap in the clouds and reflected in the young man's alabaster skin. 'Komm mit mir,' she said, digging deep into her schoolgirl German as the lighthouse beam circled above. Despite the growing gale, she heard the bell in the school's clocktower chime the midnight hour.

CHAPTER TWO

September 1965

It was risky. Very risky. It was risky in so many ways. She was a virgin. Pure. Untouched, apart from washing, and that didn't count. Margery had been caught with the handle of a hairbrush in her mouth and now that style of brush was banned or, at least, against the unbending rules updated regularly on the school noticeboard.

Was she ready? Was she afraid? Could she relax sufficiently for it not to hurt? She wanted to please him. Oh, how she wanted to please him even if it gave her no pleasure at all. Sometimes, she craved her mother's advice but unless she could talk from the grave, her mother's gentle voice would continue to be a fading memory.

The bell in the clocktower chimed the four quarters then clanged ten times. Lights out. No talking. No whispering. No listening to the tranny. No reading Teen Girl and drooling over Brian Jones and John Lennon. No bed hopping for a cuddle, even when the air was freezing.

Lily Turnbull was in her last year at Inniscliffe School for Girls and, as a senior, she had her own room. Unfortunately, she couldn't lock or bolt the door, and the back of her desk chair jammed under the knob could result in certain privileges being removed such as her Roberts transistor radio, her considerable collection of teen magazines, and her own underwear, to be replaced with regulation school issue. *Not a comfortable thought.*

At this time of year, most girls wore flannelette pyjamas to keep warm, but she had chosen a nightdress. It wasn't particularly sexy but at least it provided easy access. Time was short and she didn't want to waste it peeling off pyjama bottoms.

Where was he? Where was the man she loved more than Cliff Richard and Elvis Presley combined?

'Lily.'

His voice reminded her of the handsome hunk she'd seen in Hatari, one of the last films her mother had taken her to before the hideous disease, which nobody spoke of aloud, took her mother's life at only forty-four. Her father's reaction was to accept a job at the British Embassy in Moscow, but not before packing his twin son and daughter off to single-sex boarding schools, separated by a vast moor in the heart of *England's green and pleasant land.*

'Sorry I'm late. I couldn't get away.' He closed the door with great care.

'You mean she's here?'

'No. Thank God, no. She and Gretchen will gas on into the small hours, knowing them.'

'What held you up?'

'I was busy. Where's the light switch?'

'Leave it.'

She heard him unbuttoning his clothes and kicking off his shoes as he approached her narrow, iron bed.

'You're sure about this?' he asked, his deep

mellifluous tone almost catching in his throat.

In response, she threw back the covers.

Sylvia Cooper took a few deep breaths. Why had she allowed Gretchen to open another bottle of Burgundy? She looked up and saw the vague outline of bulbous clouds hiding the new moon ...and staggered. Her head spun so much she had to lean on the bonnet of her Sunbeam Alpine sportscar. *Damn*. She would have to ask Gretchen if she could sleep over. *No*. It was late. There'd be little traffic, especially out on the moor. Her Alpine had a soft top. She'd drive with the roof down, despite the early autumn chill. That would sober her up.

Her Twiggy-styled bob slapped her cheeks as she accelerated along the Old Military Road. She hated driving across the moor at night. It was years since the road was properly tarmacked; there were no streetlights, no cat's eyes, no white lines, just the terror of missing a bend and ending up sinking into a black bog.

She wished she hadn't bothered to visit Gretchen, a General Practitioner in the small market town of Undermere. Doubtless, one of many GPs who declined to join the National Health Service when it was first established after World War II and then piggybacked lucrative private patients on their NHS work. Sylvia had hoped Gretchen would want to give up her duties at Inniscliffe when Sylvia inherited the crumbling girls' school from her Godmother. Instead, Gretchen continually undermined her whilst never hesitating to bill for every visit, whether requested or not. At times, Sylvia wondered what had attracted the older woman to the medical profession as she seemed to have little empathy for sick children, or for people in general. Perhaps it was the Swiss-German in her. But at least she was a female doctor, which was as rare as a win on the football pools.

The blast of air as Sylvia sped through the night was decidedly chilly, and she debated whether to pull over and put the soft top back up, but she had entered the *dancing dell* and was too scared to stop. Trees in a macabre discothèque formed unnerving shapes as the wind gathered.

She needed to focus. The Eyas, one of many streams that fed the River Hawk on its way to the North Sea, was deep enough to swamp her car should she fail to take the sharp turn before rising onto its narrow stone bridge. A minute later, the dim light in a public telephone box told her she was nearly home and within another minute she swerved around the turning circle at the front of her inheritance, a poisoned chalice if ever there was one. Only a few lights were on in the neo-gothic building as she drove to the staff car park.

This was it. This was the moment Lily had dreamed about since arriving at Inniscliffe aged seventeen following her father's posting abroad. The smell of cigarettes combined with his manly odour was intoxicating.

'Are you sure?' he asked.

'Yes. Please.' She had no idea how it would feel. She'd heard from Annabelle, an older girl, who'd been expelled for keeping a stash of Parade magazines featuring young women in various stages of undress, that it was awful, like being stabbed with a stick. She'd been told stories about the hymen ripping, terrible pain, blood; but she'd not heard a word about the exquisite sensations that were taking her to a place she'd never been. The tingling began in her toes and rippled up her thighs until she gasped, enveloped by an overwhelming pulsation that went on and on.

'Are you okay?' His voice was husky, almost breathless.

'Have you?' she asked, not quite knowing how it worked.

'Not yet, but I'm fine.'

She gripped his muscled arms and searched for his eyes in the darkness. 'Take me there again. Please. Don't stop. Please.'

Sylvia flicked a switch and entered her study. She crossed to her Godmother's imposing desk, pulled open a drawer and deposited her car keys. She checked the time on her watch despite the clock in the tower striking the midnight hour. Exhaustion swept over her, and she was tempted to collapse on the worn Chesterfield sofa that was there when she was a pupil. A voice spoke in her head, and she looked up at her Godmother's portrait, painted by a local artist shortly before she died.

'You're right. Duty calls.'

Sylvia stepped out of the study into the school's cavernous entrance hall. The floor was paved with stone, worn and uneven after many years of service. To her left was a wide stone staircase carpeted in blue in an attempt to reduce the clatter of numerous pounding young feet. Now threadbare, it was one of many maintenance issues assaulting the school's beleaguered bank account. Plastered walls bounced back the clip-clop of her leather soles as she crossed the hall. She pulled open a stained-glass-panelled door, scarred from decades of children coming and going, and stepped across the lobby to a pair of heavy oak doors with bolts, top and bottom.

'Annabelle.' She spoke the name of the girl responsible for bolting and locking the front doors. Then it dawned on her that Annabelle had been expelled. She had begged Sylvia to beat her as she had been by the previous headmistress; but Sylvia had made it clear in the school prospectus that all forms of corporal punishment were forbidden. Teachers, much to their chagrin, could no longer strike knuckles with the edge of a ruler, thwack school-issue knickers with a leather slipper, smack the back of girls' heads with calloused palms or a heavy book, grab fistfuls of hair and shake vigorously; or, in a burning rage, usually after all the aforementioned punishments had been dished out, send the wretched child to the headmistress. Perhaps she should've let Old Ma Barry use her belt on Annabelle, after all. It would've saved Sylvia having to hand back next term's fees to the girl's father.

Annoyed, she slammed home the bolts then reached for an old iron key hanging on a hook screwed into the stone wall. Whoever she assigned to secure the front door needed to be tall enough to reach the top bolt. Who could she entrust? Lily in Upper Sixth? She'd only been at the school a little over a year but had shown great initiative and intelligence. Perhaps the responsibility for locking the school at night would help lift the ever-present cloud of her mother's recent passing.

Lily had heard many horror stories about sex, the worst was that a man's thing can grow to an enormous size and rip a woman apart. The only penis she had seen in the flesh was her twin brother's, and that was only from the time when they used to share a bath.

To be frank, she had yet to see her lover's, but she had most certainly enjoyed the feeling it conveyed throughout her entire body. Perhaps it was because they were in love that it felt so good. She didn't care. Tonight, may be the last time she would ever get the chance to sleep with a man and she was determined to enjoy every single moment.

Sylvia reached the half-landing and caught the toe of her shoe on the threadbare carpet. She would have to talk to the manager at the Midland Bank. He liked her. Aged twenty-nine, she still looked pretty good. People said she reminded them of the famous actress, Honor Blackman, although Sylvia didn't have quite the same husky voice. More the smooth tone of Emma Peel, played by Diana Rigg in the TV series The Avengers. For some reason, senior girls, who were allowed to watch television at the weekend, enjoyed The Avengers, most notably Annabelle. Was it the catsuit Emma Peel wore that attracted her? She hoped Annabelle's interest in the fairer sex was just a teenage thing, for her sake, but she feared it may be more deep-seated. Sylvia's late Godmother had never married, always wore brogue shoes and tweed suits, occasionally complemented with a necktie. Her hair, iron grey, never permed, was cut short for practical reasons she always said. Could she have been a lesbian? Sylvia paused. Was it such a crime that Annabelle liked looking at pictures of women? After all, what harm could one woman do to another? It wasn't like homosexuality. Unfortunately for Annabelle and the school's finances, her sin against God and woman had been exposed publicly.

This time it was taking Lily longer to reach the

magical heights. One girl told her that when a man wears Durex it's like picking one's nose with a glove on. Lily had no idea. A: she tried not to pick her nose and B: she had no other experience.

'I can't come,' the young man gasped. 'It's the rubber. I can't feel you.'

Lily hugged him harder and panted in his ear. 'Take it off.'

'I dare not,' he said.

'Take it off. It's almost impossible for a virgin to get pregnant the first time.'

He stopped. 'Are you sure?'

'I heard it somewhere. Something to do with the insides not being ready.' She felt him ease his way out of her and was sorry. Even with a prophylactic, as it was described by Miss Rooney in her previous school during an excruciating lesson in marriage and reproduction, it felt wonderful. She sensed him fiddling around and then he re-entered her. The ripple up her thighs took her by surprise and she peaked before he had barely started.

'Are you okay?' he croaked.

'God yes. *Yes. Yes! YES!!*'

Sylvia stood at the end of a dimly lit corridor and listened. She had been Head Girl when her Godmother ruled the roost and had developed an instinct for when something was not right. She held her breath.

A giggle.

She stood stock still.

A muted cry. Possibly a moan.

She looked down the long corridor. Exterior lights created strange shapes on the brown and beige battered wall. Each door opened into a dormitory containing six beds, or an individual prefect's room.

Another suppressed giggle. At this time of night there should be absolute silence. Taking care not to tread on a squeaky floorboard she tiptoed to the first door and put her ear to the jamb.

Nothing.

The noises came again but not from the first room. Maybe the second. The third door down she knew was a prefect's room, possibly Lily Turnbull's. She wasn't sure.

A gasp. Now there was absolutely no doubt. Catherine, her late Godmother, would have made no attempt to be quiet. She would have marched down the corridor throwing open every door until she located the offending girls. Each guilty child would have felt the stout woman's leathery palm on her bare buttocks. Sylvia shivered again as a horrible memory of one night flooded her mind. Her Godmother had caught her reading a copy of Lord Byron's epic poem, *Don Juan*, and regarded the poet as so salacious there was no choice but to confiscate the book and for Sylvia to be sent forthwith to Miss Barry.

'Have you read the inscription?' Sylvia asked her Godmother and was relieved to see doubt flicker across her face. 'It says, *To our darling daughter, a fellow lover of great poetry. Keep this with you at all times, and we shall never be apart. Love Mummy and Daddy.*' Her mother's best friend from when they both attended Inniscliffe as pupils, swallowed hard. She handed back the book without a word, and Sylvia saw her swipe an offending tear.

Lily could contain herself no more and screamed in delicious ecstasy until a large hand clamped across her mouth. She bit into his fleshy palm, and he yelped.

Sylvia had heard enough. A swift turn of the knob

and she flung the door open.

Silence.

She felt for the light switch and snapped it on. The view that presented was of young girls with torches hiding under bedsheets tied to bedsteads to create a canopy, a tent, a den.

'Come out,' she demanded.

No movement.

'Come out this instant.' She saw torches being switched off and the emergence of a pretty young girl called Jane, wearing pyjamas. The poor thing was shaking. Others crawled out from under the makeshift tent and looked equally scared until six girls stood in line in front of her. 'What were you doing? The truth, now.'

The girls shuffled their bare feet then Jane spoke. 'Charlotte received a mini hamper from her parents, and she was sharing it with us.'

'So, you were having a midnight feast?'

All the girls nodded.

'What are the sweets?'

Charlotte looked up. Through trembling lips, she said, 'Love Hearts, Fruit Gums, Sherbet Flying Saucers, Black Jacks, Smarties, Jelly Beans, Pink Shrimps, Aniseed Balls, Catherine Wheels, Milky Bars… um.'

'Quite a selection. Have you eaten them all?'

'We were allowed to choose one of each,' Jane said.

Sylvia turned back to Charlotte. 'Are there any flying saucers left?'

The scared little girl nodded.

'I'll have one Flying Saucer and a Love Heart.'

Charlotte's mouth dropped open.

'I'm waiting,' Sylvia said.

Charlotte pulled off a covering sheet to reveal a

perfect picnic spread of sweets, and a large metal tin in the shape of a picnic hamper. From one section she retrieved a Flying Saucer, and a Love Heart from another. She presented them to Sylvia.

'Thank you.'

The girl stood back in line and Sylvia addressed them all. 'You're fortunate it's me that has discovered you and not Old Ma Barry, I mean Miss Barry. Charlotte, it's kind of you to share your sweets but I want you all to promise me you'll have no more midnight feasts.'

The girls looked stunned.

'Do you promise?'

They all nodded vigorously.

Sylvia popped the rice paper and sherbet Flying Saucer into her mouth. 'Mmm, it's years since I had one of these. Thank you, Charlotte. Now, quickly tidy up, get to sleep, and make sure you are not late for breakfast. Miss Barry is on refectory duty.'

Rainer Herrnstadt hoped his wife wouldn't still be awake. He checked the time on his wristwatch, a Seiko Presage Automatic, given to him by Sylvia on his birthday in April. Taking great care, he eased his semi-naked body under the sheet and blankets.

'You worked late,' she mumbled.

'Go back to sleep.' His lips found her head and he kissed her hair. She moved closer to him, and he felt her hand on his chest. A gentle circling motion was the signal he'd grown to recognise after that night, nearly two years ago, when she saved his life.

In the beginning, he was so grateful to be alive that he was happy to do anything and everything she wanted until he realised that all the lovemaking was in fact baby making, and he didn't want to be a part of that. *Ja* they were married, but it was a marriage of convenience, on his part, for sure. She had insisted on doing everything right by way of alerting the authorities. Marriage was a simple solution to ensure he was given leave to stay in England. He spoke vows in the school chapel, but he wasn't in love. She was older than him for a start. Of course, not as many years as the gap between him and the schoolgirl, but that was different. He really liked her. Although, truth be told, he liked quite a few of the girls in the school.

Jumping from the fishing vessel to escape the strangulating hands of the Soviet Union was little better than suicide, and without Sylvia it would have been. He accepted that. They would stay married. If they divorced, he risked being returned to Germany, albeit the Federal German Republic not the Democratic German Republic where every move was chronicled by an over-enthusiastic secret police known as the Stasi. An organisation to which he had belonged, albeit reluctantly.

'I love you, Rainer.'

'And I love Bella.' It was a little game they played before lovemaking.

'She is very beautiful,' Sylvia whispered.

'But not as beautiful as you.' He summoned his reserves and made sure she fell asleep with a smile.

CHAPTER THREE

Miss Geraldine Tozer believed in rigorous exercise. It was late September, and the North Sea was bracing but still retained a little summer's warmth and, to top it all, the morning sun was shining. Junior girls did as they were told and were happy to play games on the sand when the tide was out, and end with a bracing dip, but senior girls were more interested in gossiping than hunting for seashells. She blew two sharp blasts on her whistle. If the older girls were not prepared to utilise the time to run around, play games, stretch their young limbs, she would take them back to the quad, where exercise would be rigorous and compulsory, with punishment for those who did not comply. She blew a long blast on her whistle and indicated that they should go back to the brick-lined passage and make their way up the steps.

'Miss Tozer,' Lily said, panting for breath. 'I cannot find Bella. I think she may have followed a scent into one of the caves.'

'Go look for her. The tide is coming in, so don't get caught.'

Lily ran off, her bare feet sinking into the soft sand

with each long stride.

'Bella,' she called.

Up ahead she could see the mouth to the largest cave along the stretch of diminishing beach, scooped out by eons of waves, probing the sheer cliff for weaknesses in the strata.

Lily stood in the gaping mouth and shivered as the first tongues of the chilly North Sea lapped around her ankles.

'Bella,' she called.

Bright sunlight made it impossible for her eyes to adjust to the dense gloom of the cave. Rivulets of water formed a stream in the soft sand which she decided to follow.

'Bella,' she called again as she stepped deeper into the vast cavern. Within seconds she was enveloped by the gloom and wished she had a torch.

'Bella,' she called again, and was relieved to hear a little yelp. 'Bella, come here, girl.' She hoped to see the happy collie bounding towards her but all she heard above the sound of breaking waves was the dog's pitiful yelp. She hurried deeper into the depths of the cave and scraped the toes of her right foot on some rocks. The pain was intense, slightly abated by the cold water that seemed to be deepening with every passing second. Her young eyes adjusted to the gloom, and she was relieved to see a glint of white teeth.

'Bella! What are you doing?' She stroked the beautiful dog's black and white fur and felt for a collar. 'Come on girl. Before we both drown.' She gently pulled the dog, then realised Bella was stuck fast, her body trapped between two rocks. She couldn't go forward or back. *How did this happen?* Lily looked around and saw the cave went up into a form of an artistic-looking spiral, creating a path to nowhere, carved by the North Sea over the centuries.

A wave broke at the mouth of the cave and swept up to the rear, almost engulfing Bella, whose bark was laced with fear. Lily slid her arms under the dog's body, digging her hands into the sand. The tips of her fingers felt a smooth dome. What was it? On one side was a round hole and another, more triangular. A jolt shot up her arm as she realised her fingers were probing a skull. She shivered but did not recoil. Instead, she lifted the collie out from between the vice of the two rocks. Another wave almost knocked her off her feet and she sank to her knees, still keeping a firm grip on Bella.

Once clear of the rocks, but with her fingers tightly gripping the dog's collar, she and Bella splashed through the deepening sea towards the bright opening.

Foamy water sucked around their legs as they picked their way towards the brick passage and steps to safety, feeling dwarfed by the cliff face rising so high above.

Her gym slip soaked, and feeling exhausted and alone, Lily and Bella emerged from the steps at the top. 'Thank you, Miss Tozer, for not waiting,' Lily said, in no rush to get back to school. Instead, she lay on the grass and enjoyed the warmth of the September sun. Bella lay beside her and licked her cheek. Any other time Lily would have recoiled and rushed to wash her face, but she was happy they both had escaped, unscathed, save for her scraped toes. At that precise moment, whilst basking in the sun and relishing her young life, she realised her plimsolls were still on the beach. Too bad. She laughed. Poor daddy. It would be another addition to her school fees. Then she felt sad. Deeply sad. She missed her twin brother who was ensconced in a boarding school on the far side of the vast moor. Too far to walk or even cycle. Not that she had a bike. *It is forbidden for girls to own or ride a bicycle for reasons of safety and decorum.* Only staff were allowed the indignity of riding to and from school, although those not residing on site usually shared cars as the twisting lanes were considered lethal for cyclists. There was an infrequent bus that stopped about a mile away from the end of her school's long drive, so she hoped she and her brother would be able to meet up soon.

'What happened?'

Lily was standing in her damp gym slip in front of her headmistress. She looked at Bella snoozing in her basket and decided to tell a white lie. 'We were playing games on the beach but when it was time to return to school, Miss Tozer noticed that Bella was missing. I volunteered to look for her. She must've followed a scent into the large cave and we both got a bit wet making our way back to the cliff steps.'

'I see.' There was an uncomfortable pause while Miss Cooper digested Lily's explanation. She looked at her watch. 'You'd better hurry and change, or you'll miss lunch.'

Lily could smell the sea on her skin as she queued with the other girls outside the refectory. She had contemplated taking a shower before changing back into her school uniform but there hadn't been enough time. The doors were opened by Miss Barry and, in silence, they all trooped into the grand hall with its vaulted ceiling, furnished with long oak tables and benches, each with a single wooden chair at one end. The girls knew exactly where to go and stood by their allotted places. Lily, as a prefect, stood by a chair.

Already seated at a long table raised on a dais, were the school's mistresses, looking similar to Leonardo da Vinci's *The Last Supper*. Their raised position afforded a good view of their pupils, ensuring the girls sat up straight and adhered to good table manners.

Miss Barry strode to the centre of the room and even the staff fell silent. She spoke in a voice that would carry to the rear stalls of a large theatre. 'Today, we shall thank the Lord with a new grace, which I will ask one of the senior girls to translate into English, so pay attention. Benedic, Domine, nos et dona tua, quae de largitate tua sumus sumpturi. Lily Turnbull.'

Lily had a feeling her Latin would be tested by the ogre and had made a point of focusing on the words. 'Bless us, Lord, and your gifts, which we are about to receive from your generosity.' It was the grace from her previous school. She decided to show-off. 'Et concede, ut illis salubriter nutriti,' she continued in Latin, 'et tibi debitum obsequium praestare valeamus, per Christum Dominum nostrum. And grant that we may be healthily nourished and able to render due obedience through Christ our Lord.' A pause. 'Or words to that effect,' she concluded.

There was an ominous silence. Everyone waited to see Miss Barry's reaction. Unsmiling, she clapped her hands, once; the shutters to the kitchen shot up, and she strode to the table at the head of the room.

The girls, slightly awkwardly, lifted their legs over the benches, smoothed their skirts, and sat down. Lily pulled out her chair and once seated, surveyed her girls who looked eager to eat. 'You may talk,' she said, and immediately the table filled with semi-whispered, excited babble.

Two girls at the end of Lily's table slid out from their benches and joined the queue at the long serving hatch. From the smell that wafted as soon as the shutters were opened, lunch was definitely fish.

'Would you like bread, Lily?' The girl next to her proffered a plate of white bread cut into quarters.

'Thank you.' Lily took two pieces and placed them on the table to the left of her fork. There were no napkins. Each table was served by two girls who rotated at each meal, so that the onerous job of collecting plates of food from the serving hatch, and gathering them up at the end, was fairly shared throughout the school term, although some girls, through manipulation and bullying, managed to avoid being seated at the serving end of the bench. Not on Lily's table, she made sure that everyone took their fair turn.

Lily was the first to be served. It was fish in a watery white parsley sauce, mashed potato, peas and carrots. She was hungry but waited until everyone had their food before giving permission for the girls to eat. Within a few minutes all bar one of the plates was empty. Lily knew Brianna Dandridge hated fish. She was about to swap her empty plate for the young girl's when Miss Barry spotted the uneaten meal. She stood behind Brianna and spoke loud enough for neighbouring tables to hear. 'I will not move until you have eaten every morsel.'

Lily watched tears roll down the young girl's cheeks. Shaking, she picked up her knife and fork and started with the potato. She had already eaten what was untouched by the white sauce, but clearly couldn't face any of the food in the fishy liquid.

Miss Barry placed her heavy hands on the terrified girl's shoulders. 'Nobody at this table can have pudding until you have finished. If you fail to finish, I will have the plate placed in the refrigerator and it will be presented to you at the next meal, and the next until every scrap is eaten. Understood?' By now, most of the room had stopped talking, aware that a drama was unfolding.

Lily recognised a bully when she saw one and Old Ma Barry was the epitome of someone who should never have been given power over young girls. Lily was tall and quite strong, but Miss Barry was powerfully built. She had the stature and physical strength that could defeat any challenger amongst the girls and the faculty.

Lily felt she had to do something. Brianna was sobbing and pudding was already being served at the other tables. The young girl would not readily be forgiven by her fellow pupils if they missed out on jam roly-poly and custard.

Determined to convey a confidence she didn't feel, Lily stood and walked up to Miss Barry. She reached over Brianna and picked up the plate, leaving the knife and fork in the young girl's hands. 'Thank goodness there's some fish left,' she said to a glowering Miss Barry. 'I nearly forgot. Miss Cooper asked me to collect any unwanted fish as it's Bella's favourite. She'll absolutely love this.' The girls at her table looked up at her with a mixture of trepidation and amazement. 'I'll pop this into the kitchen,' Lily continued in a jolly voice, 'and make sure that Bella gets it.' She looked across at the two junior girls sitting at the end of the benches. 'Rosie, Emily, hurry and get pudding before the kitchen runs out.'

'Sssssittttt down.' The two words hissed from Miss Barry's thin lips. She turned to Lily. 'Put that plate back on the table.'

Lily stared into the woman's hard-bitten face and felt sick. In the past, Miss Barry could back up her absolute authority with extreme pain. Even now she could make a young girl's life not worth living. On the back of her legs, Lily felt a momentary draught as a door opened behind her.

Miss Barry smiled, victory spreading to her pokey eyes. 'Miss Cooper is here.'

Lily's heart sank until fur rubbed against her. 'Miss Cooper, there's only a little fish left for Bella.' She didn't wait for a reply but squatted down and watched Bella consume all the fish and potato, flicking peas and carrot with her tongue until the plate was licked clean.

Lily smiled at Miss Cooper. 'She was hungry.'

Miss Cooper looked from Lily to Miss Barry and down to her happy dog. 'If anyone doesn't want their roly-poly, please keep it aside for Bella.'

Without comment, Miss Barry strode away, back to the staff table. Lily knew she had made a formidable enemy.

CHAPTER FOUR

Malcolm Cadwallader accelerated his two-tone, green and cream MG 1100 down the long drive from Hawksmead College. He was on a mission and despite the pelting rain was determined to use his free afternoon effectively. He passed two miserable-looking pupils as they pedalled up the incline in the opposite direction. Both new boys, he felt especially sorry for one who was good at English, the subject Malcolm taught, but was cursed with a terrible stutter.

At the bottom of the drive he came to a T-junction and turned right onto the Old Military Road. The car, beautifully nippy, accelerated with gusto up the hill until Malcolm had a perfect view of Hawksmoor; a vast expanse of green and purple hues, severed with jagged ridges, crisscrossed with drystone walls, spotted with clumps of trees providing windbreaks, and pocked with treacherous, stinking bogs. Hidden gullies with gushing waterfalls engorged rapidly-flowing rivulets that fed the River Hawk's serpentine course. Circling above, he spotted the rust-coloured plumage of a red kite, its long wings carrying it effortlessly as its sharp eyes sought movement from an unwary water vole or rat.

The journey to Inniscliffe School for Girls took longer than expected and it was with some relief when he turned into the school drive and roared through a forest of deciduous trees, still partly in leaf and in various shades of gold, enhanced by the late arrival of the afternoon sun.

The toot of a horn behind him from a Vauxhall Victor Estate shook him out of his reverie and he pressed the accelerator. He had reached fourth gear and quite a speed by the time he approached the turning circle in front of the imposing school. The austere façade was topped by a clock tower rising high above the impressive entrance. Another toot from behind, forced Malcolm to turn left and follow weathered wooden signs. He arrived at a large courtyard where a section was marked Staff Parking and another section, Visitor Parking. He chose a space far away from other cars and was surprised when the Vauxhall parked next to him.

Malcolm opened his door and happily stretched his long, lean frame. The driver of the Vauxhall climbed out and looked across the roof of his car. 'I presume you have an appointment?' the man asked, his voice clipped, military-precise, authoritative, below a neatly trimmed moustache.

'I rang this morning, several times, but nobody answered.'

'At the end of the drive is a phone box. Try again.'

Malcolm stood his ground despite the charmless aggression of someone who probably could have defeated Hitler single-handedly. 'Thank you, Mr...?'

'Craig. Colonel Craig. And it's *Sir* to you, sonny.'

'Good to meet you, Colonel.' Malcolm closed his door and used a key to lock it. 'I think I'll take my chances. Perhaps you would direct me to the school office?'

Colonel Craig strode around the rear of his car. 'Make the phone call.'

'Thank you for your advice.' Malcolm approached the colonel who blocked his way. Both were about the same height. The former soldier had no doubt experienced the heat of war, but Malcolm had youth. 'Colonel Craig, I understand that Sylvia Cooper is the owner and Headmistress. It is she with whom I would like to speak. I am a master at Hawksmead College. And you? What is your role here?'

Colonel Craig drew in a deep breath through his heavily forested nostrils. 'Follow me.' He turned on his heel and marched off. Malcolm almost broke into a run trying to keep up.

Sylvia was in her study looking at a bank statement that had arrived with the second delivery of mail. As soon as she saw the Midland Bank envelope her heart sank. She had been in charge of the school for almost three years and the responsibility was really weighing on her. The respectful knock was a welcome distraction and she looked up as Maureen, the school's secretary and bursar, popped her head around the open door.

'Sorry to bother you, Miss Cooper, but there's a gentleman here to see you. He says he's from Hawksmead College.'

'Thank you, Maureen. Please show him in.' A second later, Sylvia was surprised to see the smiling face of a young man, looking not much older than a sixth-former.

'Malcolm Cadwallader.' He held out his hand. 'How do you do, Miss Cooper.'

Sylvia stood and shook his hand across her expansive desk. 'How do you do Mr Cadwallader.' She gestured to an upright chair in front of her desk with a worn leather seat, then smoothed the back of her skirt as she sat back down. 'Hawksmead College?'

'Yes. I teach English.'

'And how may I help you?'

'I need a Roxane.'

'You're producing Cyrano de Bergerac?'

'Yes. We're entering the play in the interschools' competition.'

'Really?'

'A bold decision, I grant you. I thought it would add a little impetus to the cast if a girl played Roxane.'

'Mmm. Interesting.'

'Lily Turnbull's twin brother, David, told me that his sister is a wonderful actress and, according to him, perfect for the role.'

'What about her A-level exams? She's taking them next summer.'

'Valid concern. I understand from Turnbull, David, that they visit an aunt over half term. Perhaps Lily could stay here during the holiday and catch up? David tells me she's the smart twin.'

'What does that make David?'

'Keen on sports.'

Sylvia leaned back in her chair and examined the young man. 'Mr Cadwallader, I wish you had picked up the telephone as it would have saved you a wasted journey. Lily could probably do both your play and keep up with her studies, but I am not going to allow her to be placed under such pressure. You will have to find another girl to play Roxane or, may I suggest, you cast a prepubescent pupil amongst your own ranks, as

Shakespeare would have done.' She watched Malcolm deflate. 'I am sorry.' She stood and he followed suit. 'I wish you luck with the play, and the competition.'

'Thank you.' He shook her hand then reached into his inside jacket pocket. 'Here is a letter from David Turnbull for his sister. Perhaps you would kindly make sure she receives it?'

Sylvia took the handwritten envelope and placed it in her desk drawer. 'I'll see she gets it.' She smiled. 'It's been a pleasure to meet you, Mr Cadwallader. Maureen will walk you back to your car.'

He chuckled. 'I think I can find my way.'

'No doubt, but this is a girls' school. I'm sure you understand.'

'Of course.'

Malcolm drove slowly and thoughtfully across Hawksmoor. Cyrano de Bergerac by Edmond Rostand was a five-act play originally written in French and a big challenge for any school. Malcolm had his Cyrano and his Christian. What he didn't have was the third point of the triangle… Roxane. As soon as he got back to school, he would set up auditions to cast a suitable boy. Chances of finding one who could be a convincing girl *and* was able to act were remote. There was the boy in his English class who could look the part but his stutter was a definite impediment. Frustrated, he sighed and pressed the MG's accelerator.

This is the secret diary of Robert Oakes
DO NOT READ UNTIL 2065

I didn't cry today. That's progress. Or maybe it's because of my friend, Mini. We go everywhere we can together. I don't stutter when I'm with Mini. He's taught me that in the right circumstances, I can be normal. I'm not different. He's given me confidence and although I can still feel a juddering in my brain, and I still fear the letter 'W', I am more confident, but still not confident enough to raise my hand in class.

Mini has told me that the school play is *Cyrano de Bergerac*. Mr C, my English master, is producing the play. I like him, and I know he likes me because I'm good at English. But he also knows I stutter when I'm nervous. I managed to get hold of a copy of the play and read about Roxane who charms handsome Christian and his sword-fighting friend, Cyrano. The only role I have a hope of getting is Roxane. At my prep school, I was always cast as the girl. I have found a speech that I think will help get me the role. I know I can act if I can just not stutter.

I've auditioned! I stood in line and was surprised that nobody made fun of me. Perhaps they were all too nervous. Eventually, it was my turn to walk on stage. I have read the whole play several times and rehearsed my lines with Mini so there was no risk that my mind would go blank. As I stood on the stage in the grand hall, I knew that this was my one opportunity to do something special, be someone special. When I looked out into the hall, I felt Roxane imbue my body, and I became her – and she was perfect. I spoke her words, flawlessly, without a hint of a stutter, and it was the greatest feeling I have ever enjoyed in my life. When I finished, Mr C stood and clapped.

"Well done, Oakes. The best audition of the day."

I felt so good when I heard those words.

"But, I can't give you the role because I cannot take the chance on you not stuttering."

When I heard those words, I felt Roxane leave me.

"I won't stutter, sir. All the while I am Roxane I won't stutter. Please trust me, sir. I won't let you down."

Mr C asked me to read another speech which I hadn't learned. My whole body almost shook with fear as I looked at the lines. But then I felt Roxane's confidence flooding through my veins, and when I turned to speak, I knew that she was within every corner of my mind. And I got the role! I am so excited. Roxane fills me with happiness, with a joy I've not felt before.

CHAPTER FIVE

Sylvia looked at the exceptional young woman seated opposite her. In most cases, she would make a pupil stand when visiting her study. Lily Turnbull was different. She had lost her mother who, according to Lily's father, had suffered greatly right to the end. She had also, in effect, lost her father who had taken a posting at the British Embassy in Moscow. Lily had one more year of school and Sylvia was determined that she would leave with happy memories. She picked up a brown window envelope and a brass letter opener to convey a level of disinterest in what Lily was about to say.

'My father has arranged for my brother and me to stay with our Aunt Jessica during the half-term break, but I would much rather stay here and catch up on work.'

Sylvia put down the envelope and opener. 'I see.'

'Without the other girls around, I think I will be more productive.'

'The problem is, you'll be on your own. It's a golden rule that every member of staff takes a break away from here, apart from Colonel Craig, Mr Herrnstadt and me.'

'What about the cleaners?'

'They don't live within the school estate.' She reached for the letter opener. 'I'm afraid it's not on, Lily.' She picked up the half-opened envelope. 'And what about your brother? I'm sure he's very much looking forward to seeing you.'

'I want to see him, too, but I know he will understand. We're quite competitive. He always thrashes me in sport, and I'm meant to be the brainy one. Truth be told, he's every bit as smart as me, but I will never ever beat him at tennis again. He may struggle with Lacrosse, but you can bet your bottom dollar that as soon as he got the knack, he'd be scoring all the time.'

'Spend half-term with your brother, Lily. Family is important.' She observed the beautiful girl looking down at her hands. 'If there's anything else worrying you, don't hesitate to come and see me.'

Lily looked up at Sylvia, her eyes awash with tears. 'I can't fail my father. He suffered so much during mummy's illness. If I get really good results next summer, I know it will please him.'

They both heard the bell for the start of class. Lily got up from her chair.

'We haven't finished,' Sylvia said. 'Sit down.'

'It's Latin with Miss Barry. I… I can't be late.'

'I'll write a note. Better still, I'll walk with you to her class.'

'She can get very cross.'

'Don't I know it.' Sylvia pulled open a drawer and removed the handwritten envelope delivered yesterday by the English master. 'This is from your brother.' She slid it across the desk.

Lily looked a little confused. 'It's been opened.'

'Letters from home are randomly checked by staff.'

'You had no right to read a personal letter.' Lily's eyes sparkled with defiance.

Sylvia clenched her teeth and drew in a deep breath through flared nostrils. 'This is my school, and everything is my business.' She stared at the young girl. 'Do I make myself clear?'

'Yes.' Lily dropped her head and touched the rough edges of the opened envelope.

'You may read it.'

'I spoke to my brother from the phone box at the end of the drive,' Lily said, as she rotated the envelope. 'He told me that his school wants me to be in their play.'

'I refused the request.'

'Why?'

Sylvia pushed her chair back and stood. Lily also got to her feet. Both women were slender, tall, a little over a decade apart in age, and saw some of self in the other.

'Travelling for rehearsals would be a problem,' Sylvia said. 'Also, you have enough quotes to learn for your literature A-level. The Persian Princess isn't easy. I know, I played the queen when I was a pupil here.'

'You acted in a play, but won't allow me to?'

'I've given my reasons. You may go.'

'What about Old Ma Barry? I'm late for class.'

Sylvia studied the beautiful teenager. 'I'll go with you.' She opened the door. 'I'm sorry about your brother's letter. I think it must've been a nosy cleaner.'

'A cleaner?'

'Probably hoping to find a crisp, ten-bob note.'

'Hardly. My brother's not that generous.'

Sylvia rested her hand on the young woman's

shoulder. 'You may stay here during half-term on one condition.' She saw Lily's eyes open wide. 'You tell no one, apart from your family, of course.'

CHAPTER SIX

Lily was furious. She was also in pain. Her menstrual cycle was haphazard at the best of times but usually when the honour of the school was at stake, her body responded accordingly. Not this time. She had gone to her room to collect her mother's leather-bound Holy Bible and was on her way to meet the divinity master when Miss Tozer saw her wince and she was immediately dropped from the lacrosse team.

'But it's Oakwood. I have to play.'

'You know the rules, Lily. Playing an interschools match wearing a sanitary pad is not permitted. The risk of it falling out is too great.'

'Why can't I play with Tampax? You could lend me one.'

'Out of the question.'

'Don't you use tampons?'

'What I use or do not use is none of your business.'

'Miss Tozer. I have scored more goals than any other player. It's madness to exclude me for a few drops of blood.'

A group of young pupils giggled as they passed in the corridor.

'Please, Lily, don't be vulgar.'

'Why aren't we allowed tampons, anyway? It's ridiculous. I use them at home.'

Miss Tozer took a moment before replying in a loud whisper. 'Menstruation is embarrassing enough for the younger girls. The pad is a simple solution. Using a tampon requires a certain level of skill. It is also contrary to God's law.'

'God's law?'

'There is a risk that a tampon can rupture the hymen, destroying a girl's virginity.'

'But Miss Tozer, many activities can tear the hymen. Riding bikes and horses, for a start. Ballet lessons, gymnastics.'

'Nevertheless, inserting a tubular object into such a private place, however well-intentioned, is against school rules.'

'The sanitary pad won't slip, Miss Tozer. I promise.'

'Villagers from Crowford will be arriving soon to support the school. I cannot risk an embarrassing episode.'

'Won't losing to Oakwood be a bit more embarrassing?'

Miss Tozer sighed. 'According to my chart, your period is not due to start yet.'

Lily smiled. 'Exactly. Therefore, according to your chart, I can play.' At that very moment she experienced a particularly sharp stab and doubled over.

'I am sorry you are in such discomfort. Perhaps you should consult Dr Bircher.'

Lily swallowed and forced herself upright. 'Who is going to be captain?'

'I haven't decided yet.'

Another stab of pain forced her to gasp.

'Now you know why menstruation is called the curse.'

Lily looked the games mistress in the eye. 'I feel cursed, that's for sure.'

'Support our girls from the sidelines. Hearing you cheer them on will inspire more goals.'

Lily glanced at her watch. 'I am due to meet Reverend Longden in Form 5B.' One of the best decisions Miss Cooper had made, in Lily's eyes, was to ask the young Methodist minister from the Parish of Crowford to become the school chaplain. It meant his Sundays were pretty busy; he officiated early matins at the school followed by a morning service at his Methodist Church, and at 5 pm, Evensong. During the week, he would care for his parishioners and also teach divinity at Advanced level to a few senior girls of which one was Lily. In her first year at Inniscliffe, she had opted to study Latin, Biology and English at A-level but when the new minister arrived at the beginning of her final year, she felt so inspired by his first Sunday sermon that she added divinity to her busy study schedule. Aged eight, she had joined the Scripture Union and enjoyed reading stories and analyses of the life of Jesus, so studying for divinity at A-level, she felt, would help her gain a place reading Philosophy at a top university. Of course, sex before marriage was a sin and she knew that her relations with a married man may condemn her to eternal damnation, but she hoped and believed that God loved a sinner and that, in time, He would forgive her.

'Why are you meeting the Reverend Longden on Saturday?' Miss Tozer asked. 'Isn't it his one day off?'

'I asked if he would clarify a couple of issues regarding Paul's First Letter to the Corinthians for my divinity A-level. He said he would as he's coming to watch the match. Did you know he was a keen sportsman when at school?'

'I can't say I did, but he has a strong physique.'

'He told me his proudest moment was when Bradfield College was playing a cricket match against Haileybury. Their captain thwacked the ball for a certain six. Reverend Longden ran for the boundary and owing to his great height and length of arm, caught the ball with one hand. He said it stung like hell, but it won them the match.' She looked intently at the games' mistress. 'What reason should I give the Reverend for not playing, today? Sorry, sir, I'm skipping lacrosse as I've got a visit from Aunt Flo?'

'Simply tell him you've been dropped from the team. It's not a lie as you have.'

'What's wrong with telling him I'm on the rag and not allowed to play?'

'Under no circumstances discuss menstruation in his presence.'

'Why not? Jesus cured a woman with menstrual problems.' Lily opened her bible. 'I'm studying the Gospels and remember seeing a section written by Luke.' She flicked a few gossamer-thin pages. 'Here it is, chapter eight, verse forty-three.'

'Don't tell me... Jesus turned blood into wine!'

Lily looked intently at Miss Tozer. 'I am surprised. That is an irreverent joke, but quite funny, albeit unrepeatable.' She ran her finger down the fine print. 'And a woman having an issue of blood for twelve years, who had spent all her resources consulting physicians, but none could heal her, came behind Jesus and touched the border of his garment. Immediately her issue of blood stanched. Jesus said, Who touched me? When all denied, Peter said, Master, the multitude throng thee and press thee, and yet thou sayest, Who touched me? And Jesus replied, Somebody hath touched me: for I perceive that virtue is gone out of me. Trembling, the woman came forward and fell to her knees. She declared unto him before all the people present why she had touched his garment, and how she was healed immediately. And he said unto her, Daughter, be of good comfort: thy faith hath made thee whole; go in peace.' Lily smiled at Miss Tozer. 'Reverend Longden is the next best thing to Jesus, so I may just touch his garment.'

'Don't you dare! He's a man and men do not want to know about such things.' She glanced at her watch. 'I must go and let Sarah Pothecary know she is now in the team.'

Lily arrived in the cold, deserted classroom. It was one of the smallest in the school as very few girls took divinity A-level. She sat at the end of a row of stained desks. All wooden and all joined together in an iron train that incorporated excruciatingly uncomfortable seats and an inkwell that would be filled on Monday with blue ink powder mixed with water, which always clogged her fountain pen.

At the front of the classroom placed on a low dais were a large desk and chair. A blackboard was fixed to the wall behind. For a moment, she thought about the girls in years gone-by who had sat at the desks, petrified by fear, and whose intelligence and education would be frittered away as secretaries supporting less-intelligent bosses.

Windows to one side offered a perfect view of the lacrosse field of play. She looked at her mother's watch. Her teammates would expect her support, but to witness their struggle when she couldn't pick up her stick and help, would be more painful than her menstrual cramps. She went to the windows, turned one of the metal handles, and breathed in the refreshing air.

'I think we have about fifteen minutes before you need to change and warm up.'

Lily shut the window and looked at the Reverend William Longden. He was very tall and wore a three-piece worsted suit with the strap of a worn leather satchel over one shoulder. It was clear from his domed forehead he was an utter brainbox, but not in a smug, superior kind of way. Whenever he passed on yet another gold nugget of information to his class, not necessarily about the bible, but about the world in general, he always conveyed it with charm and a twinkle in his eyes.

'Unfortunately, I'm not in the team, today, sir.'

'I'm sorry to hear that.' He skirted the nearest row of desks to the door as he unbuckled his satchel. 'I have brought a thermos. As you are not playing, perhaps you would care to share a cheese and pickle sandwich and a cup of tea.'

Lily didn't know how to respond.

'Mrs May, my housekeeper at the manse, always overestimates the capacity of my stomach. She is such a dear and so very kind to believe that I will fade away without sufficient sustenance, that she always caters as if I were two.'

'Two?' Lily laughed.

'Two people, not a toddler.'

She smiled. 'Nobody would take you for a toddler.'

He laid out a cloth napkin on a desk and unwrapped the greaseproof paper from one of the rounds of sandwiches.

'I have to confess,' Lily said. 'As a reserve player, I was excused lunch so as not to be weighed down by suet pudding. My stomach is definitely rumbling.'

'Then I trust you will tuck in.'

Lily picked up a sandwich quarter and sat on a desk, resting her feet on the seat in front.

Reverend Longden unscrewed the cup at the top of the thermos flask to reveal a second, smaller cup. He placed them both on the desk and unscrewed the stopper. 'In all my life,' he said, 'I have yet to discover a beverage that comes close to the magnificent taste of Tetley tea, brewed with loose leaves, at the insistence of my housekeeper.'

'I love tea.' She watched him pour the steaming brew already mixed with milk into the two cups.

'Do you take sugar?'

'I don't, but it's fine if it's already sweetened.'

'It's not. My father lost most of his teeth to cane sugar. I try to reduce my consumption.'

'My mother weaned us off sweet drinks from an early age. She was health conscious.'

'Miss Cooper told me about your loss. If at any time you feel overwhelmed, I hope you will come to me.'

'Can you bring my mother back to life?' She regretted her question, immediately.

He picked up the smaller of the two cups and placed it within her reach. 'I do not have a panacea for your grief,' he said. 'Nobody does. Every death, wounds; but it's how we bind those wounds that can make a difference to our pain.'

Such a clever man, she thought, as she bit into her sandwich.

Lily was surprised by how many people had come

to watch the match. Apart from pupils, many were family and friends of those who worked at the school, both mistresses and staff, and saw beating Oakwood in lacrosse as a matter of honour. She was pleased Reverend Longden had insisted she wear her coat, although the press of onlookers acted as a windbreak. The school chaplain was fortunate. His great height afforded him a perfect view of the pitch, whereas Lily found the heads and hats in front of her, frustrating.

'I am sorry not to see you play, today,' Reverend Longden said. 'Perhaps, if one of the girls on your team sprains an ankle, you could go on as a substitute?'

Lily laughed. 'Oh, that's very Malory Towers.'

'Malory Towers?'

'They're books set in a girls' boarding school written by Enid Blyton. All fun and frolics and nothing like Inniscliffe, I can assure you.'

'Perhaps I can borrow one from the school library?'

Lily laughed again. 'That would certainly raise a few eyebrows.'

A moment's pause. 'I think you had better explain the rules of lacrosse,' the Reverend said. 'I know the game was created by tribes in Canada, but I have no knowledge of how it is played.'

'It's similar to football.'

'Rugby football?'

'More like soccer with sticks, and twelve on a team instead of eleven.'

'There appears to be an open area of play behind each goal.'

'Up to seven attacking players can be within the thirty yard line and that includes behind the goal.'

'What's your normal position?'

'Captain Attack the girls call me.'

'Is there much physical contact?'

'No more than in Rugby Union.'

The Reverend hooted, attracting the attention of fellow onlookers. The blast of Miss Tozer's whistle quietened the crowd. As much as Lily was disappointed not to be on the pitch, ready to cradle the rubber ball all the way to the back of Oakwood's net, she did find it strangely pleasing to be in the company of the tall divinity master.

CHAPTER SEVEN

It was tough lying to her friends but eventually the school emptied of girls, collected by their parents for a week of respite, away from draughty corridors, icy washrooms, hard toilet paper.

Lily's first job, once she was sure everyone had gone, was to carry the Dansette record player from the prefects' lounge to her study bedroom. A second visit was required to collect the 45s she especially liked, and the long playing 33s. She was looking forward to hearing lots of pop music at maximum volume. The Beatles were her favourite group of all time. There were others she loved including Sonny & Cher – the coolest couple ever on TV. She'd seen them on Top of the Pops singing their number one hit, *I Got You Babe*. She also liked The Kinks and had bought *Tired of Waiting for You*. And Bob Dylan… she really hoped he was right when he sang, *The Times They Are a-Changin'* but she didn't think so. Of course, Elvis Presley was King. Her mother had loved his rock 'n' roll – Elvis the Pelvis he was called - but since her mummy's passing, Lily had listened more to his beautiful ballads especially *Crying in the Chapel*, and her mother's favourite, *Wooden Heart*.

Lily stared at her biology textbook with its illustration of a dissected frog and decided to play a record. She looked through the singles, all in paper sleeves to protect them from scratching, although many were scratched already, causing the needle to jump. She decided to stack eight records and took a few moments to work out the order. Elvis would be first with *Can't Help Falling in Love* from the film Blue Hawaii, which Lily hadn't seen. Unusually, she also liked the B-side, *Rock-A-Hula Baby*. B-sides were rarely any good, although *Rock-A-Hula Baby* was fun to dance to with the other girls. Next on the stack was *Terry* sung by Twinkle. Lily knew all the words and promised her daddy that she would never go out with a boy who demanded she ride pillion on his motorbike or scooter. *Concrete and Clay* by Unit 4 + 2 was next. She wasn't sure about the song, but it encouraged her to sing at full volume. *For your Love* by the Yardbirds – sweet but short, then *Ticket to Ride* by The Beatles, of course. Elvis again with *Crying in the Chapel,* then *Mr Tambourine Man* by The Byrds. Finally, *Satisfaction* by The Rolling Stones. She preferred John Lennon to Mick Jagger but Mick did have raw, dangerous sex appeal.

Later, as the music was so loud, she didn't hear Sylvia come into her room and jumped when she tapped her on the shoulder. Lily hastily turned down the volume. 'Sorry about that.'

'I hope it is accompanying a good morning's work.'

'Oh yes. It relaxes me and I focus more.'

'Interesting.' Sylvia's eyes wandered around Lily's room finally resting on her desk. 'Biology, I see.'

'I prefer flora and fauna to dissected animals, but it does give me a chance to draw, which I enjoy.'

'Well, I'm off to Undermere to collect vaccinations

from Doctor Bircher. Her fridge has broken. I'll be out most of the morning.'

'Safe journey.'

Sylvia smiled. 'There's food in my private kitchen should you get hungry.'

'Thank you.'

Lily observed Sylvia as she strode out of the room, leaving the door wide open. She waited a few seconds then spun the knob on the record player. Mick Jagger could still get *no satisfaction*. Too right, thought Lily as she danced around the room in her blue jeans and striped, crew-neck sweater, happily singing along. With the music at top volume, she went over to the open door and looked left and right. After a quick check, she walked down the long corridor and peered out of a window into the central quadrangle.

As she expected, it was deserted.

At the far end of the next corridor, she turned left and headed for the back stairs that led down to the private kitchen and one of three rear entrances.

She opened a door onto the car park and watched the Sunbeam Alpine roar off leaving behind Colonel Craig's Vauxhall estate. She waited until she could no longer hear the car then closed the door.

The school was suddenly eerily quiet. She took a deep breath and ran. Panting, she arrived at the top of the stairs to the main entrance hall.

Empty.

She hurried down another corridor until she reached a heavy door, lined with leather and studded in brass. A large sign screwed to the wall read, *Entry Forbidden*.

Lily reached for the decorative handle and slowly pushed it down. The door opened, held back by a heavy wool curtain, fixed to a brass rail above the entrance. Through the thick fabric, she could hear Marlene Dietrich's husky, seductive voice.

'Why do you like her?' Lily had asked when she heard him humming one of Dietrich's wartime hits, the first time she had entered his private lair. 'She's old. The past.'

He had fixed her with his bright blue eyes and held her shoulders. 'Marie Magdalene Dietrich is everything that is good about the Fatherland.'

'But she rejected Germany for America.'

'No. She rejected Nazi Germany for the Free World. She never turned her back on true Germans, especially political dissidents, and German Jews. During the war, she went to the Front and performed concerts for American soldiers. Decent Germans understood her courage and that she was fighting for their freedom too. *Lili Marleen*, recorded in both English and German, is a love song that was popular with both Allied and German troops. Dietrich sang it as Lili Marlene. This year, she was awarded the Israeli Medallion of Valour. She is a remarkable woman.'

'What did your father do in the war?'

Rainer broke away and lit a cigarette with a battered, flip top steel lighter. 'This is all I have of his. He was shot down over the English Channel in 1944. His body washed up on a beach near Broadstairs, Kent. I was three when my mother told me he was not coming home.'

'Where were you living?'

'Berlin.' He sucked hard on his cigarette. 'When the Russians arrived in '45 they raped my eleven-year-old sister and my mother. So, we Germans got our just desserts.'

'Better than a gas chamber.'

Rainer took another deep drag. 'My mother was born in Vienna to a Jewish family. She fell in love with my father, and he took her to Berlin where she was baptised as a Christian. After my father died, she was honoured as the wife of a war hero. She won't tell me what she did during those terrible years in Berlin, but I know she was part of the attempt to assassinate Hitler. Her name was given to the Gestapo, but she was warned in time, and we fled to a secret address in East Berlin.'

'Is she still alive?'

'Yes. She lives with my sister under Soviet occupation.' He stubbed out his cigarette into an overflowing onyx ashtray.

Lily pulled aside the curtain and stepped into the strange room. Despite daylight streaming through leaded lights, two bright spotlights shone down on three wooden school desks, battered and stained, where Rainer worked. Several more desks were dotted around the room amongst many items of school equipment including a narrow iron bed with a stained mattress.

Rainer's back was to her. She watched him, bent over, fully focused.

'Hello.'

He jumped. 'Was zum Teufel?'

She saw that his desk was covered in yellowing sheets of paper. There was a jam jar with assorted fountain pens, and numerous bottles of inks. But what attracted her eye was a large, cantilevered magnifying glass with a weighted stand and an adjustable arm.

He looked flustered. 'What are you doing here?'

She smiled and walked as seductively as she knew

how up to him. 'I thought you might like some company.'

He took a deep breath, stood, and gripped her arms. 'Please go. This is my private place. I have work to do.'

'Marking German tests?' She tried to look over his shoulder.

'Yes, and no.' He stepped aside and let Lily see his mess of papers and documents. 'The work I do is top secret. I cannot say more.' He cupped her face in his hands. 'Please do not betray my confidence. I beg you.'

She smiled. 'I won't. But on one condition.'

Sylvia bounced around a bend and knew instantly she had a puncture. Damn. She was already using the spare. The numerous ruts and potholes on the Old Military Road were playing havoc with her Alpine. The car was too refined for such rough and ready tarmac. Ah well, Colonel Craig will sort it out for her. She glanced at her watch. Half an hour's walk back to school, call Gretchen, and get on with balancing the books. An impossible task, but she was determined that the day was not going to be a complete waste. She looked at her court shoes. They were about to be ruined.

'Don't you have a heater?' Lily was lying naked on a worn chaise longue with a gossamer thin veil artistically draped over her.

'Heat burns out creativity.' Rainer was sitting on a stool with a large pad on his lap, drawing Lily with a stub of pencil.

'Am I to freeze my nether regions just for a sketch? I thought I deserved oils.'

'First, liebling, I make sure I have all the correct proportions in pencil before I commence with charcoal, unless you want to have große Brüste und fette Oberschenkel.'

'I think I've been inoculated against that!'

'You are very funny.'

'My mother told me I have a queer sense of humour.'

Rainer got up from the stool and placed the pad and pencil on the seat. He looked at Lily and she felt a surge. Since that amazing night, she had acted upon many urges alone in her room, then had knelt by her bed to pray for forgiveness. In her former school, Miss Rooney had made it clear that self-gratification was against the teachings of Christ.

'As for adultery and fornication,' Miss Rooney had said, 'they are an abomination and will send you straight to hell.' She had slammed the palm of her hand down on her thigh as she paced about and eyed the young girls seated before her. Young girls who had yet to experience their first period and were still reading books by Enid Blyton.

Well, Lily thought, hell it shall be because she was hooked on the greatest drug of all and despite her belief in God, she would rather face His wrath than become a dried-up old prune like Miss Rooney.

Rainer knelt in front of her, and she felt his warm tobacco breath... so intoxicating. 'You are beautiful,' he said.

'Make love to me,' she whispered.

'An artist sleeping with his model is a cliché, is it not?'

'Call it the Spark effect.'

'I don't understand.'

'Muriel Spark... she wrote The Prime of Miss Jean Brodie. It's a novella set in a girls' school. If they ever make it into a film, I want to play Sandy.'

'Sandy?'

'She's the smartest girl in the Brodie set and has an affair with the art master.'

'Who is very handsome, no doubt.'

'Of course. Unfortunately, Sandy ends their affair and becomes a Roman Catholic nun.'

He chuckled. 'Is that your destiny?'

She shrugged. 'Que sera, sera, whatever will be, will be.' She let the veil slip, exposing a youthful breast. 'My fate is in your hands.'

He repositioned the veil and stepped back.

She forced a smile. 'So, it's a nunnery for me then?'

He looked at her. 'I cannot imagine loving anyone more than I do you.'

'What about Sylvia?'

'She saved my life and has given me a future out of reach of the Russian bear.'

Lily wrapped the gauze tightly around her and stood. 'I'd better go.'

'Please stay. I owe Sylvia, but I want you.' He pushed her gently down onto the chaise longue and knelt before her.

'Colonel Craig, I am in your debt,' Sylvia said, surprisingly warm after her long walk and suffering from very painful feet. She handed him her car keys. 'What will you do?'

'I'll prop your car on two jacks and drive both punctured tyres to Hanbury's garage. I'll then return and fit the repaired tyre and place the spare in the boot. I'll drive my car back here and together we can retrieve your Alpine.'

'You're a diamond, thank you.' She gave him a kiss on the cheek, then looked at her scuffed shoes. 'Right, well I'd better get on.' She watched him stride to his car, whistling the Colonel Bogey March. It was her Godmother who had employed the former army colonel after the war when jobs were scarce. Why he had stayed in such a menial job after so many years, she had no idea.

Sylvia entered through one of the rear doors to the school and was enveloped by silence. She enjoyed the lack of schoolgirl babble during the holidays, but never got used to the impenetrable shadows the gothic building cast as soon as the sun dipped below the high escarpment that carved through Hawksmoor. Happily, there was still plenty of daylight as she marched down one of the long corridors that looked out onto the central quad, comforted by Bella's panting presence and the knowledge that both Rainer and Lily were beavering away in their separate rooms.

At first Lily thought it was disgusting, but once Rainer got going, she prayed he would never stop. The bearded men in cassocks who denounced women for enjoying life's greatest pleasure could all go hang. Rainer was infusing her with ripples of joy that spread to her very extremities until the exquisite pain became almost unbearable. She gripped his thick hair in her fists as wave after wave pulsed through her entire being.

It took a long time before she was able to open her eyes and look at her lover. He smiled and kissed her cheek. 'What about you?' she gasped, her voice, husky, almost cracking.

'I'm fine. Giving pleasure to another is the greatest gift. And I don't want to make us a baby, just yet.'

'But one day, we will. Yes?'

'One day, perhaps.' He pushed himself onto his feet.

'Get dressed. Sylvia will have left us some lunch.'

She reached for his hand. 'Make love to me. I won't get pregnant. My period has only just ended.' She let her fingertips seek out what she desired and was pleased to feel his response.

Later, Lily followed Rainer into a part of the school she'd never been. It was a large kitchen by domestic standards but tiny in comparison to the school's food production factory, next to the refectory. But what surprised her, was seeing Miss Cooper, as she was still called despite her marriage to Rainer, cutting a beetroot for a winter salad.

'Good. You're both here.'

Rainer walked around a scrubbed pine table laid for lunch and kissed his wife on the cheek. Lily hadn't seen much of Miss Cooper following the greatest night of her life but after the experience she'd just enjoyed, relished, loved with every fibre of her being, seeing her headmistress in the same room as Rainer was a little disconcerting. If she had known Sylvia was back, she'd have had a quick shower.

Sylvia placed the salad and a plate of cooked meats on the table. She smiled at Lily. 'We have sülzwurst, German sausage; flönz, smoked blood sausage – very tasty; and Black Forest ham.' She reached for a bowl of shredded white cabbage. 'And this is sauerkraut. Rainer's speciality.'

'My mother's recipe,' he said, as he pulled out a chair and sat down.

Sylvia picked up a large jar of pickled gherkins and tried to twist open the metal lid. She handed the jar to Rainer. 'Hopefully, you have some strength left after all your hard work.'

Lily felt her cheeks burning as she sat down at the

table.

'We're out of coal,' Sylvia continued, 'otherwise I would have cooked lunch.'

Lily looked past Sylvia to a cast-iron range, set within a recessed arch with a flue leading into a chimney, where food was once cooked over logs on an open grate. Black smoke still stained the surrounding stone. 'I can get more coal after lunch, if you tell me where to go,' she offered, to assuage the guilt she felt.

Sylvia smiled. 'Thank you, Lily. That is most kind.'

'What about Colonel Craig?' Rainer asked. 'Is he not joining us?'

'Unfortunately, a puncture altered my plans. The colonel kindly volunteered to sort it out.' Sylvia turned and pulled open a drawer in a pine bureau.

Lily and Rainer exchanged an apprehensive glance.

'What goes hand in hand with love is loyalty.' Sylvia spoke without looking at Lily or Rainer. 'Betrayal of that love hurts above all else.' She selected a wide-bladed knife. 'The realisation that what one holds dear has evaporated in another's arms is crushing and drives all reason from a once sane mind.' She turned, and a ceiling light flashed in the shiny steel blade.

Lily pushed her chair back and stood. Rainer reached for her hand, but she pulled it away. 'You will elicit no apology from me,' Lily said to Sylvia. 'I am neither ashamed nor sorry. I will not beg for mercy. I have lived these last weeks more than ten of your lifetimes. Nothing you can do will make me regret my actions.'

Sylvia stabbed the point of the knife into the kitchen table causing Rainer to leap to his feet. 'Mein Gott im Himmel!'

Sylvia took her hand away from the knife. 'Damn,

I've forgotten what comes next.'

'What is this?' Rainer asked looking from Sylvia to Lily and back to Sylvia.

Sylvia pulled the knife out of the scarred pine and examined the cut. 'It's the final scene from the play Lily is studying for A-level. I performed it here in the school eleven years ago, to great acclaim I might add.' Sylvia replaced the knife in the bureau drawer and sat down at the table. Rainer, still looking shocked, also sat down, followed by Lily.

Sylvia smiled at Lily. 'Please, help yourself.'

'Thank you.' Lily reached for the bowl of salad. 'I do have one question,' she said. 'Why doesn't the Persian Princess use the knife to kill her mother instead of killing herself?'

Sylvia picked up a jug of water. 'She knows she will never be reunited with the man she loves. Her stepmother has given her the kind way out.' She filled three glass tumblers.

'I would have killed the stepmother first,' Lily said, 'then myself.'

'What about a hero?' Rainer asked. 'A handsome young man who saves the princess. It's the ending the audience wants. No?'

Sylvia looked at him. 'The play is a tragedy. It has to have a tragic ending.'

'Why?'

'Because tragedies do, and that's what the writer wrote.' Sylvia reached for the salad bowl. 'Anyway, what makes you think that the lover would choose the princess over his queen?'

Rainer shrugged. 'She's younger.'

'But he knows the queen holds his fate in her hands. At any moment she can have him banished to a foreign land.'

For an uncomfortable moment, there was silence.

'Do start, Lily,' Sylvia said. 'You don't need to wait for a clap of hands, here.'

Lily pushed open a rear door and was dismayed to see that dark clouds had brought twilight on early. In her hand was an empty copper coal scuttle. She had been directed to turn right, head towards the netball court and the entrance was down some steps where there was a wooden door and a light switch on the left upon entry.

'Isn't there an entrance inside by the school kitchen?' Lily asked.

'Colonel Craig fitted a couple of bolts on the door so the cellar cannot be accessed.'

'Why? Every time you need coal you have to go the long way around.'

'Have you ever heard of Primula Susan Rollo? She was a friend of my mother's in the Women's Auxiliary Air Force, during the war. My parents were guests at her wedding to the famous actor, David Niven. They married in 1940. It was a tricky time for everyone but Primmie, as she was called, was generous and kind to my mother, despite being much younger. She always remembered her birthday and gave me presents on mine. I still have her birthday cards signed, *with love always, Primmie & David.*'

'I remember him in The Guns of Navarone,' Lily said. 'Mummy and daddy took my brother and me. He is a good actor. But what have they got to do with locking the door to the cellar?'

'After the war, Primmie went to Hollywood to be with David. They were invited to a gathering hosted by the late Tyrone Power and his French wife,

Annabella. After dinner, to entertain themselves, someone suggested that they play sardines. Do you know the game?'

'Is it where someone hides and then everyone looks for them? When each person finds them, they hide with them. If it's in a cupboard, it can get pretty crowded and strangely intimate.'

'Quite. We know how permissive Hollywood actors can be.'

'But what has this got to do with locking the cellar door?'

'Primmie was selected as the one to hide. To make it harder, they turned off all the lights. Primmie didn't know the house and was feeling her way along a corridor when her hand rested on a door handle. She pushed the door open and stepped into a void. It was a door to a cellar with very steep steps.'

'I see.' Lily thought for a moment. 'Thank you for explaining it to me.'

'Securing the coal cellar door was one of the very first things I did when I took over the school.'

Lily nodded. 'Last question… was Primmie all right?'

Sylvia looked at her. 'No. She died. She was my age. In fact, a year younger than I am now. It was tragic.'

Lily was stunned. 'I'm so sorry.' She picked up the copper coal scuttle. 'Thank you. Thank you for being cautious.' She almost laughed. 'You've probably saved my life!'

'I am a guardian to all my pupils.'

The outside steps down to the coal cellar were fortunately shallow but her heart still thumped in anticipation. A few weeds hung on to nooks and crannies despite the recent wintry weather. She gripped the pocked handrail and the cold chilled her hand. She was just getting coal, she told herself. Even rats don't like coal, so the fear was simply in her mind.

In the dwindling daylight, the door looked weather-beaten. She turned the old knob and pushed it open and heard the clang of an iron key falling onto the stone floor. The blackness of the subterranean room oppressed her, and it took every ounce of courage not to drop the copper scuttle and run. She felt for the light switch, terrified that some monster would grab her hand. A bulb flickered and the immense coal cellar was revealed. Aged oak beams supported the floor above and, across the vast space, she could just make out the steps that she knew led up to the door by the kitchen. Sylvia was right; they were steep and clearly an accident waiting to happen. The cellar walls were brick-lined, barely discernible under the coal dust. The stone floor was also thick with coal dust and covered in scattered pieces. To one side, near the chute where the coal was delivered, was a small pile and a shovel. The bulb flickered again. Ancient wiring. Better hurry.

She did not enjoy the feeling of being in a dungeon or the crunch under her shoes. After, she would clean her soles on the grass. The dented scuttle clanged almost like a bell when she placed it on the floor. She reached for the shovel's wooden handle and did not enjoy the feeling of ground coal dust in her clean palms. Taking a firm grip of the handle with both hands, she scraped the steel scoop under the pile of coal and dropped half of the pieces on the floor as she tried to direct them into the scuttle. She took another shovel full and the same happened again. She decided she didn't care. It was a quick way of working. She liked the echo within the cavernous cellar and gave full throat to one of her favourite hymns, *We plough the fields and scatter the good seed on the ground*, taking pleasure in changing the words. '*We scoop the coal and scatter across the cellar floor. It doesn't really matter, it's such a dirty chore.*'

Happy that the scuttle could take no more coal, she threw the shovel down and reached for the scuttle handle. It was incredibly heavy, and she wondered whether she'd even be able to carry it up the steps.

She put the scuttle down and decided to clear up the coal she had wantonly scattered. The metal edge of the shovel scraped the stone floor and made the kind of noise that affected the nerves of her teeth. This time she made feminised grunts to the melody of the Chain Gang song by Sam Cooke. '*Ooh Ahh, Ooh Ahh, working in the cellar, Ooh Ahh, Ooh Ahh, sleeping with my fella.*' She scooped and tossed the pieces of coal onto the main pile, almost enjoying the horrendous scraping noise. Finally, she stood back and admired her tidying up. Satisfied, she leaned the shovel against a wooden pillar and brushed the palms of her hands together.

Job done, she reached for the scuttle and was plunged into darkness. It closed in on her and was so impenetrable, it made no difference whether her eyes were open or closed. Her heart pounded as she took a few deep breaths to control her rising panic.

Calmed, she felt confident she knew where the door was and the light switch. She didn't think there were any pillars blocking her route. She held out her hands like a blind person and took a first tentative step. How far was it? Ten paces? Fifteen? She took another step. And another. Confident. Her hands outstretched, she increased her pace until her palms felt decades of coal dust on the surface of the bricks. She slid them along not sure whether the switch was to the left or right, or where the wooden door was. She told herself, it didn't matter which way she went, she would eventually find the door and could get out. She hated the feel of coal on her hands and the taste in her mouth. Why hadn't she brought a torch? She kept sliding her hands along the bricks and finally her fingers found the light switch. It was off, which was odd. She pushed it down and expected the bulb to flicker on as it had before. Nothing. Never mind. She was right by the door. Her fingertips ran over the ancient wood until they located the old knob. She turned it and pulled.

It didn't budge.

She twisted it the other way and pulled again.

The door was jammed shut. Was it locked?

She felt with her shoe for the key she'd heard fall on the floor when she first walked in. Where was it?

On her knees she swept her palms over the worn stones in ever widening arcs, tears falling silently as she frantically searched.

Had someone come, picked up the key and deliberately locked her in? Who would do such a thing?

Total and utter darkness shrouded her in terror, and she imagined all manner of horrors and monsters.

She cried, and sobbed, and wailed. Her gut convulsed as she clawed the door, kept turning the handle, pulling and pushing, hammering her fists on the solid wood.

She knew she had to get a grip. Across the cellar were the steps and the bolted door. Even if she couldn't get it open, someone would eventually hear her banging.

To get to the steps required another walk with her hands outstretched. The monsters were all in her head, she told herself.

Or were they?

Had someone locked the door and remained in the cellar? Were they listening to her sobs and enjoying her terror? Would they suddenly pounce?

She held her breath as best she could and listened, but the silence of the cellar was drowned out by the pounding of her heart.

Her only hope were the steps. She rushed forward and slammed into a pillar, her hands fortunately sufficiently out front to prevent her face from being flattened, but not enough to stop herself falling backwards onto the floor and banging her elbow, which sent electric shocks through her arm.

She got up and crawled across the stone slabs, slowly and determinedly towards the steps. This time her sense of direction was spot on, and it was with relief she felt the first step. She crawled up, step by step, finally getting to her feet when she felt the wooden door at the top. There was a knob but no keyhole. Relief flooded through her veins. Her fingers found a bolt and she slid it back quite easily. The knob turned but the door wouldn't open. She felt for another bolt at the base. It slid back with no problem. She reached again for the knob, turned it and the door swung open. If she hadn't had a firm grip on the knob, she would have fallen the way Primmie had fallen at that party in Hollywood.

She stepped into the gloom of the corridor which led to the main kitchen.

Fearing she looked an absolute sight, she knew she

had a choice. She could return to Sylvia empty handed or she could go back in the cellar and retrieve the coal scuttle.

She found a switch which turned on the corridor lights and looked down the steep steps into the cellar. A cool breeze carried the smell of coal dust. She heard a noise. She listened. The cellar light flickered on. So that was it. Someone wanted to frighten her. Enraged, she gripped the handrail and hurried down the steps. Whoever it was, her adrenalin-fuelled muscles would tear them apart.

At the bottom of the steps, she stopped as suddenly as though slamming into a pillar.

Rainer was holding the copper scuttle.

'Lily!' he said, clearly shocked. 'What in God's name has happened to you?'

'Rainer? Do you hate me? Is that why you played the trick?'

'What are you talking about?'

'Someone turned off the light and locked the door. I was left in pitch black.'

'The door wasn't locked when I arrived, and the light clearly works.' He put the coal scuttle down and moved towards her. 'It is a scary place. I hate coming down here to collect coal.'

'Someone tried to frighten me on purpose.'

'Who would do that?'

She looked at him, intently. 'Was it you?'

'Liebling. I would never do anything to harm you.'

She took a deep breath, hating the taste of the coal dust. 'Someone locked that door and must've unscrewed the lightbulb.'

'Well, it wasn't me.'

Lily took another unpleasant breath. 'Why are you

here? I said I would get the coal.'

'I went to the kitchen to make a coffee, saw the coal scuttle was gone, and thought I would come and help.'

She looked at the man who had taken her to a place that morning she never imagined, possible. Someone she regarded as heaven-sent.

He sighed. 'I may as well take the shortcut up the steps, seeing as you've unbolted the door.' He picked up the coal scuttle.

'You promise it wasn't you?' she asked, her voice as weak as she felt.

'With all my heart.'

Lily went straight to the washroom and undressed there. Her clothes needed to be machine washed, and she most definitely needed a shower.

She thought about what Rainer had said and decided to believe him. She had not imagined the door being locked or the bulb not working. Human hands had deliberately set about to frighten her, but whose?

Could it have been Sylvia wanting revenge? Had she guessed what Rainer and Lily had been up to? No, Sylvia was her headmistress and would not do such a thing.

Who else could it have been? Colonel Craig? For all his faults he was a war hero. She may not like him, but she believed he played cricket with a straight bat.

Glorious hot water streamed over her hair, and she delighted in washing away all the coal dust. She thought about coal tar soap and wondered why people bought it. Even wrapped up it stank of coal. She'd heard that it was good for the skin but after her experience in the cellar, whatever its cleansing and antiseptic properties, washing her body with it was not something she would ever entertain. Although, frankly, the school's red carbolic soap was not much less unpleasant.

'You locked her in the cellar, didn't you?' Rainer almost dropped the heavy coal scuttle as he placed it by the range.

Sylvia was standing by the window with her back to Rainer. 'She's lucky I didn't push her down the steps,' she said. 'A few minutes in the dark is nothing compared to seeing you both at lunch oozing sexual pheromones.' She sniffed as tears came. 'I didn't plan it.' Her voice was small. 'I went to help her collect the coal and saw her scattering it with gay abandon. I spotted the door key on the floor and was about to put it back in the lock when I was consumed by rage. I locked the door and unscrewed the light bulb a couple of turns.'

'You imprisoned her? How could you, Sylvia?'

'She wasn't imprisoned. I waited until I heard her crawling up the steps before I left.'

'After all she's suffered, it was cruel. I did not take you to be vengeful.'

She turned to him. 'You hurt me, Rainer. You really hurt me.' She pulled out a chair and slumped down at the table. 'I know. You're right. It was nasty and unnecessary.' She looked up at her husband. 'I was jealous. I will make it up to her. Please don't let her know it was me.'

He sat down beside her, took her hand and examined her palm. 'The light bulb must've been hot.'

'I used the sleeve of my sweater.' She looked at him, her face smeared with tears. 'How did you know?'

'When the light didn't work, I was puzzled, as I put a new bulb in last week. I tightened it up, it came on; it was obvious someone had fiddled with it.'

'Lily trusts me. Please don't tell her.'

'She knows somebody set out to scare her. Unfortunately, there aren't many suspects.'

CHAPTER EIGHT

The remaining days of half term saw Lily working hard on her A-levels in the morning, although frequently dreaming of a life with Rainer, and going for long walks with Miss Cooper in the afternoon, accompanied by an inquisitive Bella. She liked the headmistress and felt sorry for her. Rainer was clearly in love with Lily, and she knew, one day, Miss Cooper would have her heart broken.

She still had no idea who had locked her in the coal cellar. As much as she tried to persuade herself that she was unaffected by the trauma, she slept with her light on and did everything she could to avoid the dark. That was the big disadvantage to being almost alone at school; the vast, gothic building was more than a little spooky especially at night in a gale. Until she was locked in the cellar, Lily was not bothered by the long, poorly-lit corridors, creaking timbers, or the howl of the wind whipping off the North Sea. But lights that were usually on when night drew in were turned off to save costs, turning benign passageways into menacing alleys.

By the end of half-term, she looked forward to the return of her fellow pupils. There had been no more trysts with Rainer, who now kept his workroom door locked. Despite it being only seven-thirty on Saturday evening, winter darkness wrapped her in its suffocating cloak. She felt tired and alone and sought her narrow bed, snuggling under the sheet and blankets. But, before sleep could overtake her, a memory of Old Ma Barry's hideous voice rang through her head like a discordant bell.

'Stand by your bed, girl,' the evil crone had demanded.

Lily was naturally tidy and confident that her dormitory room would pass the surprise inspection.

'When did you last sweep the floor?'

'This morning, Miss Barry.'

'Eyes forward,' yelled the school's Sergeant Major.

Out of the corner of Lily's eye she observed Miss Barry running her sausage-like fingers over various surfaces looking for dust.

'What do you call this?' Lily heard the woman bark her question from behind.

'May I move my head, miss?'

'Don't be insolent, girl.'

'Are you referring to my bed, miss?'

'Where are the hospital corners?'

Lily looked at her bed which was smooth, flat, neat. 'Hospital corners?'

Old Ma Barry grabbed the blanket and sheets from the base of the bed and pulled them away from the mattress. 'Observe.'

Lily stood back, annoyed that the woman's grubby hands were touching her bed clothes.

'Lift the mattress at the bottom corner,' barked the Latin mistress, 'and tuck the sheet under all the way to the base.' Lily watched the woman stride to the other side of the bed. 'Repeat,' she said. 'At the base, you will observe a triangular shaped excess sheet. Tuck neatly under the mattress. Same process with the blanket.'

'Thank you very much for showing me.'

Old Ma Barry pulled the sheet from the base of the bed. 'Now you do it.'

'What about at the head end of the bed?'

Miss Barry looked at her, puzzled. 'Head end? It's hidden by the wall and your pillow. Don't make work for yourself, or you'll end up a *puella defututa*.'

Lily knew what the Latin meant but chose to ignore the barb. Miss Barry watched her make the bed three times before she was satisfied. Fortunately, the old crone had gone to wherever witches go for their holidays and so Lily didn't have to worry about making her bed during half term, with or without hospital corners.

She contemplated the Latin insult – *worn-out whore* – and debated whether Old Ma Barry knew about her liaison with Rainer. Thinking of the times she had spent with her handsome lover made her happy, and as she lay in bed, light on, listening to the growing gale, she pondered seeking solace with her fingers. Her brother had once told her that at his school there was a lot of what he called wanking at night, although she'd heard it more commonly referred to as self-abuse. She wondered what aspect of that self-induced pleasure could be considered abuse? Or why it was denounced as being so bad when almost everyone did it, although many begged forgiveness from the Almighty once the amazing sensations had subsided. She heard gossip that some girls did it to each other, not because they desired women, just that it was nice to have someone else look after their needs. She'd asked her brother whether it was the same at his school, but he thought not, although a few seniors did strike up unusual friendships with some of the younger boys, he said. Her brother also described a popular pursuit at his school called *ragging*. Two boys would wrestle until one managed to get hold of the other's scrotum. At that point the boy would surrender. All very odd she thought, and she couldn't imagine the same pastime occurring at her school.

She fantasised being with Rainer and let her fingertips slide up her nightdress. Although nothing she could do to herself would match the pleasure of making love to her handsome German, it was still a jolly good nightcap that would send her off into a deep sleep.

Guttural voices barked orders. What was going on? She was wearing stained and worn garments over a ripped buttoned blouse. Her left arm hurt. She pulled up the sleeve and was shocked to see a triangle followed by a row of five jagged numbers. How did that happen?

Her door burst open and a girl, stick thin, rushed in. She grabbed Lily's shirt. 'Hurry, we must hurry. Roll call.'

Lily searched for her slippers and found a worn-out pair of leather shoes. Dragged, cajoled, they joined other girls hurrying down the corridor, all wearing the same striped overgarments and all looking haunted and scared.

In the quad they lined up in rows as the cold truly bit through their feeble clothing. Teachers, Lily didn't recognise, prowled the group, prodding, feeling, slapping, selecting. Clumps of hair were grabbed as girls were dragged away.

'What is happening?' Lily whispered to her new friend.

'Don't speak!' was the hissed retort.

A shadow fell across Lily and a leather boot pressed down on her foot. The solid woman wore a worsted skirt and tailored jacket. Her face was shrouded in shadow. 'Komm mit mir,' she ordered, and walked off. Lily was about to follow when a hand gripped her arm.

'Stay.'

A baton hammered her back and Lily crumpled to her knees. Unable to stand, she was dragged to a place she'd never been and forced to lie on a table with leather straps. Belted in, she stared up at a bright light. A woman, in a white medical coat, peered down at her. Lily recognised her younger face ...and screamed.

The room was pitch black when Lily forced herself awake; her nightdress was soaked. She pulled the bed clothes tightly around her and wished Rainer would come. *Damn.* Despite sweating, she was desperate for a pee. She resisted the pressure but fearful of the consequences, threw back the covers. A cold draught made her shiver as she wrapped around her dressing gown and her feet sought her slippers.

She opened the bedroom door. What was that music? It was a woman's voice, sweet and young, but too soft to make out the words. In a strange way it was comforting. She hurried to the loo and experienced pure relief as she settled on the wooden seat and listened to her flow. For a moment she almost nodded off, until the slam of a door made her jump.

'Hello. Anyone there?' she called. The howl of the wind responded. She pulled the chain and slid back the bolt. Why had she locked it?

Water cascading from the basin tap was icy cold.

She had been trained to wash her hands by her mother and despite other girls skipping the ritual she always went through the cleansing process. She found a clean section of towel hanging on a wall-mounted roller and dried off. In the mirror, she checked her high plait was still in place – *why*? She was just going back to bed. The door swung open behind her.

'What are you doing here, girl?'

The woman was tall, well-built, with sturdy bones, flint-grey eyes, and wearing a tweed suit and brogues.

'Dr Bircher, I... I...'

'Answer my question.' Her accent carried a strong Teutonic tone.

'Ich war auf der Toilette und wasche mir jetzt die Hände.'

'Did I ask you to answer in German?'

'I was being polite. I thought you would like to hear your language spoken as there aren't many Germans living in England.'

'I am Swiss-German. Don't make that mistake again.'

Lily looked into the woman's eyes and shivered. Dr Bircher scared her. 'Why are you here in the middle of the night?' she asked the stout woman, her voice conveying a slight quiver.

'That is none of your business and it's only eight o'clock.' She strode to a cubicle and Lily heard the bolt slide home.

Bumping into the German doctor, *Swiss*-German doctor, had unnerved her, and she dreaded the thought of the big-handed woman sticking a needle in her arm. She reached for the door's brass handle and pulled it open. The shock of what she saw was like a punch from Henry Cooper and she keeled over backwards onto the unyielding tiled floor.

A bright beam blinded her eye. She felt the lid on her other eye being lifted and she turned her head to avoid the light.

'She must rest,' Dr Bircher said. 'I'll call by after surgery in the morning to check on her. I don't think she's fractured her skull, but it is a possibility. In the meantime, aspirin as prescribed on the bottle.'

Lily waited for the doctor to leave her bedroom before opening her eyes and was surprised to see Rainer looking down at her.

'How are you feeling?'

'A bit grotty. What happened? How did I get here?'

'Dr Bircher and I carried you. You are surprisingly heavy. Perhaps you should cut back on sponge pudding and custard.'

Miss Cooper came to the side of the bed. 'You've got a little colour back. It's a good sign. I'll go and get some aspirin. It'll help with the headache.'

Rainer waited for Sylvia to go then sat on the edge of the bed. He took her hand. 'I was worried. You were out, cold.'

'Kiss me.'

Rainer looked at the open door. 'She'll be back in a minute.'

'Kiss me.'

He smiled. 'You are so beautiful.' Another quick glance at the open door and then their lips touched. She wanted the moment to last forever.

All too quickly Lily was left alone with her sore head. There was a definite lump, but the skin wasn't broken. Her hair, in a French plait, had helped to cushion the thump. She didn't have the least idea why she'd fallen.

Did she faint? Did something scare her? Somehow, she managed to sleep and was surprised by the time in the morning when she finally awoke, desperate again for the lavatory.

She was also desperate for a shower, despite her head still feeling very tender, and hoped there was still plenty of hot water. Fortunately, it was scalding and soon the whole washroom was full of steam, or water vapour as she knew it was correctly called.

Wet and pink, the cold tiled floor was almost welcome as she walked towards the basins, wrapping a towel around her, although there was nobody to see. The wall mirrors dripped with condensation highlighting a finger-drawing of a lily.

She took a breath. Had someone watched her shower? Was it Rainer? Her headmistress? The German doctor? And then it dawned on her. One of the girls before half term must have drawn it with a soapy finger. She smiled and squeezed toothpaste onto her brush. After a thorough workout around her mouth, she spat for a final time, looked up and used her hand to wipe away the flower.

In the blurred reflection, was the image of someone standing behind her. She spun on her bare soles to face whoever it was. Embarrassed, she realised it was her own dressing gown hanging on a hook. Heart pounding, she slipped it on and removed the towel. Perhaps the bang on the head had done more than she realised. She looked in the mirror again and this time she saw a girl standing in the corner. She whirled round. The girl was an inverted floor mop in a metal bucket with its long strands resembling hair.

What was going on? She needed to get a grip. So far, her wheeze to stay on at half term to see Rainer for illicit lovemaking had cost her a bang on the head, a suspicious headmistress, and the feeling that she was being watched at every turn. Fortunately, the walk back to her bedroom helped her recover some of her equilibrium and she felt a little confidence returning.

Later that day, she was staring out of her window across the lush sward towards the edge of the cliff and the vast expanse of the North Sea when the first cars arrived carrying staff and pupils. Banging doors, excited chatter, screams of laughter, and general commotion rapidly returned. It was a relief when Lily was able to be alone in her room after lights out.

Sleep came and she dreamed that she was a child again, with her mother and brother. They were skiing, the air was biting, and she shivered. White mountains turned grey, and she was back in her dormitory room, alone and cold for the covers had fallen on the floor. She pulled them back over her and tried to return to the dream where her mother's face and voice had been so vivid. She was ten when she went skiing for the first and only time and although she loved the beauty of the mountains and the prettiness of the Austrian Tyrol, skiing was not a sport she would ever enjoy. Of course, her brother was sensational.

In 1958, skiing holidays were very much for the privileged few with a pioneering spirit. Her parents had been going for several years when they decided to take Lily and her brother. They had driven to Dover and caught a ferry to Ostend where they left their car. Skiing involved packing many warm clothes, so their suitcases were large and very heavy. Lily and her brother did their best to help but they saw how much effort it took their parents to carry the cases between where the taxi dropped them and the train.

Her father had booked a private compartment in a sleeper. A corridor ran the length of the carriage with compartments to one side, each with a sliding door and blinds over the interior windows for privacy.

It was very exciting looking out of the carriage window as they passed through many towns and cities in Belgium. She remembered feeling nervous when two men in uniform slid open the compartment door and asked her father for their passports. She and David did not have their own; their names had been added to their parents'. It surprised her how long the inspector took examining the passports before handing them back with a *Vielen Dank.*

'Were they the Gestapo?' her brother had asked once the compartment door had slid shut.

'I doubt it,' their father had replied. 'Most of them fled to South America at the end of the war, but they were old enough to have fought.'

At night, the train guard came into their cabin and opened up the bunkbeds. Lily was too excited to sleep and loved seeing the snow-covered stations as the train trundled through West Germany. She remembered they had wonderful names such as Erlingshofen, Sielenbach, and Rosenhein. When they arrived in the Austrian city of Wörgl, the train waited for a while and Lily finally fell asleep, to be vigorously woken by her parents.

'Wake up,' her father said. 'Hurry. We have to get off.' Her parents hastily packed the small bags that were Lily and her brother's responsibility. Struggling with the heavy suitcases, they carried them with difficulty down the train's corridor to a door at the end. Her father opened it, and Lily felt an icy blast. 'Lily, David, jump down onto the platform.' Lily went first and landed in deep, soft snow that went up to her armpits. David followed. She noticed that they seemed to be the only people getting off the train in the middle of the night and that it wasn't even a station. They were standing between tracks. Her father swung one of the large suitcases into the snow and was reaching for the second when Lily heard shouting. She watched her father jump off the train and grab the suitcase he'd just thrown out. 'Get back on,' he yelled. The snow was so deep and fluffy it was difficult for Lily and David to move quickly. A guard stepped down, grabbed David, lifted him up and put him in the carriage. The train began to move as her father placed the heavy suitcase back through the open door, which her mother dragged in. The train was gaining speed as the guard lifted Lily up and placed her back in the carriage. She marvelled at his strength. He hauled himself in and helped her father who was hanging on to the handrail. When everyone was safely aboard, the door was slammed shut, and Lily heard her mother mutter unusual words under her breath.

'The train was not due to stop there,' said Lily's breathless father. 'The next station is ours.' Both her parents looked stressed, but David seemed to have thoroughly enjoyed the little excursion.

It was still dark when they arrived in Kitzbühel railway station, and bitingly cold. Lily was a bit nervous getting off the train in case it was the wrong stop, but her father assured her that Kitzbühel was their holiday destination. A taxi, with metal chains wrapped around its tyres, took them to a chalet-style hotel in the centre of the pretty town. Lily and her twin were to share one room, and her parents another. They were all hungry, and agreed it was best to have breakfast first and then a sleep. They would sort out boot and ski hire later.

Breakfast was strange but tasty. Lily remembered liking the white rolls and the apricot jam. She and David begged their parents to arrange ski hire immediately, and get on the slopes, but were ordered to go back to their room and rest.

It was gone eleven when their mother woke them up. Lily and David got dressed in their new ski clothes which included thermal underwear, two pairs of socks, ski pants, and a bright pink anorak for Lily and a bright blue and white anorak for David. They each had a pair of leather mittens, sturdy shoes, and a woolly pompom hat.

When they stepped out of the hotel, it was snowing and Kitzbühel's main street looked enchanting. Their first port of call was ski hire and fitting ski boots. It took quite a while to sort out the footwear. Lily's boots felt very uncomfortable, but the man in the shop assured her father, in German, that she would get used to them.

Next came selecting wooden skis and ski poles. Lily was told to stretch her arm above her head as that would be the right length of skis for her. Unfortunately, owing to high demand over the Christmas holiday, they could only hire skis without safety bindings, although they would be able to swap them in a couple of days.

Laden with skis and ski poles, they set off for the tourist office where her father purchased tickets for the ski lifts. They were supplied on elasticated string and attached to the zip fasteners on their anoraks. Each time they were to go on a lift, a hole would be punched in the ticket until it was all used up. Tickets for ski school were also purchased. It was too late to attend ski school that day, but they were told to arrive at the nursery slopes by 9.30 the following morning so that Lily and David could be assigned to a class. By now it was early afternoon, and the winter sun was already dipping towards the mountain peaks.

'Let's treat ourselves to an Austrian tea,' their father said. Burdened by skis and boots, the family of four trudged in the icy snow past shops selling the latest fashions, perfumes, watches, and jewellery, with prices marked in Austrian schillings. They parked their skis and poles in a special rack for the purpose and entered Café Praxmair carrying their boots. Lily was immediately entranced by the atmosphere. They were led to a wooden table by a young blonde woman wearing a traditional Tyrolean white blouse, embroidered bodice, full skirt, and white cotton and lace embroidered apron. The effect seemed to mesmerise her father, and Lily could understand why.

Café Praxmair was full of many wonders including apfelsaft, a deliciously fizzy apple drink; and apfelstrudel, an apple pastry sprinkled with powdered sugar and served with whipped cream. The contrast of the tart apple with light, fluffy pastry was truly tasty.

'Thank you, daddy,' Lily said. 'This is the best holiday, ever.'

'Tomorrow, can we go up the Hahnenkamm?' her brother asked their father who was tackling an enormous slice of Black Forest gateau. He smiled. 'By the end of the holiday, you'll be a downhill racer but, tomorrow, you two will be on the nursery slopes until you get your ski legs.'

'How high is the Hahnenkamm?' David asked.

'It's over five and a half thousand feet above sea

level,' their father replied.

David was not satisfied with that answer. 'But how high is it above Kitzbühel?'

'That is a good question,' their father said. 'Let's do the arithmetic. If the peak of the mountain is five and a half thousand feet above sea level and Kitzbühel is two and a half thousand feet above sea level, how high is the mountain above Praxmair's?'

'Do you mean above the roof, or the floor?' Lily chimed in.

Her parents laughed. 'Approximately,' her father said.

'The peak is three thousand feet above us,' Lily quickly worked out.

'Correct,' replied her father.

'That is so annoying,' David whined. 'I was just doing the subtraction.'

'In your head?' Lily's mother asked. 'Perhaps you would explain it to me. I'm not sure how to do it.'

'Imagine, mum,' David said, all enthused. 'Imagine five thousand, five hundred written above two thousand five hundred. Start from right and go left. Zero from zero is zero. Zero from zero is zero. Five from five is zero. Two from five is three plus the three zeros and it's three thousand. Simple'

'Bravo,' said their mother. 'Thank you for explaining it so well.'

'It's good to know my taxed income has gone to good use,' their father said, and their mother chuckled, leaving the children puzzled.

A group of men appeared in traditional Austrian dress with leather shorts, Lily discovered were called lederhosen; and white shirts with sleeves rolled up, knee-high woollen socks, and felt hats with a feather.

They had an assortment of music-making tools including a piano accordion, cow bells in many sizes, a large two-person saw, and a pine tree trunk.

The piano accordion's bellows were expanded and contracted creating the most wonderful chord that caught everyone's attention. Within seconds the café was filled with intoxicating sounds of sawing wood, ringing cowbells, and the voices of men singing and yodelling. Lily didn't know the language at all, but she was desperate to join in.

Praxmair's instantly became her most favourite place in the world, full of laughter, music, cakes and cigarette smoke.

The following morning, she and David carried their skis to the slopes where their parents sorted out a beginners' class. Putting on the skis required the bindings to be adjusted, which their father did for them.

'Remember,' he said when they were ready. 'These skis do not have a snap release, so be careful.'

Lily and her brother joined a line of tiny children at least half their age and were listening to the instructor who was speaking German, when their father tapped her on the shoulder and explained that she and her brother were not starting in the advanced class. The beginners were a rag tag group of adults, in brightly coloured anoraks, who looked as nervous as they did uncomfortable. The instructor for the novices spoke in broken English, much to Lily's relief, and spent the first hour of the class teaching them how to sidestep up a gentle slope and snowplough down. It was hard work but quite enjoyable, especially when one of the grown-ups caught an outside edge and tumbled head-over-skis and couldn't get up. One time, Lily laughed so much she lost her balance and fell over onto almost flat snow. Still giggling, she tried to get up but needed the instructor and her brother to help her.

'It is einfach to get up on hill,' the instructor said. 'Gravity does good *verk*.'

She liked the closeness of the lean Austrian, who had lifted her with ease; an emotion she didn't understand at age ten. He wore the ski instructors' traditional red sweater and anorak, clear to see against snow, and grey ski pants. He had sparkling blue eyes, dark brown hair, but a voice, to her ears, a little like a robot.

'What is your name?' she asked.

'Torger. And you kleiner engel?'

'Lilian,' she said, perplexed by her own embarrassment. 'Lily.'

She soon discovered that Torger was right; it was much easier to get up after a fall on a slope, although gravity often caused her skis to carry on sliding and she would fall all over again, once crashing into Torger.

'Stop below me, mädchen. Always better,' he said, still holding onto her until he was sure she was not going to fall again.

The first lift Torger led them to, was not an easy climb for any of the beginners who slipped and fell as they tried to manoeuvre up the short slope to the entrance of the concrete and wood construction. Lily followed David as each had their ski pass clipped by an attendant; tiny triangles of coloured card adding to the mound by his boots. The noise from the engine that powered a large wheel above their heads, was surprisingly loud and a little scary, but she supposed it was all part of the joy of skiing.

Finally, it was Lily's turn. She shuffled over rubber mats, placing her skis within the parallel ruts in the snow beside a tall ski instructor who had pushed ahead of her. The lift operator waited for the next swinging wooden T-bar to go around the wheel and pulled it down from the cable above. He placed the central bar between Lily and her fellow traveller, the curved ends below the man's backside. For Lily, it meant that the T-bar instead of being at the top of her legs was halfway up her back, held in place by her armpit. Next time, she vowed, she would only share a T-bar with someone her size. There was one advantage, however, to being dragged up the mountain with an experienced skier; every time her skis veered away from the snow tracks, the strong man would grab hold of her until her skis landed back on the snow, parallel again.

At the top of the lift, the slope was really steep. The T-bar dug into her back as it took almost her entire weight. They reached the crest of the hillock and to her horror, she realised she was about to go way too fast downhill to level ground where her classmates were waiting. If she fell, people on the draglift behind would crash into her.

Her drag-lift partner pulled the wooden T-bar away, making sure that the inertia reel took it safely up to the cable above, before skiing down to his class. She tried to emulate his easy skill and nearly fell before snowploughing to a halt by her classmates of fearful-looking adults.

'Follow me, tally ho,' called their instructor as he skied off. Lily decided that the best way to learn was to screw up her courage and get on with it. David seemed to have developed the knack of turning and stopping fairly easily, but she found snowplough turns very awkward. After a couple of runs, her confidence grew together with her skill, both on the T-bar and sliding downhill.

Near the end of the morning class, snow was falling heavily, making it much harder for her to turn and stop. It was quite easy to look good on flattened piste; but trying to turn where the snow was deep or had been pushed into a mound by many skiers was decidedly tricky.

There was one more run before she and David were to meet their parents for lunch, and she was determined to ski with elan. Snow was coming down thick and heavy and she was scared of losing touch with her class. All thought of skiing with elan went out of her mind - she just wanted to get to the bottom, take off her skis and have a hot chocolate with lots of squirty cream.

And then she fell. She heard her shin bone crack before shooting shards of pain overwhelmed her senses. The agony was so sharp, so intense, it took a few seconds before she could scream. Terror flooded her mind as hot blades of pain stabbed through to her core, overwhelming all conscious thought.

Through her misty goggles and blurred eyes, she saw David waving his arms frantically, bellowing for help.

It took an age before the blood wagon arrived, as her mother had described the metal sleigh that was controlled by two skiers. Her leg was put in a temporary splint, and she was lifted into the sleigh. They wrapped her in a blanket, strapped her in tightly, and covered her with a waterproof sheet that clipped to the sides.

The pain in her leg was so bad, the speed the skiers travelled didn't bother her at all. She was eventually lifted from the sleigh, crying with pain and fear, and taken in an ambulance to a nunnery, or that's what it seemed to her. The nurses were Roman Catholic nuns and not very friendly, probably because she cried and screamed so much. Fortunately, they had enough compassion to give her a painkiller before taking an X-ray of her broken leg. Somewhile later, a doctor came and after looking at the processed x-ray on a wall-mounted light box, without saying a word, pulled her leg. The pain shot up to another level and Lily wondered whether she had reached maximum. No pleading, no tears had any effect on the doctor who seemed to resent her presence.

Finally, the medication did its job, and the pain subsided. Her leg was carefully bandaged and wet Plaster of Paris, applied. It took a while for the young nun in a full-length habit and apron to apply the plaster but when she had finished, Lily received her first smile of encouragement.

It was dark by the time her worried parents arrived with David to visit her. For the next few days her mother stayed by her bed, and they played card games and chess to while away the time. But the nights were long and very lonely, and the nuns were always scary.

Once she was out of hospital and had learned to use crutches, she and her mother spent the days telling each other stories, reading whatever they could find in English, and spending teatime in Café Praxmair. She loved the drinks and cakes but most of all she loved the Tyrolian folk songs, and the schuhplattler dancing when men in lederhosen would slap their shoes, thighs, and sometimes each other's bottoms, much to

Lily's amusement.

At the end of the fortnight's holiday, she was more than ready to go home. Her plaster cast made moving around very difficult and washing properly was almost impossible. Back in England, the plaster cast was removed in the local cottage hospital and her leg x-rayed again.

'Good job,' said the doctor. 'Those krauts knew what they were doing.'

Lily mentioned that they were Austrians, not krauts, but the difference seemed to be lost on the doctor.

By Spring, her leg was fully healed although at times, when she least expected it, a stabbing pain would shoot up her shin.

Since her mother's death she yearned for those happy times when they were a whole family. She missed her mother, terribly, and would never forget how much she cared for Lily especially during those long days in Kitzbühel.

Half asleep, Lily got off her bed in her dormitory room to retrieve the flannel sheet and blankets that had fallen on the floor and felt an unwelcome desire. *Damn.* She'd have to brave the corridor. She reached for her dressing gown hanging on the back of the door and put it on. As she tied the cord, she heard strange soulful singing. Her brain still fogged, she opened the door and looked out into the corridor but couldn't tell where the singing was coming from. It seemed almost more in her head than via her ears.

The bell in the clocktower struck two and all went quiet, even the girl standing at the far end of the dimly-lit corridor was mute. Lily had no idea who she was, but there were plenty of girls in the school she didn't know. As a prefect, it was Lily's job to look out for younger girls and so she padded down the corridor towards her, wondering why the girl was still dressed in school uniform, and not pyjamas.

'You'd better get to bed before anyone, less benevolent, sees you.'

Up close, Lily could see that the girl's long dark hair framed a face, pale as alabaster; her full, sultry lips were cherry red, and her sunken eyes, luminescent green. She was small, skinny, possibly fourteen, and standing stock still.

'What is your name?'

The girl didn't respond. She turned and Lily followed her down the corridor to the washroom until she merged into the shadows.

Puzzled by the girl's silence, Lily pushed open the door and was surprised to see that the lights were off. She flicked a switch and neon tubes flickered into life. Where was the girl? Very odd. She entered a cubicle and braced her cheeks for the cold seat.

This is the secret diary of Robert Oakes
DO NOT READ UNTIL 2065

Today, we started rehearsing. A boy called Hart is playing Cyrano and he is very good. He doesn't like me, as a person, but when I become Roxane, he changes towards me. I'm a good actor. As Robert, I stutter, but when I am Roxane, it's like she's taken over my mind and body. I am her. I love her. She is beautiful and clever and sweet. The play has five acts, and Roxane is in four of them. I love her so much. I want to be her forever.

Mr C fired a starting pistol during rehearsal for a

battle scene, and it gave me such a shock that my knees buckled under me. He was cross that I'd over reacted, but I could tell that he regretted his words. At lunchtime, he said that he was giving us the afternoon off to learn lines and to rest. I didn't know what to do. Roxane knows all her lines. She is confident in a way that I will never be. As I was walking back to the bike shed, Mr C called out to me from his car and invited me to go home with him for tea. He drives an MG 1100, the same as my mother does, so it's nice to get into a familiar car. I like Mr C because he says kind things.

We drove to a house on the outskirts of Hawksmead. It's a nice place, smaller than my home but very cosy. It's nice to be in a homely environment after being so cold but, in a way, it made me yearn for home even more. He made a pot of tea and also put out biscuits and a jam sponge cake. He's not married and looks young. We had a good conversation about the play and how it was coming along. I am impressed by his plans for the set and am so excited to be part of something so big and so special. I sat on the sofa, and Mr C put the tray with the tea things down on the coffee table. I didn't stutter once. Not once. He made me feel so comfortable and he really does like my Roxane. He kept talking about her. It may be hard for you to believe, but people see me differently now. When they look at me, I think they see Roxane – I don't mind why people are nice. I just want them to be nice.

There is talk of two older boys who are missing. They were canoeing on the River Hawk. The heavy autumnal rain has swollen the river, and they can't be found. Mini said that the river swept the boys down to the humpback bridge where a man saw them trying to grip the slippery stones. Mini said that neither boy was wearing a life jacket as it was too difficult to use the paddles with one on.

CHAPTER NINE

Malcolm Cadwallader, the youngest member of teaching staff at Hawksmead College, volunteered to be the one to break the sad news. He owed it to the young man, and the young woman. Mr Gibbs, the school's headmaster, had been totally inadequate at Monday morning assembly when he announced the death of two pupils who were in their final year. He had followed his crass announcement with a clap of his frostbitten hands, from his time as a mountaineer in Nepal, and declared it was to be Monday as usual. Apart from many of the boys' peers being in shock, Malcolm knew that David Turnbull's mother was dead from cancer and his father far away working for the Foreign Office in Moscow. That left his twin sibling to face the shock and grief, alone.

The morning was glorious as Malcolm gunned the responsive MG 1100 and, despite his dark mission, the silvery green moorland hues lifted his spirits. In the far distance he could see the Ridgeway and promised himself that he would walk it one day.

The size of the vast moor and the condition of the terrible road always surprised him, so it took longer than he had envisaged to arrive at the end of the long drive that led to Inniscliffe School for Girls. He glanced at the faded sign and pressed the accelerator, changing from second to third gear as he raced along the narrow, forested lane. When he reached the turning circle in front of the main entrance, he headed for the car park.

He had not shut the driver's door before his presence was challenged.

'Do you have an appointment?' The question was fired at him by Colonel Craig, standing with a long-handled shovel and wearing heavy, worsted, outdoor working clothes.

'My reason for being here is of a very serious nature and not suitable for conveying via telephone.'

Craig sniffed hard. 'Follow me.' He leant his shovel none too gently against the side of the MG and marched off.

Malcolm did as he was commanded and followed Colonel Craig into the school and down lengthy corridors to the Head's study. The retired army officer rapped on the wooden door and immediately opened it.

'Miss Cooper. The man from the other school is back. It appears to be serious.'

Malcolm almost saluted Colonel Craig and entered the spacious study, far bigger than the staff room in Hawksmead College, and a lot less smoky. He looked at the young woman, dwarfed by her vast desk.

'Good morning, Mr Cadwallader. How may I help you?'

'I am…' Malcolm hesitated and half-turned to the military man, ready for action, standing a pace or two behind him.

Sylvia smiled. 'Thank you, Colonel Craig.' He gave a

brief nod and gently closed the door.

'Please take a seat.' Sylvia gestured to the old oak and leather chair in front of her desk. She could only be a few years older than Malcolm and yet, despite meeting her for the second time, he felt his stomach tighten, as if he were a petrified pupil.

'Miss Cooper, I am the bearer of very bad news.' He took a few seconds to sit down. 'On the weekend, David Turnbull, and one other boy, drowned in a canoeing accident on the River Hawk.'

'David Turnbull? Lily's brother?'

'Regrettably.'

Malcolm saw the woman's face blanch. When she found her voice, it was thin, strained. 'What should I do?'

'Would you like me to tell her? It may help coming from a stranger.' He watched Miss Cooper shift in her chair. 'I can answer her questions,' he continued, 'although I know little of the circumstances.'

Lily was sitting in the quad thinking about Rainer and contemplating whether it was worth the risk trying to be with him again when she saw Colonel Craig striding towards her. What did the old man want, apart from a fumble behind the gym?

'Miss Turnbull, Miss Cooper requests your attendance in her study.'

Lily felt her heart sink and swallowed hard. 'Do you know why? I was just about to er... um...'

'Follow me,' he ordered.

'It's okay, Colonel, I do know the way.'

The colonel's boots echoed as he marched ahead of her down the long, tiled corridor towards the main entrance hall.

'How many people did you kill in the war, Colonel?' she asked his back.

'War is a horrible thing. Pray we never see its like again.'

'Did you shoot many Germans? Young men like Rainer?'

'It's not a cowboy shoot-out.' He knocked on the Head's door and swung it open.

Lily hesitated before entering and was surprised to see a young man standing by the marble mantelpiece.

'Thank you, Colonel,' Miss Cooper said. 'Kindly close the door.'

Lily noticed the Colonel's reluctance to leave. Clearly, this was something big.

'Lily, I would like to introduce you to Mr Cadwallader. He's a master at your brother's school.'

She looked at the tall man, and if she hadn't been in love with Rainer, he would certainly have piqued her interest. His clothes were fuddy-duddy, but there was something about his hair, his eyes, his slim athletic physique that appealed to her awakened senses.

He gestured to the chair in front of Miss Cooper's desk. 'Miss Turnbull, Lily, please sit down'

She ignored his invitation and waited.

He cleared his throat. 'It is, um...' He cleared his throat again, then his words came out in a rush. 'It is with great regret I must inform you of the death of your brother, David.'

Her knees buckled and she would have fallen if the young man had not reached out and guided her to the chair. A glass of water found its way into her hand, and she took a sip without thinking. She wanted to form a question but the pressure within her chest made her gasp for breath.

'You'll have many questions, Miss Turnbull,' he continued, 'and I will seek answers for you over the coming days. It is a terrible shock and a great tragedy.'

Eyes blurred by tears, she looked at the young schoolmaster. 'How? How could it happen?'

'As you know, Hawksmead College is a school renowned for its outward-bound activities. Your brother and another boy were canoeing on the River Hawk. The strength of the flow was underestimated and neither boy was wearing a life preserver. We don't know what happened, but their canoes capsized, and the river took them. The police are investigating.'

'I want to see him.'

There was no response.

'Will you take me to my brother?' She read enough in the schoolmaster's eyes to know the truth. 'Where is he?'

Mr Cadwallader swallowed. 'They are still searching. I'll let you know as soon as I have news.'

Silence. 'I must call my father.' She thought about her one and only parent now in Moscow. 'Would you tell him?' she asked her headmistress, who shuffled in her chair. 'I don't think I can.' Tears came as her whole being was consumed by grief. How could her brother be dead? He was strong, athletic, a good swimmer.

It took at least a couple of minutes before the first wave of grief subsided. She looked up at the young man's concerned face. 'I want to help with the search.'

'I don't think that's a good idea,' Mr Cadwallader immediately responded.

'Please. I want to know everything. I have to know.'

'If your headmistress agrees, I can drive you to the humpback bridge where David was last seen.'

'Thank you.' It came out in little more than a

whisper.

The road was quite bumpy, but it didn't bother Lily. Her eyes were looking out at the vast expanse of Hawksmoor not registering the crisscross of drystone walls, clumps of wind-battered trees, or the jagged ridge that looked as sharp as a circular saw.

They drove in silence, past a pub with a weird name she didn't quite catch and headed down a long hill, swerving around potholes in the worn tarmac. A sign indicated they were approaching a school.

'I'll take you up to the college first so that you can get a feel for the moorland landscape and the river.' They turned into what looked like a country lane and headed up a narrow winding road, lined with ditches, hedgerows, and trees mostly shorn of leaves, not that Lily was paying any attention.

They arrived at a large, gravelled apron in front of a forbidding, Victorian structure. She gasped. 'I had no idea this is where daddy sent my brother. It looks like an asylum.'

Mr Cadwallader pulled the car to a gentle halt. 'It was built over a hundred years ago to house the homeless. That sounds benign. It was a workhouse, in many ways a slave camp. Men, women and children were sent here for the crime of being penniless. In return for a roof and what passed for food, they worked the land, and died from malnutrition, disease, and the cold. Cruel times.'

'Is it any less cruel, today, Mr Cadwallader?'

The kindly man turned to Lily. 'There will be an inquiry into what happened.' He waited a moment, then accelerated away.

Malcolm knew he was ill-equipped to offer the

pretty young girl sitting next to him any form of counselling. He drove with care towards the stone bridge over the River Hawk, the northern gateway to Hawksmead, a once thriving community built in the late eighteenth century to serve its textile mill; and now a tired, oversized village of rundown houses for the millworkers. He slowed as they approached the narrow, humpback bridge and parked where there was pedestrian access to the river via a tow path. They both got out and for a moment stood in awe at the roar of water rushing through the stone arches, the river too high and too ferocious for a boat to pass under.

Malcolm decided that Lily deserved the truth, unalloyed. 'Your brother didn't have a chance. He was seen trying to get a grip of the stone buttress, but the force of water was too great. I am so sorry.'

'And the other boy?'

'He was seen clinging to a tree, but he was taken, too. He was swept into the channel that leads to the mill's waterwheel where his body was recovered.'

She nodded. 'Thank you for telling me. I doubt I will ever know a time when I am not thinking about the terror my brother faced.' She turned to him. 'Do you believe in God?'

Malcolm was taken aback by the question and didn't know how to answer. 'Yes. I do. At least, I want to.'

'I don't.' She looked at the bridge and they both stared at the merciless torrent.

'Hello sir.'

Malcolm looked round at a young boy on his bike who was cycling with a friend up to the school.

'Hello Oakes. How is Roxane coming along?' Malcolm turned to Lily. 'Young Oakes is to play Roxane in Cyrano de Bergerac.' He turned back to the boy. 'I'll see you at rehearsal after school.'

'Yes sir.' They watched the two pupils, wearing corduroy shorts and heavy sweaters, cycle over the humpback bridge.

'He's a talented actor,' Malcolm said, almost wittering on to fill the awkward void. 'Stutters like a machinegun in class but when on stage, something magical happens and he's rather good.' He smiled, but could tell she wasn't listening.

After a few moments she said, 'I hope I never see this place again.'

Lily barely noticed the drive back to Inniscliffe. She was still in shock and knew a tsunami of grief was building. Her family home, just off King's Road in Chelsea, had been let, with photo albums and personal possessions boxed-up in a mews garage her father rented near The Boltons. She had nothing of her brother's apart from a photo of the twins taken with their mother on holiday in Alderney, a couple of years before their mother died. Four years on, two out of the family of four were gone forever. She couldn't cry. All she wanted was to be enveloped in Rainer's arms and be transported to a place far, far away.

It was getting dark when the nice schoolmaster dropped her off by a rear entrance to the school. He insisted on writing down a telephone number where he could be reached. 'Just in case,' he said.

'Thank you. I know it wasn't easy being with me.' She watched him drive away and was sure he was looking at her in his rearview mirror.

'Good. He's gone.'

Startled, she stared up into Colonel Craig's craggy face. 'You could learn a lot from him,' she said, and marched off, knowing he was staring at her, probably boiling with rage and sexual desire.

She hurried down a corridor, took the stairs at the end two at a time and rushed back to her bedroom.

The door was ajar. She had made a point of closing it.

Taking care to make no noise she pushed it wide open. A hinge squeaked. She switched on the centre light. The room was empty. She peered behind the door and bent down to look under her bed. To the left of the window was an old oak wardrobe. Perhaps someone was hiding in there?

'Lily,' Rainer said, from behind her.

She turned and wrapped her arms around his neck. 'I've missed you.'

'Sylvia told me. I am so sorry. What can I do?'

'I love you, Rainer. You're all I have.'

'Sylvia and I will take care of you.'

'Take me away. Far away.' She felt his resistance and pulled back to look into his eyes.

'I am married,' he said as he prised himself free of her arms. 'This school is my life. I have nothing to offer.'

'We can get jobs. Make our own way.'

'I cannot do that. For the sake of the school's reputation, we must end it.'

A knock.

Lily jumped.

Miss Cooper entered through the open doorway. 'The colonel told me you were back.' Her tone was gentle.

Lily looked from Sylvia to Rainer and back to Sylvia.

'What about my father?' she managed to ask. 'Did you speak to him?'

'Yes. He is going to write.'

'Write?' Lily was truly shocked.

'Please excuse me.' Rainer stepped towards the door. 'You have our sincere condolences. Miss Cooper and I...'

Sylvia interrupted. 'Don't you have German papers to mark?'

'Ja.' He left the room without saying another word.

'My father's going to write?' Lily asked, angrily.

Sylvia approached her. 'Until they...' She hesitated. 'Until they find your brother, your father will remain in Moscow. He sees no point in returning and has asked me to act in loco parentis.'

Now it hit her. The grief came from deep within and her whole being convulsed. She fell to her knees and cried for her mother, her twin brother, and for herself. Her father could offer no comfort. Her friends were scattered, and the love of her life had left her. She had nothing. No one. She wanted to die.

It was late the following morning when Lily was able to open her eyes. She was in bed still dressed in the clothes she was wearing the day before. The last twenty-four hours seemed like a dream, a nightmare. Was her brother really gone? Would she never see him ever again?

Pressure from her full bladder made her get out of bed and hurry down the corridor to the washroom. She pushed past girls rushing back and forth between lessons and only just made it. After pulling the chain she decided to have a shower despite not having brought her towel.

Hot water cascading over swollen eyelids felt good and she was almost content as she dabbed herself dry with a muddy towel she'd found balled-up under a bench.

She turned to the mirrors above the washbasins and saw they were all steamed up, with the name *Eva*, written by a finger, clearly visible on each one. Interesting name; definitely not typically English. Someone was having fun.

Almost naked, carrying her bundle of clothes, she ran along the corridor to her room, hoping she would not run into Colonel Craig.

But the person she saw standing by the window, filled her with even greater dread.

'I've been waiting for you,' Dr Bircher said. 'My sincere condolences.'

'Thank you.' Lily tried her best to make sure she was fully covered at the front. 'Please wait outside until I'm dressed.'

'I am here to examine you,' came the guttural response. 'Close the door and lie on the bed.'

Lily looked at the stout doctor, carrying her black medical bag, and knew this was a battle she couldn't win. 'I'll just put on some things.'

'No. Lie on the bed. Full examination.'

'I'm sure Miss Cooper did not suggest a full examination.'

'You are under my care. I decide.'

Reluctantly, Lily closed the door and lay on the bed, using a worn blouse to partly cover herself.

Dr Bircher placed her bag on the floor and opened it. She took out a clear glass bottle and unscrewed the cap.

Lily could smell alcohol. 'Why do you need surgical spirit?'

'To sterilise my hands.' She poured the liquid into one palm, placed the open bottle on Lily's bedside table and rubbed her hands together. She bent down and removed a metal tube from her bag, unscrewed the top, and squeezed cream into her palm. She placed the tube next to the bottle on the table. 'Lie back. Open legs.'

'What?'

'Are you a virgin? Have you had intercourse?'

Lily bit her lip. 'No, I mean, I'm not a virgin. I've had intercourse.'

'And the other party is…?'

Lily swallowed. 'Rainer.'

Dr Bircher smiled. It was cold, ruthless. 'That is what I will report to your headmistress.'

She felt sick.

'What precautions did you take?' the doctor asked.

'We were careful.'

Dr Bircher waved her hand, dismissively. 'Get dressed and pack.'

'Please don't tell her.'

'Too late for that, meine kleine Schlampe.'

Lily watched the doctor rub the cream into her hands and replace the items in her bag. 'Were you really going to give me an examination?'

'What do you think?'

'Why are you doing this?'

Dr Bircher looked intently at Lily. 'Colonel Craig has had his eye on you for some time. He knows what the German boy has been up to. You have put the school's reputation and financial future at risk. Were you to become pregnant, the scandal could close the school and Colonel Craig, and the rest of the staff would lose their jobs. Your brother's death, though tragic, offers an honourable smoke screen for your early departure.'

Lily had one last throw of the dice. 'Who is Eva?' The immediate change in Dr Bircher's composure surprised her.

'Why do you want to know?' Her tone was aggressive, but also seemed laced with genuine fear.

'Tell me about her.'

Dr Bircher closed the bag. 'She attended here many years ago.'

'And...?'

'And nothing.'

Lily got off the bed and reached for her dressing gown. 'Fine, I'll ask Miss Cooper about her.'

Dr Bircher sniffed hard. 'Eva attended here long before Miss Cooper took over as headmistress, although they were pupils together. She won't remember her. Eva was younger.'

'Then there must be another Eva in the school.'

'There isn't. I would know.' Her eyes were hard as flint. 'You crossed the line, Lily. As with loss of virginity, there is no going back.' She opened the door. 'You have my sympathy.' Lily listened to the clump of her shoes as the doctor strode down the corridor.

She had no idea what to do. Her father had just heard that his only beloved son had drowned and now he was to learn that his little princess was a harlot. Her mother's cancer had broken his heart. No wonder he didn't want to leave Moscow and face reality. All the time he stayed in the Soviet Union he could pretend that everything was fine and dandy in England.

Where could she go? Who would have her? Who would want a meine kleine Schlampe? She looked at her dog-eared copy of *The Prime of Miss Jean Brodie* sitting on her bedside table and picked it up. The cover was an illustration of a weird tree, a white silhouette of a woman, and six girls sitting on the ground, listening. There was a time when she imagined attending Marcia Blaine School for Girls and sleeping with the dishy art master. She had seen it as exciting and life-affirming. Not anymore. Now she saw Jean Brodie as just another woman who tried to disguise her own failings by manipulating others.

She hurried over to her window, opened it, felt an icy blast and threw the paperback as hard as she possibly could, not looking to see where it landed.

'Lily.'

She had been so lost in her own misery she hadn't heard the clip-clop of Miss Cooper's heels.

'I came to see how you are.'

'Don't worry. I won't make a fuss.'

'About what?'

'About the truth Dr Mengele extracted from me.'

'Mengele? You mean Dr Bircher?'

'Has she spoken to you?'

'Yes.' Sylvia closed the door. 'I intend to terminate her contract with the school.'

'When?'

'After Christmas. I would appreciate it if you would keep the information to yourself.'

Lily thought for a moment. 'And me? When do I get my marching orders?'

'You are family. This is your home, until your father comes to collect you after your final exams.'

'I thought you hated me,' Lily said, her voice soft. 'It was you who locked me in the cellar, wasn't it?'

Sylvia sighed and looked away. 'Rainer is a handsome young man who needed a safe place to live, far from prying communist eyes. Marriage helped speed along his application to stay. We care for each other, but I have had to accept that our relationship is unbalanced; that he's not Romeo to my Juliet.' She turned to face Lily. 'I was hurt. Rainer has had his flings, but I could tell that his affection for you was different to how he felt about me, and I was jealous. I am sorry and will do all that I can to make it up to you.'

'What happens now?' Lily asked.

'We go on, I as headmistress and you as a school prefect, a pupil, nothing more.'

Lily nodded. 'I understand.'

Sylvia smiled. 'Get dressed. You must be hungry. Come to my private kitchen and have something to eat.'

CHAPTER TEN

Malcolm was concerned. Although the school play was not directly affected by the loss of the two boys in the river, they were in the same school year as his Cyrano and Christian. Fortunately, his Roxane seemed unaffected and was clearly going to be the star of the show. The boy's costume was coming along well, thanks to Bridget West, a dab hand with her Singer sewing machine, and the mother of a day boy who was playing Roxane's duenna. But he was worried about David Turnbull's twin sister. He feared that the grief she was enduring with her father so far away could have unforeseeable consequences. In truth, he liked her, not as a schoolmaster, but as a young man liking a young woman, who was clearly more mature than her years. He formulated a plan to see her again then abandoned it, ashamed of his desire. She was a schoolgirl, vulnerable and probably scared for her future. He sighed. His love-life was going nowhere. Almost without exception, the staff at Hawksmead College was male apart from a few dowagers in the kitchen, and not even a desperate pupil would fantasise about any of them.

Word came from the police about Turnbull's body,

which suited his headmaster who was keen for the school to get back to normal as soon as possible. An idea sprang to Malcolm's mind which he decided to act upon before the voice of conscience interfered. He jumped into his MG and drove a bit too fast over the humpback bridge at the north end of Hawksmead and turned into the short drive that led to the college's offsite boarding house. He spoke to the house matron who, in truth, was quite attractive, and with her help, recruited two senior boys who were sent up to the attic to retrieve David Turnbull's empty trunk. He and matron packed Turnbull's clean clothes; his muddy rugby kit was set aside for washing and would go in the spares box. Malcolm gathered up personal items from the boy's bedside locker which included framed photos of his family. He felt vindicated, as such personal items most certainly needed to be delivered to the boy's twin sister.

'What about the other boy?' Malcolm asked. 'Should we pack his things, too?'

'His parents have requested that nothing is returned.' The house matron blinked back tears. 'It is tragic. I have known these boys since they were thirteen. And now they are gone, and soon without a trace, apart from a few school photos. It is tragic. Deeply tragic.'

In a satchel, Malcolm discovered a pen and pencil case and Turnbull's slide rule. Maths was not Malcolm's forte, but he had learned at school how to use a slide rule for multiplying, dividing, and working out the square root of a number. The slide rule had cost David's father thirty shillings so it, too, should be passed on to Lily, although she probably already had one.

Once the trunk was packed, it was no easy task getting it down the stairs, along a corridor and down more stairs to the front door. Fortunately, he had been able to park his car near the main entrance and with matron's muscle, jam it into the rear. At the other end he would definitely need assistance and dreaded asking the wretched Colonel Craig.

He thanked matron for all her help and got in his car. His hand hovered by the ignition key. Should he stop by a call box and make an appointment with the headmistress? The risk was getting fobbed off. He started the engine and decided to just show up. He had a free afternoon and only needed to be back for rehearsal of the school play after tea at 6.30 pm. Plenty of time to talk to Lily and try and make a good impression.

The drive across the moor was uneventful and quite boring. As dramatic as the scenery was, his thoughts kept returning to the beautiful, grief-stricken young girl. He knew she was vulnerable and, at only eighteen, not yet a legal adult, but he could not contain his feelings. Within his heart and despite all the obstacles, he had to try and woo her.

Sitting alone in her room, Lily was finding it increasingly hard to focus on schoolwork. She knew it made sense to protect her future and get good A-level grades in her exams next year, but her mind kept going back to the great adventures she had shared with her brother. Now half of her was gone. All that work he'd put in trying to match her academic success had been a waste of time, a waste of his short life. She cried. She wept. She tried to rise above it, but grief came as often as the great rollers pounded the base of the sheer cliffs.

There was a knock on her open door. 'Mr Cadwallader is here to see you.' Colonel Craig's tone was surprisingly gentle. Standing next to him was the friendly schoolmaster. Between them, they carried a trunk with D. L. Turnbull etched on the lid. 'He's brought your brother's things. Where shall we put it?'

Flustered, Lily leapt to her feet. 'Anywhere. By the wall behind the door.' She watched as they placed the heavy trunk on the floor.

'Right, we'll be off,' Colonel Craig said.

'I would like a few moments with Lily,' Mr Cadwallader rejoined.

'All right,' replied the colonel, not moving.

'Alone, if you wouldn't mind,' Malcolm mumbled.

'I do mind. Absolutely out of the question.'

Lily drew in a deep breath. 'Colonel Craig, please go and consult Miss Cooper if you're concerned about my safety with regard to Mr Cadwallader. But bear in mind, I have already spent time alone with my late brother's English master.'

Colonel Craig looked from Lily to Malcolm, sniffed what appeared to be a bad smell and half turned. 'I shall wait in the corridor. Five minutes.'

'Thank you, Colonel,' Malcolm said. He reached for the doorknob, and as soon as the former soldier had left the room, closed the door firmly behind him.

'I loathe that man,' Lily whispered.

'He's not in my top ten, either,' Malcolm responded.

'It's good of you to deliver the trunk, personally.'

'I have news.'

This was it. This was confirmation.

'Your brother has been found and is with the coroner. There will be an inquest, but it may be quite a while before they release him for burial.'

Lily looked at her unmade bed. 'Excuse me.' Fat tears fell as she straightened up the base sheet, puffed her pillow, and tidied the top sheet and blankets. She scrubbed her cheeks with the heel of her hands and gestured to her bed. 'Please sit.'

The tall young man walked around the base of the bed and sat near the foot. She reclaimed her desk chair and took a deep breath as she sniffed. 'How is Cyrano coming along?' she asked.

There was a momentary pause. 'Surprisingly well.'

'Why surprisingly, Mr Cadwallader?'

'Would you mind calling me by my Christian name? It's Malcolm.'

'And I'm Lily, as you know.'

'I wanted you to play Roxane. Your brother told me you have a natural gift for theatre.'

'If I'd had a choice, I would've accepted.' She looked intently at the schoolmaster sitting at the end of her bed. 'How old are you, Malcolm?'

'Twenty-five.'

'Did you always want to be a teacher?'

He shook his head. 'No. But, it's a good interim job until I find my true calling.'

'Which is?'

'Something creative. Perhaps advertising.' He stood and she followed suit. 'I am so sorry about your brother. His passing has really shaken us all.'

'Thank you. You're very kind.' She decided to reward the handsome young Englishman with a kiss on the cheek.

He swallowed. 'You have a number where I can be reached, if you need anything, or just want to talk. I can jump in the car, anytime… apart from when I'm in class or rehearsing the play, of course.'

She smiled, surprised by how much she liked the young man. He did not have Rainer's roguish charm, but he was charming and handsome, nonetheless.

'I am deeply sorry about David,' Malcolm said. 'I didn't know him well, but please be assured, he had many friends who miss him, greatly.'

There was a loud rap on the door, and it opened.

CHAPTER ELEVEN

'I'll take Bella for a walk,' Rainer said.

Sylvia looked up from the bank statement on her study desk, printed mostly in red. 'I walked her this morning,' she responded.

'I need air, and I need company.'

Sylvia looked at Bella who was sleeping peacefully in her basket. 'She won't thank me.'

Rainer reached for the leather lead hanging on the back of the office door. 'Komm her, mein süßer Schatz.'

Bella didn't move.

Sylvia stood. 'Bella, walkies.' The dog opened her eyes and within a split second was bouncing around the room, barking with excitement. Sylvia pointed at Rainer. 'You bring her back, clean. It's muddy out there.'

'Ja, mein Führer!' He clicked the lead onto Bella's collar and smiled at Sylvia. 'We'll see you later.'

They left the school by the main entrance and headed for the long drive, shrouded by woodland and dark shadows. Bella was keen to run and pulled hard on her short leash. Rainer paid her no attention. He was worried. During half term he was concerned that Sylvia's jealousy regarding his relationship with

Lily had driven his wife to act in a rash and cruel manner but now, since the death of Lily's brother, she had changed, and not in a good way. Six months after his arrival at Inniscliffe, he had enjoyed nightly trysts with plumply-humply Hannah, a gorgeous sixteen-year-old he couldn't resist. Sylvia found out and the girl was instantly expelled, even though she was the child of immigrants who'd fled from Poland. Sylvia had followed up the swift expulsion with renewed nightly demands, but the exact opposite was happening now. Rainer had deployed all his considerable charm and confident sex appeal to woo his wife but had been soundly rebuffed, not with the usual excuses but with plain, unalloyed lack of interest. If Sylvia initiated divorce proceedings on the grounds of his infidelity, Rainer's comfortable life in England would come to a rapid end, with a good chance he would be deported. Although many immigrants were arriving from former British colonies, the war was still too fresh, too sore for an exception to be made for a German. Somehow, he had to repair the damage with Sylvia as he may need her help and support with a new, more serious problem.

Twenty minutes later he and Bella arrived at the end of the drive and headed for the red telephone box. He looped Bella's lead over the stump of a broken tree branch and pulled open the heavy door. He looked at the telephone sitting on a shelf above several weighty directories and picked up the receiver. His finger poised over the circular metal dial. He knew the number but decided to check the note just in case. The letter was written in German, an innocuous missive from his aunt who was living in Leipzig. His training in the *Ministerium für Staatssicherheit*, the

East German Ministry for State Security commonly known as the Stasi, had been thorough and although Sylvia had seen the letter, only he could understand its shocking message. His aunt in Leipzig did not exist but he recognised the scrawl and knew the hand would have been coerced to copy the carefully worded message. What was most alarming was the fact his address and pseudonym were known. Someone had talked.

He fished in his trouser pocket and looked at the coins in his hand. There were several copper pennies, ha'pennies, a silver sixpence, a silver shilling, and a silver half crown. The telephone number, hidden in his aunt's letter, was based in London so he was going to make a trunk call, which would cost a lot. He decided to feed in all the copper coins followed by the sixpence in a separate slot. Heart pounding, he dialled the number. Within a few rings he heard a voice.

'It is Rainer.'

'Hallo. Hallo.'

'It is Rainer.' The person didn't seem to hear him, then he realised what was wrong and pushed in the chrome button beside the large letter A. His coins clattered into the metal box. 'It is Rainer.'

The words that came back were few and fatal. His heart sank. The life he'd come to know, and love, was over.

He let Bella off the lead and trudged back along the wooded drive. Thirty minutes later, the winter sun was setting and bathed the front of the school in a golden light. The solution to his plight lay within his own hands, but only if he was prepared to do the unthinkable. And, if he did, would he get away with it?

'You're very glum. Bad news?'

Rainer looked sharply at his wife across the pine table in their private kitchen.

'The letter from your aunt. Is she ill?'

'No. All is well. Her kind words reminded me how much I miss my family, my country.'

'You miss home.'

'This is my home, thanks to you. But I do miss my mother and sister.' He laughed. Gallows humour. 'Life is not straightforward in Germany. *My* part of Germany.'

'The Russian bear casts a long shadow.'

He nodded and pulled out a chair. 'How is Lily? I've not spoken to her, as per your instruction.'

Sylvia placed a steaming bowl of beef stew in front of him. 'She's coping, I believe. Her father telephoned me from Moscow.'

Rainer's rumbling stomach clenched. 'What did he want?'

'He can't come home for Christmas and asked us to keep his daughter safe.'

'Safe?'

'For an additional fee.'

'What did you say?'

'I told him, she needs to see her father and should fly to be with him over Christmas.'

Rainer banged his fist on the table and the bowl of stew almost jumped. 'No. It is too dangerous to go to Russia. She must stay here.'

Sylvia scooped up a large mound of mashed potato and carefully placed it in Rainer's bowl. 'I agree, but on one condition. You give me your word you will not resume your relationship.'

'I give you my word.'

'Fine.' Sylvia ladled the beef stew into another bowl

and added the potato. She sat down opposite Rainer. 'Her father has given me his private number in the embassy. I'll ask her to call him, and he can break the news to her.'

They ate in silence.

Rainer finished his food and placed his spoon in the bowl. 'There's an east wind coming.'

'Yes, it is getting colder and the cost of oil for the boilers is going up.'

'I need a cheque. You haven't paid me at all this term.'

'It's your punishment,' she said, 'and the school cannot afford to pay you or me. We are only just keeping our heads above water as it is. I've had to let the bursar go.'

'I want my money. You owe me.'

'I owe you nothing; whereas you owe me everything.'

He stood and his chair legs scraped the tiled floor. 'I have to go back to East Berlin.'

Sylvia looked shocked. 'Why? They will arrest you.'

'My mother and sister are in danger. If I return, I can protect them.'

'From what?'

'The secret police.'

'The Stasi?'

He nodded. 'They have asked me to commit a crime here in England. If I refuse, bad things will happen to my family.'

'What crime?'

He paused. 'Murder.'

Sylvia's mouth dropped open.

'If I stay and don't do their bidding, they will punish my mother and sister. I have to get back and smuggle them to the West.'

'The same way you got here?'

'In summer, it would have been possible but there's a Siberian winter coming our way. They'd never make it to shore.'

'How will you get across the iron curtain?'

'I'll think of something, but I need money.'

He saw Sylvia's shoulders drop as a sigh escaped her lips. 'I'll visit the bank, tomorrow.'

'Thank you, liebling.' He watched her finish the remnants of her stew.

She put her spoon down and looked at him. 'We're out of coal.'

He peered over her shoulder at the range. 'Is there none in the bucket?'

'I used the last.'

He sighed. 'Can you not ask Colonel Craig? He actually gets paid for working.'

'And the ash tray is full.'

'The ash will be hot.'

'It will have cooled by the time you've fetched the coal.'

He looked at her – it was not just the ash that was cooling.

CHAPTER TWELVE

It was bitterly cold that November Sunday. The kind of cold that freezes condensation on the inside of windowpanes. Lily wondered if it was even too cold for sex, although sex was definitely off the cards.

A letter had arrived in the usual way and although she had learned mail was often read and sometimes censored, a particularly pleasing missive had got through. Following the compulsory attendance in chapel led by the lovely Reverend Longden, Lily set off for what she hoped would be a day of adventure. To disguise her intentions, she mingled with girls at the front of the school whose only entertainment was to go for a walk in the woods or along the cliff path. There was nowhere else to go without a car; outings with family were strictly regulated as was every other aspect of school life, if not by the headmistress, then by over-enthusiastic staff who relished exercising their power. Lily knew she had an insurance policy in Sylvia that ensured her protection from the likes of Old Ma Barry, who would happily slap despite the no-hitting rule, but Lily was still careful to mingle with other girls as they ambled down the long school drive. An unbending rule was that girls had to wear the school uniform at all times. As it was so cold, Lily wore a thermal vest, standard white blouse and blue V-neck sweater but instead of the regulation blue tunic with the school's emblem embroidered for all to see, she wore a red-leather miniskirt that was at least four inches above her knees. Below her knees, and not covered by her duffle coat, were school issue long, blue socks.

As soon as the group was out of sight of any inquisitive eyes, Lily broke free and started jogging, hoping that the others did not feel as energetic. The biting air bit into the tissue of her lungs and she was panting by the time she reached the red telephone box. Parked close by was the green and cream MG 1100 with smoke puffing from its exhaust. She hurried over to the passenger side, but Malcolm beat her to it.

'Good morning,' he said, opening the door.

'Good morning, sir.' She slipped into the front seat, and he carefully closed the door. As he settled in beside her, she felt a kind of glow that was nothing to do with her run or the warm air blowing from the car's heater.

'Where are we going?' she asked, slightly breathlessly.

'I have booked a table for lunch at a pub I know out on the moor. I thought we could have a little walk and then warm up with a Sunday roast.'

She smiled. 'Thank you. Sounds lovely.'

Colonel Craig had enjoyed following Lily. He'd used his army training to track her, hidden from view in the woods. His thoughts were a mix of disgust and concern. Disgust at his own base urges for the nubile tramp, and concern about what she might say to the young man. He had disliked the cocky schoolmaster on sight. He'd not had to fight in a war. He'd not had to pick up a rifle and strip it down and reassemble it blindfold. He'd not even been in the catering corps, thanks to conscription being abolished.

The colonel waited for the two-tone MG to disappear from view then hurried to the phone box. He pulled open the door and fed in a few copper pennies. He knew the number off by heart and spun the dial.

'Hallo.' When he heard her voice, his gut tightened. He may have sought relief elsewhere on occasion, but she was a woman he loved and admired above all men and would go to the ends of the earth to protect.

Lily wished she could drive. It looked such fun. She admired the way Malcolm was able to smoothly change gear and how his right foot worked seamlessly between the accelerator and brake pedal, in harmony with his left foot depressing the clutch. Her father drove a Mercedes-Benz 220 SE automatic, which she thought was boring in comparison.

'I like your car,' Lily said, thrilled by its peppiness.

'It was designed by Alec Issigonis, the gentleman who designed the Mini.'

'It's a good ride.'

'The brilliant suspension is thanks to Alex Moulton. The same chap who created the small-wheeled Moulton bicycle, which also has front and rear suspension.'

'You know a lot.'

Malcolm laughed as they crested a hill giving them an amazing view of Hawksmoor. 'I know very little about very little, but only because it interests me.'

'You have a university degree. It means you're clever.'

'At Oxford I met people who actually understood

quantum physics. All I understood was the meaning of the words quantum and physics but certainly not how it applies to energy, matter, or Einstein's theory of relativity.'

'I have always wondered about that theory of his.'

'Me too. When I was a boy, my father told me that the gravitational pull of the moon is the reason we have high and low tides. How is that possible?'

'I think the moon does the heavy lifting,' Lily said, enjoying the freshness of their conversation, 'but the sun's gravity has an impact, as does our planet's.'

'There are more things in heaven and earth, Horatio, than are dreamt of in your philosophy.'

Lily laughed. 'I know that quote. It comes after Hamlet and Horatio have seen the ghost of Hamlet's father.'

'Shakespeare was trying to add credibility to Hamlet's father coming back from the dead,' Malcolm said, enthusiastically, 'by telling the audience that there are many things in our world we cannot see, hear or touch.'

He swerved into the small car park of a former coaching inn and they came to a stop. 'Nobody can prove God exists,' he continued, as he turned off the engine, 'and yet half the world believes He does.'

'Reverend Longden, the chaplain at our school, is a believer, and he's very clever.'

'Perhaps you will introduce me.' Malcolm pulled up the handbrake.

'Do you believe in ghosts?' Lily asked.

His hand paused by the door lever. 'I have an open mind. In fact, I have an open mind about most things. Would you care to walk before lunch or after?'

'After. I'm starving. Cook was ill so Old Ma Barry

was in charge of breakfast. The fried bread was inedible.'

'Well, the Rorty Crankle has an excellent reputation for Sunday roasts.'

'What about beef steak and pineapple rings?'

He looked at her. 'You must have a craving for iron and vitamin C. It'll be the school diet; not enough nutrients.' He opened his door and hurried around to her side.

'I won't be drinking as I'm driving,' he said as they strolled to the front entrance, 'but you most certainly can partake in a glass of red to go with your steak.'

'I'm only eighteen.'

'Even though you are too young to vote, you are old enough in law to buy your own alcohol.'

'Really? I hadn't appreciated that, not that I've had a chance.'

'Of course, if you get drunk, I, as the responsible adult, will feel the long arm of the law.'

'Even out here?' She looked at the vast wilderness.

'You're right. It is a bit of a cycle ride for our local bobby.'

'Sadly, I shall have to decline the wine. If Old Ma Barry gets a whiff of it on my breath, there will be hell to pay.'

'So, you do believe in God.'

'I believe in the Devil.' They both laughed as he held the door open for her.

'Rorty Crankle, funny name,' she said, looking around the cosy, dark-wood interior.

'Some say it means Happy Corner in Anglo-Saxon,' Malcolm responded, 'although I think the translation is somewhat bawdier.'

'The original name was The Dirty Habit,'

announced a gravelly voice from behind the bar. 'Monks, wearing habits, used to stop off to refresh themselves.'

CHAPTER THIRTEEN

Rainer was used to cold weather, but it felt truly polar, as cutting as a Bavarian winter. There was no snow, almost no visible ice, but a wind chill, driving down the temperature.

He missed his midnight trysts with Lily; her warm, soft, delectable body promised so much and delivered even more.

'Herr Herrnstadt.' The colonel's two words were clipped and precise.

Rainer looked at the tall, weathered man cleaning Sylvia's Sunbeam Alpine.

'Colonel, next time you want a chat, don't leave a cryptic note. Come and talk to me. I have no secrets left to conceal from Sylvia.'

'Unfortunately, you do.'

Rheumy eyes fixed on the young man. No doubt some fatherly advice was coming his way. 'Okay, I'm all frozen ears.'

Colonel Craig turned off the outside tap and dropped the rubber hose he was holding.

'Don't you feel the cold?' Rainer asked.

'I read the letter from your aunt in Leipzig.'

It was a punch to his solar plexus. 'Why would you

do that?'

'When you washed up on the shore and Sylvia took you in, no questions asked, I was approached by Her Majesty's Government with a request that I keep an eye on you. They could not allow a former Stasi officer to run around the English countryside unchecked. The Soviet Union has many spies in the United Kingdom and my job, as ex-military intelligence, is to make sure you're not one of them.'

'I'm not.'

'As far as I can tell, that is the truth; and until you received that letter purporting to be from your aunt in Leipzig, the authorities were content for you to live here and continue to forge documents in your little hideaway.'

Rainer knew the game was up. 'I loathe Mother Russia, but I am a loyal German, not to the Soviet cold war machine, but to the new Germany. A Germany that sees former enemies as friends.'

'Which is why you were led to believe that the work you undertook was commissioned by the Federal Republic of Germany whereas, in fact, you have been undertaking, I might say, brilliant work for Her Majesty's Government, to which I am the conduit.'

Rainer could hardly breathe. There was no point lying. The jig was up. The British were more on the ball than the German national soccer team. 'I am not a spy. My reason for coming to England was genuine.'

'There are very few ideological spies. Most are coerced one way or another. You have family in East Germany, East Berlin.'

'Why are you talking about this now? Does Sylvia know what you really do?'

'Of course not. I was only approached following

your arrival. Prior to that, I was simply the school's janitor.'

Rainer felt his new life slipping away. 'Am I to be deported?'

'The letter from your aunt. Was it written by her?'

'It is in my mother's hand but dictated by another.'

Colonel Craig sniffed. 'I assume you read between the lines?'

Rainer nodded.

'What have they asked you to do?'

A cigarette found its way between Rainer's lips, and he fired up his late-father's lighter. The smoke warmed his lungs and calmed his nerves. He looked intently at the colonel. 'I have to get my mother and sister to the West.'

Colonel Craig fixed his grey eyes on the young German. 'What is the job? I presume it has to do with Lily Turnbull, the daughter of a diplomat currently in Moscow. A man who has already lost his only son.'

Rainer slumped against the Sunbeam and felt the cold shoot up his arm like an electric shock. He reeled away. Colonel Craig reached out to steady him. 'I have to get my sister and mother out of Berlin. Can you help me?'

Colonel Craig looked at the young man. 'Are you responsible for the death of the girl's brother?'

Rainer was shocked. 'How can you think such a thing? Wasn't it an accident?'

Colonel Craig kept his eyes fixed on Rainer. 'Do I need to worry about Lily?'

Rainer shook his head. 'I would never hurt her.'

'Even at the expense of your mother and sister?'

'That is why I have to get them out. They could be sent to a gulag.'

Colonel Craig took a drag on Rainer's cigarette and handed it back. 'There is a simple solution to your problem.'

'Tell me.'

'Return to East Berlin.'

He thought for a moment. 'I intend to, but to get my family out.'

'I'll see what I can do my end.' Colonel Craig picked up the hose. 'The documents you are currently creating, when completed, do not need to be hidden in the woods. You may give them directly to me.' He turned on the tap. 'Last thought, keep your hands well away from young Miss Turnbull. The situation, re your marriage, is tenuous. Now is not the time to rock the boat. I hope I make myself clear.' He pointed the hose at Sylvia's little sports car.

CHAPTER FOURTEEN

The MG 1100 was driven by its front wheels which Malcolm liked. He felt he had full control over the vehicle, especially in tricky conditions. The car's heater had little effect on the air temperature within; without, it was raw, and he felt for the boys inadequately protected from the elements in their corduroy shorts as they cycled to school that Monday morning along the Old Military Road.

He was grateful for his teaching job as it meant he could stay at home with his parents in Mint Cottage. Living with mater and pater did cramp his romantic ambitions but it enabled him to save for his first home. He was happy with his plan to work in advertising, which was an exciting profession and, from all accounts, very lucrative, but he didn't want to move to the heart of the industry in London. The City of Manchester looked to him to be growing fast with plenty of businesses seeking ways to promote their products and services. Malcolm had many attributes that he was confident would secure him a good position within a local advertising agency. For a start he had a First in English from a top university, a fine way of speaking, and a tall, lean frame that carried clothes well. Yes, he had to admit, he was a classic Englishman, determined to go places. He was also an Englishman in love.

Lunch at the Rorty Crankle Inn on the moor in the company of Lily Turnbull had been one of the happiest moments in all his twenty-five years. Simply put, she was truly stunning. In his eyes, pure perfection. She reminded him of the film star Deborah Kerr in the way she spoke, but more like Grace Kelly in the way she looked. There was no doubt, nature had been very kind even if the world had not.

'Do you have plans for when you've completed your A-levels?' he asked, as she picked up her glass of Coca-Cola and put it to her lips; lips that he longed to kiss. She put her drink down and fixed him with her wonderful eyes. 'What would you suggest?'

Her question surprised him. 'I think the world is your oyster,' he said. 'Does university appeal?'

'I want to formulate my own views. I have had enough of old people spouting old thoughts. Times they are a-changing.' She smiled and he marvelled at her brilliance. He was enchanted but knew he needed to focus. 'Do you like Bob Dylan?' she asked, slightly tilting her head.

He nodded. Popular music was good turf to venture upon. 'Yes. He's very cool.'

'What is your taste in music?'

'I would say, it is a little eclectic. I like The Beatles, but I also like ballads. Have you heard of The Righteous Brothers?'

'Yes. They can sing, but they don't really speak to me.' She took a sip of her Coke.

'Speak to you?' he questioned.

'They don't have any of the bad boy about them.'

Malcolm laughed. 'I see.' In his heart he saw a wild and beautiful young woman sitting across from a buttoned-up, straitlaced man. 'Do you think they are a bit too square with their short hair and smart suits?'

'I like square,' she said.

Now Malcolm was confused and did not have a ready response.

'There are two types of boys,' she said. 'The ones parents like and the ones that smoke pot, protest against the bomb, and play guitar.'

Malcolm was now out of his depth and decided to change gender. 'What about women? Do you like Petula Clark?'

'My father does.'

That hurt! He soldiered on. 'Joan Baez? She's like Bob Dylan.'

'*There but for fortune…*,' she said. 'I love the guitar intro, and the lyrics really strike home. Her voice is so perfect, so rich, it makes me shiver.'

He nodded. 'I agree. To be frank, I also like Nancy Sinatra, pun not intended.'

'Pun?'

'Frank, her father?' He raised an eyebrow.

'Frank who?'

'Sinatra.'

She shrugged. 'I don't know him.'

Malcolm chuckled. 'Why should you?' There was a pause. Not quite awkward, but he felt he had to fill it with something clever. 'Peter Noone. Name the group.'

'I do not have the least idea, but I know he's not in the Rolling Stones.'

'Herman's Hermits.'

'I've heard them on Radio Luxemburg. *I'm into something good*, I think.'

He hoped she truly felt that. Somehow, he had to keep their relationship ticking over until she left school, and he could really stake his claim.

She smiled. 'I like you, Malcolm. You're very funny.'

'I try.' He laughed and looked deeply into her eyes and knew he had fallen for her hook, line, and sinker.

Lunch concluded too quickly. Outside the pub, by his car, he wanted to take her in his arms but didn't want to scare her by coming on too strong. Later, when she insisted he drop her at the end of the drive leading up to her school, he was desperate they part with a romantic kiss. But where was his courage?

He leaned across in the gloom of his car and found her cheek. 'May I see you again?' he whispered.

She squeezed his hand. 'Write to me.' Her voice was angelic, almost seductive.

'I will.'

He leapt out to open her door, but she was too quick.

'Goodbye Malcolm.' He watched her hurry away until the darkness took her.

The drive back to Mint Cottage was a mix of fevered excitement and fear. Fear that, somehow, she would slip through his fingers. If she did, he knew it would affect the rest of his life.

At Sunday-night supper with his parents, he tried to suppress his emotions, but they were still buzzing that Monday morning on his way to pick up costumes for Cyrano de Bergerac.

He glanced at his watch as he approached the stone, humpback bridge – the northern gateway to Hawksmead. It was only wide enough for a single vehicle, so Malcolm always slowed as he drove onto the ancient structure. The MG climbed the hump and to his stark horror, he saw his Roxane and another boy lying on the thin strip of tarmac ahead of him. Wisely, he wasn't driving fast so could easily stop in time. He pressed the brake pedal, but there was no response. He pressed it hard. Still nothing. He tried to steer, but he was a passenger in the driver's seat. Panic set in and he stamped the brake with both feet. One boy, his Roxane, managed to roll out of the car's path, but the other boy was not so lucky. He disappeared from Malcolm's view and acted as a cushion when the MG slid into a stone wall on the south side of the bridge.

Malcolm didn't move. He knew he'd just killed the boy. He applied the handbrake, turned the ignition key and forced his hand to open the driver's door. His bones felt like lead. As he eased his way out of the car, the sole of his right foot shot out from under him, and he crashed onto the road.

Black ice.

Rainwater, landing on frozen tarmac had turned to glass. Crystal clear, it was impossible to see. Holding the door as he got to his feet, Malcolm became aware that another vehicle was approaching the bridge. He eased his way around the nose of his car and his worst fear was realised. The thirteen-year-old schoolboy was dead. His eyes were open, and the freezing temperature was already creating an opaque film.

Malcolm fell to his knees as the first wave of grief and guilt hit him. The same wave would come many times throughout his life, a golden future blighted forever. As for the boy he'd killed, there was nothing he could do for him except have sufficient backbone to visit his parents.

This is the secret diary of Robert Oakes
DO NOT READ UNTIL 2065

There's been a terrible accident. I'm almost too sad to write it down, but you've helped me a lot, you person reading this in 2065 – your understanding has given me courage when I needed it most.

This morning, it was particularly cold on the moor. Condensation on the window panes of our dorm had frozen on the inside. I dressed up as warmly as I could then Mini and I went down to the shed to collect our bikes. My teeth chattered as we pedalled. The cold went through my gloves, and my bare knees have never been so blue. There was a dense mist across the moor, and the school formed only a faint outline. As we approached the humpback bridge over the River Hawk, the road looked like a black satin ribbon. Mini came alongside me, pedalling hard. As we cycled together onto the bridge, without warning, our wheels slid out from under us, and we landed hard on what I learned to be black ice.

We were both in shock, our knees bruised and bleeding. What had happened? It took a moment or two for us to be aware of a car coming towards us, sliding uncontrollably on the ice. I rolled as close as I could to the side of the bridge but Mini was not so quick. The car scooped him up, and I heard his bones crack as he was crushed between the bumper and the stone wall. The MG 1100 was badly damaged, and I'd never seen a schoolmaster cry until that terrible moment.

Later that catastrophic Monday, following a formal interview and written statement in Hawksmead Police Station, Malcolm went to see Mr Gibbs, the school's headmaster.

'The boy I killed, is, was the best friend of Robert Oakes, who is playing Roxane in Cyrano de Bergerac. He will be in complete shock; I doubt he can continue in the role. Out of kindness and respect, we must cancel the play.'

Mr Gibbs rubbed the stubs of his frostbitten fingers. 'Out of the question. It is not in the boy's or the school's interest for him to wallow in misery. For the sake of the entire cast, it is vital that we all hold our heads up, square our shoulders, and march on. Cyrano de Bergerac will continue with you as director, or with me. Your choice.'

CHAPTER FIFTEEN

Friday, November 12, 1954

The corridor was poorly lit, which is what they hoped. If they met a member of staff or a pupil their story was simple. Colonel Craig had heard a sound and had requested the school's in-house doctor to go and see what the problem was. He hadn't wanted to disturb the headmistress.

Dr Müller knew exactly which room to visit and was banking on the girls being asleep. Colonel Craig reached for the door handle, but Dr Müller gestured for him to wait. She placed her leather bag on the floor and carefully unbuckled its two straps. She removed a glass bottle and a gauze pad.

'Don't breathe,' she said, her voice guttural. The rubber bung came out with an audible pop and the open neck was immediately covered by the gauze pad. She nodded to the colonel.

He reached for the dented, brass doorknob and turned it. There was a slight creak from the hinges. He opened the door wide and stepped aside to allow the doctor to enter. He followed her to one of four beds and watched as Dr Müller covered the mouth and nose of one of the pupils. The teenage girl, struggled under the weight of the doctor but her cries were muffled.

Soon, she fell limp. Dr Müller pulled back the bed clothes and Colonel Craig scooped up the lifeless body until he had her securely over his left shoulder.

Dr Müller replaced the bottle of chloroform in her medical bag together with the gauze and gathered up a pair of walking shoes from under the bed. She reached for a school tunic draped over the end of the bed and unhooked one of four coats from the back of the dormitory door. She didn't care whose coat it was.

Once the door was closed the colonel spoke. 'How long before she wakes?'

'If she stirs, I will give her more. Komm, lass uns gehen.'

Their sturdy shoes clip-clopped on the floorboards as Colonel Craig, burdened by the unconscious girl, tried to keep up with Dr Müller.

The air was bitterly cold when they stepped into the school car park from a rear entrance. The girl moaned; her bare skin solely protected by her flannelette nightdress.

'Give her more,' demanded the colonel.

'Nobody will hear her,' responded the doctor, 'and I want her to be conscious. I want her to know it's me, Doktor Herta Oberheuser. I want her to know she has not escaped Reichsführer-SS Heinrich Himmler's Final Solution.'

Colonel Craig, feeling the weight of the slight girl on his shoulder watched Dr Müller place her medical bag and the girl's clothes in the boot of her car. She picked up the girl's heavy walking shoes and placed one shoe in her own armpit. With her free hands, she eased the laces and pulled the tongue of the second shoe and slid it onto the girl's bare foot.

'Why bother with shoes?' Colonel Craig asked, now

really feeling the weight.

'Nobody walks in bare feet unless they have to.' She pulled the laces tight and tied them in a bow. She retrieved the second shoe from her armpit and pushed the girl's icy-cold foot into it. The hard heel, made of plied wood, kicked up and split open Dr Müller's lips. She gasped and staggered back as Colonel Craig fought the wriggling body.

The metal taste of blood filled the doctor's mouth. Enraged, she picked up the shoe that had flown off and through bleeding lips hissed, 'Let's go. We've wasted enough time.' She returned to the boot of her car, removed a large torch, and carefully lowered the lid. Aided by the beam they headed out of the car park. The wriggling girl on Craig's shoulder screamed for help but the howling wind driving inland from the North Sea, whipped away her cries. Above, the beam of the lighthouse swept high over the cliff to far across the ocean.

The girl's wriggling got more violent forcing Colonel Craig to lose his grip. She slid from his shoulder and slumped onto the uneven grass, cushioning her fall.

Dr Müller threw the second shoe as hard as she could and hoped it had flown beyond the edge of the cliff. She dropped the torch and grabbed one of the girl's ankles with both of her strong hands. She had to use all her strength to hold on.

'We'll drag her,' she gasped, ignoring the girl's screams.

Colonel Craig had to kneel on the other flailing leg before he could get a purchase on her ankle. With their back to the cliff edge. They dragged the wriggling teenage girl over the uneven turf, exposing her naked torso to the cutting wind until they were within six feet of the cliff edge.

Colonel Craig looked at the doctor and in the fleeting moonlight, saw her face smeared with blood. 'It ends here?'

'Ja. Herta Oberheuser dies with the Jewess.'

'Grab her wrists,' he ordered.

Dr Müller picked up the heavy torch and brought it with as much force as she could muster into the side of the girl's head. Almost instantly her wriggling abated and became involuntary spasms. The doctor flung the torch down and grabbed the girl's wrists. 'I wanted her awake. I wanted her to know to the last second.'

'The war is over, Gretchen,' said the Colonel. 'I am doing this to protect you, not because I wish to harm the Jew, although I care nothing for her.'

Dr Müller sniffed and together they dragged the semi-conscious girl to the edge of the cliff. 'What will happen to her body?'

'Sea creatures have voracious appetites.'

Dr Müller released her grip on the two wrists and Colonel Craig let go of the girl's legs.

'Eins, zwei, drei,' Dr Müller said, and together they rolled the girl over the cliff edge.

For a moment, they stood still, the bitter wind in their faces. 'If she catches a wave, the sea might save her,' Dr Müller said.

'No, she's dead. It's not high tide for another hour.'

Dr Müller turned her back to the wind and spat blood and saliva. Colonel Craig picked up the broken torch. 'So, what's the story?'

'I'll spread the rumour that she was not happy and has probably returned to the Deutsche Demokratische Republik.'

'Why would she choose to live in East Germany? Israel is more likely.'

'Nobody will care.'

'Her body may be discovered,' the colonel said, panting for breath.

Dr Müller wiped her mouth on the sleeve of her worsted coat. 'If they find her body, then her depression, which she talked to me about in confidence, clearly led to her tragic suicide.'

'And the clothes in your car boot?'

'Can you burn them? In Ravensbrück, that's what we did to the Jews. Best way to destroy evidence.'

'I have a better idea. I'll remove the plastic buttons and dispose of her clothes in one of the septic tanks.'

'Das ist eine beschissene Lösung.'

And they laughed and laughed and laughed.

CHAPTER SIXTEEN

Friday, November 12, 1965

Under normal circumstances, she would ask Sylvia, Miss Cooper, if she could use her office phone, but Lily wanted privacy. Technically, it was against school rules to go to the public phone box at the end of the ridiculously long drive, but she had to know what was going on. Her new friend, who she hoped would become more than that, had just disappeared – no letters, no phone call, nothing. She'd used her last postage stamp writing to him, but there was no reply. Something must have happened. Or had she simply misread the signs? She checked her mother's watch. She had time before tea, which she could not afford to miss as her absence would be immediately noted.

The door to the box was heavy and it slammed shut behind her. She fished in her coin purse and removed four pennies and a sixpence, just in case she needed it. She placed the coins on top of the coin box and looked at the piece of paper Malcolm had given her when he broke the news about her brother. The receiver felt cold and heavy, and she didn't much like putting it to her ear. She fed the coin box four pennies then stuck her finger into the circular metal dial. Within a few rings she heard a woman's voice and pressed button A. The coins clattered down.

'May I speak to Mr Cadwallader, please?'

'I'm afraid Mr Cadwallader is unavailable. Would you care to leave a message?'

Lily thought for a moment. 'Please let him know that I was enquiring after his health.'

'And you are?'

'Lily Turnbull.'

There was a pause. 'Are you related to the late David Turnbull?'

It hit her hard and her reply was little better than a croak. 'He is my twin. He was my brother.'

Another pause. 'I am so sorry. I will ensure Mr Cadwallader receives your message.'

'Thank you.'

'Goodbye.'

'No! Wait. Please. Did you know my brother?' Lily heard the woman draw breath.

'Yes. He was a remarkable young man. His tragic accident has affected us all, deeply.'

A wave of emotion overwhelmed her, and the receiver slipped from her hand. She had never felt more wretched. Somehow, she had to speak to Malcolm. She ended the call as best she could and through her blurred eyes, dialled a three-digit number.

'Hello, directory enquiries. Name please.'

'Cadwallader.'

'There is a Cadwallader listed at Mint Cottage.'

'That's the one.'

'I'm afraid it's ex-directory.'

'Ex-directory? I don't understand.'

'The number is not listed in the public directory.'

'Can you see the number?'

'Yes.'

'Please give it to me. I went to their house for dinner. They know me. I know all their names.'

'I'm sorry, caller. I am not at liberty to pass on the telephone number.'

Lily was desperate. 'Could you ring the number?'

'Thank you caller. Goodbye.' She heard a click and the line went dead. She looked at the remaining coins in her purse and slotted another four pennies into the box.

'Hawksmead College.' It was not the voice she was expecting. She pushed button A and the coins clattered down.

'Hello, it's Lily Turnbull. I rang a few minutes ago to speak to Mr Cadwallader.'

'Have you permission to use the public phone box?'

'I'm sorry, I don't understand.'

'You are a pupil where my sister-in-law is a school mistress, and I know for a fact that the public phone box is not to be used without the express permission of a member of staff.'

Lily swallowed hard. 'May I ask to whom I am speaking?'

'I am Mrs Barry. Your school's Latin teacher is my husband's sister.' Lily felt sick. She replaced the handset.

A bitter nor' easterly prickled her exposed face as she trudged back to school. Trees, shorn of leaves, swayed their bony branches to the wind's macabre moan. Grey clouds blotted out the waning sun and brought twilight on early. Since the death of her mother, Lily had felt isolated even in company. Now her brother was gone, truly gone, and her father lost in his own misery, she felt the loneliness of unremitting grief.

Her blonde hair whipped her salt-stained cheeks. Just eighteen, all she wanted was to join her brother and be enveloped in the arms of their mother; to be a family, again. Rainer had provided solace, even love, but was now keeping his distance, clearly afraid for his marriage. Malcolm had seemed the perfect gentleman, perfect husband material, but now he, too, had washed his hands of her.

The girl stood someway ahead, backlit by pinpricks of yellow emitting from the school's floodlights. A pleated tunic clung to her thin frame and her dark hair contrasted with her deathly pallor. For a moment, Lily broke step, not frightened, but surprised. Overwhelmed by a desire for companionship, she battled the cutting wind as she ran to embrace the girl.

Headlights whited her vision followed by the blast of a car's horn. She threw herself onto a mossy verge and rolled into a ditch full of crackling leaves.

A shape she recognised roared past.

Shaken but unhurt, she brushed herself down then looked for the young girl.

'Hello,' she called, knowing her cry was swallowed by the rush of arctic air. Perhaps the girl was in a ditch? Without a torch, a search was almost pointless, but she searched anyway. The wind continued to slice into her bones until her teeth chattered and she could look no more.

Sylvia stared at the latest delivery from the Royal Mail and knew this was a nettle she had to grasp. Local suppliers would have to extend the school further credit, or the girls wouldn't eat. Her bank manager was already proving to be a bit of a nuisance. Any day, he could withdraw the overdraft facility and close the school.

Could sex be the answer?

Could she seduce him into extending her loan? Or seduce him and then blackmail him? She smiled. That was a plot straight out of The Saint starring the delectable Roger Moore. No. Sex and blackmail would not do. The knock on her door was a welcome interruption.

'Enter.'

She observed the knob turn and heard the creek of hinges before seeing a rosy young face. 'Lily. Why aren't you in tea?'

'Does Dr Bircher drive a large car? A Morris Oxford I think?'

'She does. Why is that a concern of yours?'

'She tried to run me over.'

'Here, at the school?'

'Down the drive.'

'What were you doing down the drive?'

'I wanted to make a phone call, in private.'

'I see.'

'I rang my brother's school for news. I hoped to speak to Mr Cadwallader. He said he would keep me updated but I've not heard from him for over a week. Would you telephone him for me?'

Sylvia considered the request. 'Are you and Mr Cadwallader romantically involved?' She waited for Lily to reply and saw conflict etched across her brow.

'He is a kind man,' Lily said.

Sylvia picked up her Parker pen and unscrewed the lid. She made a note in her desk diary. 'I'll let you know.' She looked at her wristwatch. 'You'll get detention for missing tea.'

Instead of hurrying to the door, Lily sat on the chair in front of the large desk. 'Do you know a girl called

Eva?'

'Eva?' It struck a discordant note in Sylvia's head. 'Eva?'

'Yes. I'm a bit worried about her.'

'Surname?'

'I don't know.'

'Well, next time you see her, send her to me.'

'She still wears the old school uniform.'

'How old?'

Lily shrugged. 'It just looks different.'

Sylvia gave the young woman seated opposite a long, hard stare. 'What is this really about, Lily?'

'I saw a girl, who I think is called Eva, in Dr Bircher's headlights, before I was forced to dive out of the way. I tried to find her.'

Sylvia pulled open a drawer and used both hands to lift out a leather-bound volume with Record and Roll Book embossed in worn gold leaf. She placed the giant tome on her desk. 'In 1897, our first pupil was Jean Walker. She went to China.'

'Like Gladys Aylward?'

'A lot earlier than the remarkable Miss Aylward, but equally brave. Her grandson is the school's chaplain.' She looked down at the book and carefully turned a large section of pages. Black indelible ink gave way to Royal Blue Quink, the desk light reflecting its copper base in her Godmother's round hand. 'I take great pride in learning the names of all my girls and Eva does not ring a recent bell.' She continued to carefully turn pages, admiring her Godmother's stylish script.

'She's got dark, straight hair,' Lily said. 'And light coloured eyes, full lips and a curved nose. She reminded me of Anne Frank.'

Sylvia's head snapped up and she looked sharply at

Lily.

'Did I say something wrong?' Lily asked.

'Anne Frank?' Sylvia questioned.

'Sort of,' Lily replied.

'I do recall a young Jewish girl, very pretty, who spoke English beautifully, with better grammar than some of the teaching staff. She was also fluent in German, which seemed to annoy Dr Müller who had recently arrived at the school.'

'Müller?' queried Lily.

'Müller was Dr Bircher's maiden name before she married a solicitor in Undermere.' Sylvia turned back a few pages of tightly-written entries in the Record and Roll Book and ran her clipped fingernail down the columns. 'Eva Reimann. She left here without her guardian giving notice in 1954, during Michaelmas.' She looked at Lily. 'She was younger than me; from Hungary, I believe. Kind, and clever in the way Jews often are.'

As Head Girl, Sylvia had done her best to protect Eva from both pupils and staff who seemed agin her. A few months after Sylvia left Inniscliffe for the last time, she heard that the poor girl had disappeared. Her Godmother had reported Eva missing to the authorities but with no evidence to the contrary, it was assumed that she was typical of many refugees who took British hospitality and then left without a word of thanks. Her Godmother informed the charity that was contributing to the girl's fees, and the school returned to normal.

'Do you know what happened to her?' Lily asked.

Sylvia closed the book and waved away floating dust. 'My Godmother, who was headmistress, said very little. I was no longer a pupil.'

'What about the police?'

'I don't recall much comment. Looking back, it does seem a little odd.'

'She can't be the Eva I saw today. Would you look again?' Lily gestured to the closed book.

Sylvia took a breath. 'There is no girl called Eva currently attending the school.' She watched Lily deflate. 'When you see her, ask her name.'

Lily nodded. She looked at her mother's watch. 'Do you know who's taking tea?'

Sylvia smiled. 'I'll speak to Miss Barry.'

'Thank you.'

Lily wished she wasn't awake, but she was. The wind that hailed from Siberia was rattling her windows and slicing an icy path to her bed. She had no choice but to throw back the covers and wiggle her toes into her fluffy slippers. The room felt oppressively dark. Almost blind, she followed a faint glow emitting from a gap in the curtains, confident that nothing lay in her path. As she approached the casement windows, the curtains billowed and almost gripped her in a macabre embrace. She fought off the grasping arms and went to close the open window. Through the leaded panes she could see a three-quarter moon, occasionally blotted out by scudding clouds.

She shut the window, but icy gusts forced their way through gaps in the metal frames.

Damn! She needed the loo. *Cold air and gravity*.

She checked the windows were all fully shut and pulled the curtains, making sure they were properly closed, plunging her room back into darkness.

It was almost a relief when she stepped out into the corridor. Night lighting, though sombre, comforted her as she ran to the washroom. She opened the door and flicked the switch. Neon strips hummed as they burst into life. She chose her usual cubicle but changed her mind when she saw several drips on the seat and not a scrap of toilet paper. Opening and closing doors, she finally found a dry seat and enough sheets of Bronco paper on the roll.

Once the pressure was off, the desire to sleep was overwhelming. Her chin dropped and she dreamed of playing rounders with her brother and mother. The joyous memory ended when she woke in a heap on the cold floor. She struggled to her feet and pulled down her nightdress. The rubber handle on the long toilet chain swung like a pendulum. Why was it moving? Probably another draught. She reached for it and pulled the chain, hating the sound of rushing water from the cistern swirling around the toilet bowl.

Washing her hands, she made a point of not looking into the wall mirror. She splashed icy water onto her face, to ensure she was fully awake. She didn't trust her mind to tell the difference, and the visions terrified her.

The journey back to her room was mercifully uneventful. Suddenly exhausted, she was keen to snuggle into her bed and get at least another couple of hours' sleep. She closed the door and in almost pitch black peeled off her dressing gown and draped it over the bed's blankets. Extra warmth was definitely needed as were her socks and thermal vest.

BANG!

Her bedroom door had blown open and slammed against her brother's trunk, causing her curtains to billow as tendrils of freezing air embraced her. The door swung shut and she was overwhelmed by blackness.

Someone was crying.

Almost whimpering with fear, she felt for the light switch.

The bulb exploded and shards of fine glass scattered.

A moonbeam found a gap between racing clouds, picking out sharp fragments strewn across the floor.

The gale swung open her window and the curtains flailed. She felt for her day shoes and slipped them on without doing up the laces. Glass crunched under foot as she approached the open window and reached out into the bitter void to close it. Below, standing on the sward, was a small figure looking up.

Was she dreaming? Another nightmare?

The small figure turned away and ran towards speckles of white.

Where was she going?

There was only the cliff and the steps down to the shore.

Not trusting her instincts, or what she thought she saw, Lily secured the window and closed the curtains. She ignored the broken bulb under her feet and after kicking off her shoes almost fell into bed.

Emotionally drained, sleep still managed to elude her, although when the bell rang announcing the first class of day, she was dead to the world and didn't want to wake up.

Groggy, she slipped on her dressing gown and slippers and trudged to the washroom. There was going to be hell to pay for missing breakfast, but she didn't really care. She was certain Eva had a message for her, whoever she was, and one way or another she was determined to get it.

Or was the death of her brother affecting the

balance of her mind? She entered a cubicle and was about to sit down when she was overwhelmed with nausea and only just managed to fall to her knees before she vomited.

CHAPTER SEVENTEEN

Checkpoint Charlie, as it was named by the Cold War Allies, was one of several border crossings that linked West Berlin to East Berlin, within the former capital city that lay deep within Soviet-controlled East Germany. Since its erection in 1961, the Berlin Wall was a jagged scar that separated the Soviet sector of the war-torn city from the French, British and American sectors. Apart from barbed-wire fencing, attack dogs, mined ditches, high concrete panels, and searchlights, there was also the shoot to kill order issued to guards in watchtowers that was carried out with few exceptions. Rainer had heard of successful escapes via tunnels, but the Stasi now used devices that could trace sounds of digging.

Christmas was really the only time to try and free his mother and sister as the border was open to West Germans visiting friends and family. Despite Christmas *good will*, car boots were thoroughly checked when leaving East Berlin to make sure there were no additional passengers. The only way out, was for his mother and sister to walk from East to West at one of nine border crossings, using forged passports with fake entry stamps. He was confident his talent as a forger, able to replicate the paper, watermarks, stamps and ink would pass the closest inspection. Many excellent forged passports failed because the paper used to print the photograph was wrong. Looking too new, too unused, too unthumbed was another giveaway. He collected dust from untouched corners of the Victorian school and used an electric fan within a cardboard box to blow the dust onto the relevant document. Most of the dust would be brushed away but a few motes, trapped within nooks and crannies, were visible if the document was ever examined under a magnifying glass. The last detail were the fingerprints. Passports are handled by police, border guards and various inspectors leaving behind traces of multiple fingerprints on the cover and pages. The fingerprints had to be from anonymous male hands, untraceable, but the smudges clearly visible if the passport was ever dusted for fingerprints.

The reason he had given for entering East Berlin was to visit an old friend, who had to be a real person with a real address. Once the truth behind his visit was out, Rainer knew his old friend would be treated harshly. German interrogation techniques had not been forgotten or abandoned by the Stasi, short for Staatssicherheit, the East German state security service. He was still amazed by how utterly cruel Germans were to fellow Germans. Surely, what they did in the war to the enemy and, most notably, to European Jews would have been enough to last any country a hundred years, but the same bullies that were more than happy to join the Gestapo seemed equally at home plying their methods in the dungeons below Stasi Headquarters in Normannenstraße, a massive complex of buildings employing over seven thousand personnel of which Rainer had been one. Its headquarters were in East Berlin, controlled by Erich Mielke who used his Stalinist skills to form a highly efficient espionage organisation, considered more brutal than Hitler's dreaded SS. Farmers in East Germany were particularly vulnerable to the Red Jackboot. Successful, family-owned farms were forced into becoming collectives, causing many farmers to flee East Germany to the West. The drain of farmers and workers seeking a better life in West Germany became so great, it was the reason why Mielke ordered a fence to be built throughout the entire border with West Germany, and a wall to be constructed in Berlin, with orders that anyone fleeing was to be arrested, or shot.

Internationally, the Stasi was considered to be one of the most efficient spying organisations in the world. Former Nazis, residing in West Germany, were coerced into spying for the German Democratic Republic, or their new identities would be revealed to Mossad, Israel's intelligence agency, who would abduct or kill them. Mielke also trained and armed terrorists in Western Europe, and Far-Left guerrillas in Latin America.

Rainer had seen firsthand how brutal the Stasi could be and was in no doubt as to what would happen to him were he to be caught travelling in East Berlin under a false passport. He also knew that he could not make direct contact with his mother and sister. There were Stasi civilian spies everywhere, especially in apartment buildings, offices, factories, universities and hospitals. All visitors, family or friends, were recorded and reported to Stasi HQ with exact times and dates, noted. His mother and sister would be under constant surveillance. Their telephone would be tapped, and all correspondence opened. Both churchgoers, he knew that their church would be watched by Stasi officers and the congregation observed by informants. Even if he managed to break into the apartment where his mother and sister resided, he was confident that the Stasi would have placed eavesdropping devices.

His heart pounded as he waited for his own passport to be stamped on the East German side of the crossing point, named *Charlie* by the Allies as part of the Radiotelephony Spelling Alphabet. He had forged his West German passport with materials supplied by the ever watchful Colonel Craig. Hidden in the lining of his suit, were two more passports he had forged with the same entry stamp. Getting photos of his mother and sister had been the biggest issue. They had to be faked. Fortunately, Sylvia agreed to dress for the occasion and wore a wig, Leichner stage make-up, and clothes that Rainer found at the back of her wardrobe. He was confident that the photo purporting to be his mother, was convincing enough. His sister was more of a challenge, but a girl called Veronica, who worked in the school as a cleaner, bore a passing resemblance and with a change of hairstyle and clothes, and a fiver in her grasping hand, he hoped her passport photo would bear close inspection.

Rainer stood by the white hut, where passports and entry visas were checked by East German border guards, and tried to look nonchalant. The discussion over his passport was taking too long. He ran through all the details and images Colonel Craig had supplied to him, to reassure himself that he had not made a detectable error.

The guard emerged from the hut and handed Rainer his passport. He could feel several pairs of eyes observing him.

'Entry declined, du kleiner Besserwisser.'

'Why?' Rainer sensed fingers curling around triggers as they waited for his next move, which could easily be his last.

'This border crossing is for foreign diplomats, not for Germans.'

'I don't understand.'

The guard looked at him as though talking to a fool. 'You must cross at the Bösebrücke bridge.'

'My friend lives near here,' he said. 'His address is on the entry document. I can almost see his apartment.'

The guard leaned forward. 'Go to Bösebrücke bridge, or we'll shoot you for being a time-wasting idiot.'

Rainer nodded and walked back towards the American sector where his passport was examined again. At least he could compliment himself on the quality of his workmanship.

By the time he was back in the West, the cold had bitten through his inadequate clothing, and he needed a hot drink. Café Adler was conveniently located near Checkpoint Charlie and, as most of the customers were Yanks, he was confident it would serve reasonable coffee.

Warmed by an excellent brew, he sat at a table with a clear view of the intersection that linked the Allied West with the Soviet East. He could see the barricades erected on the East German side that forced vehicles to take a slow zigzag route, preventing cars speeding across the intersection to the American sector.

He knew Checkpoint Charlie was the wrong border

crossing for a German living in the West. He had hoped his simpleton act would see him ushered through with a boot up his backside, but it was worth a shot, and his forgeries had proved to be convincing. He also knew that if he had had to make a run for it back to the West, *gung ho* American soldiers were more likely to give him covering fire than the diplomatic French at Bornholmer Straße checkpoint. In truth, the curvature of the Bösebrücke iron bridge made it impossible to see the Stasi checkpoint from the French sector, making a hasty retreat nigh impossible.

He lit a Winston cigarette from a pack he'd bought that morning and took a deep lungful in preparation for the hour-long walk he was about to take to Bornholmer Straße. Was it to be his last hour of freedom?

It was a strange kind of relief when, once again, he was walking along the familiar streets in East Berlin. Not much had changed. The concrete wall was an impenetrable barrier that entirely encircled the Allied sectors. One of the only ways into West Berlin from West Germany was via a designated trainline that trundled through the Democratic German Republic to West Berlin. At the border between West Germany and Soviet East Germany, the driver and guards were changed, and inspection of passports and papers carried out.

Another route was by road, but that was fraught with risk as accidents could easily happen, whether deliberate or not.

The one designated airport, Tempelhof, was restricted by the Soviets to a handful of international airlines that only foreign visitors and West Berliners were permitted to use.

Rainer knew that every minute he remained in East Berlin, the risk of being apprehended multiplied. As a member of the Stasi, he did all he could to sabotage operations against fellow Germans, often shredding vital documents that he knew were lying in wait to be used by prosecutors in trials for treason. It was dangerous work, but he could not stand by and watch former members of the Hitler Youth persecute fellow Germans through a network of civilian informants.

He hoped his cloth cap, worsted coat and stubbly beard was sufficient disguise. Without it, he would be recognised by old colleagues whom he knew patrolled the streets in civilian clothes, armed with Walther PPKs under their coats. Rainer had been trained to spot agents passing messages via dead drops or brush pasts. A dead drop wouldn't work for his mother and sister as they had no idea of his plans. His one hope was to plant the forged passports on either his mother or sister and for them to realise their purpose. Direct communication was impossible.

To confuse anyone watching him, he changed his hat, often, and wore different styles of spectacles. Simply altering his look, although crucial, was not enough. How he carried himself was equally important: his posture, his gait, his eyes. If he looked down, anyone observing may think he was plotting something. Glancing over his shoulder was also out of the question. Only the guilty ever did that.

Did his mother still work in the same office? Did she still share the same little apartment with his sister? There was no way of knowing for certain. He yearned for rain as nobody likes being out in a downpour even the Stasi. Fortunately, dark clouds hastened the winter night.

When he saw her, it sent a shock through his system. His mother looked older, more tired than he remembered. Across the street, lurking in a doorway, was a man with a cigarette and newspaper in hand. Rainer knew the man's eyes were focused on his mother. He waited for the traffic lights to change and joined others, wrapped up against the cold, hurrying home. His mother would be going in another direction which meant the man with his eyes on her would have his back to Rainer.

Taking care to mingle as best he could, he followed the Stasi agent. Sleet was turning to snow which pleased Rainer and for a moment, the few Christmas lights created an enchanting scene. Within minutes, snow covered the pavement and helped to muffle his footsteps. He had considered many plans, but each one would point the finger at his mother and sister. He needed to divert the Stasi officer without arousing suspicion.

Ahead, he could see his mother bundled up against the snow now falling heavily. Almost without warning she turned and seemed to disappear. The Stasi agent broke into a run and Rainer had no choice but to run, too. He had to catch up if his plan was to work. The man disappeared in the same place his mother had.

A long flight of steps led down and were poorly lit, already with a good covering of snow. Ahead, his mother was holding the rusted handrail as she carefully navigated the steps, forcing the Stasi officer to slow.

Rainer cried out, 'Oh nein, pass auf!'

Ahead he saw the Stasi agent hesitate and half turn

as Rainer landed on his back, hurling the man down the steps, with Rainer tumbling behind. The agent took the brunt of Rainer's weight, and he heard the man's skull crack against the edge of a stone step, the snow not yet thick enough to cushion the blow.

Hearing the kerfuffle, his mother turned and climbed the steps to help. Ensuring that the Stasi agent was at least unconscious if not dead, Rainer held out his hand and proffered the passports to his mother. 'Mama, nimm das. Sie werden Sie sicher über die Grenze bringen. Zögern Sie nicht. *Mum, take this. They will get you safely across the border. Don't hesitate.*' Reluctantly, his mother took the passports and, without a word, continued down the steps.

Rainer looked at the Stasi agent and knew he was dead. He recognised him as Siegfried Dietzel, a former friend who had trained with him. Guilt would overwhelm him in the coming years but now was not the time for such an indulgence.

Snow continued to fall.

With luck, the death of the agent would look like an accident, although the Stasi rarely believed in accidents, or coincidence.

CHAPTER EIGHTEEN

Lily felt abandoned by men she thought had cared for her. Rainer had disappeared without saying goodbye. Her schoolmaster friend, who looked so promising and seemed so kind, had also disappeared without a word of explanation. Her wonderful brother was dead, and her father was in Moscow, hiding from the torment of loss.

'I've not seen Rainer. Is he all right?' Lily dared to ask her headmistress.

'He went away.'

'For how long?'

Sylvia hesitated as she sucked in air through her teeth. 'I don't know. He said he had to get away to think things through. He'll be back for Christmas.'

Even Colonel Craig refused to answer her questions as to Rainer's whereabouts, despite Lily using her limited arsenal of flirting techniques.

'I do not have the least idea, miss.'

'Would you tell me if you knew?'

'I doubt it.'

'Can you at least tell me whether you know or not?' She felt his penetrating gaze drop below her eyes. 'If you tell me all you know, I'll show you my bosom.'

Colonel Craig burst out laughing and ended up having a coughing fit, which Lily hoped would see him to an early grave.

No such luck. He recovered, lit a cigarette and blew smoke in her direction, still chuckling and coughing.

Insulted, and feeling very low, she flounced back to her room. When the tea bell went, she decided to go to bed and hang the consequences.

Sometime later, when she woke, she was surprised to see she was wearing striped pyjamas, which was odd, as her pyjamas were pink and in the wash. The door burst open, and several girls, whom Lily didn't recognise, called to her in a language she didn't know. She was hauled out of bed and, barefoot, almost dragged along the corridor to where numerous girls were waiting, all subdued, gaunt, emaciated and wearing the same striped pyjamas – torn, stained, blooded.

Bulky women in serge jackets and pleated skirts shouted in German. 'Ihr sollt entlaust warden!'

A heavy hand landed on Lily's back, and she was shoved with the others into the school showers. They were so closely jammed, Lily felt she was being crushed. A familiar face she recognised turned and looked at her. Acrid smoke filled the room, and it caught in the back of her throat. She tried to scream but nothing came out.

'Wake up!'

Someone was shaking her, but she was too scared to open her eyes.

'Lily, you're having a bad dream.'

She looked up at Sylvia, but her mouth was too dry to speak.

'You were screaming the place down.' She pulled

back the bed covers. 'And you're soaked.'

Lily tried to speak. Several girls were standing in the corridor looking in.

'Don't talk now,' Sylvia said. 'You're in a right state. I'll get matron to turn your mattress and change your bedding.'

Her kind words could not erase the hard-bitten faces Lily had seen who seemed to relish the terror they imposed on their emaciated victims.

'Come with me to the shower.'

Lily found her voice ...and screamed.

CHAPTER NINETEEN

Cyrano de Bergerac was a big success and Malcolm's Roxane had truly excelled. Since the terrible accident on the bridge, Malcolm had focused all his attention on the young boy who had lost his friend. Fortunately, playing Roxane had been at least something of a panacea. In some ways Malcolm was confused by his own feelings for the boy. He wanted to encourage him, but when playing Roxane, he reminded Malcolm of Lily Turnbull and engendered emotions that were similar and uncomfortable.

Cutting himself off from Lily was his punishment. It was his self-flagellation. He had killed a boy and despite the black ice, he felt an overwhelming need to suffer. The accident on the bridge had robbed him of any hope of happiness. His purpose, as he saw it now, was to look after Robert Oakes, help him flourish, and protect him from some of the thugs that attended the school.

The morning after the triumph of the last performance of Cyrano de Bergerac, Malcolm had expected to see his Roxane at breakfast, enjoying the praise of other boys but none, when questioned, had seen him. He decided to check that Robert Oakes was all right and jumped into his parents' Rover 80. He drove a bit too fast in his anxiety to get to the school boarding house, on the south side of the fateful humpback bridge.

He pulled into the short drive that led to the early Victorian building, its dark windows revealing nothing of the horrors that had been perpetrated within its walls over the decades.

Inside the large, oak-panelled entrance hall, he was struck by the silence. He knew Robert Oakes slept in one of the dormitories at the top of the boarding house and decided to check if he was still up there.

Young and fit, Malcolm tackled the stairs two at a time that led up to a half-landing and split left to the showers, and right to the common room and dormitories. He bounded up to the right and almost broke into a run as he hurried down the long corridor. At the end were stairs that led up to the top floor.

> This is the secret diary of Robert Oakes
> DO NOT READ UNTIL 2065

My performance of Roxane received a standing ovation. Not once did I stutter when I spoke my lines. My parents are staying in a hotel in Undermere and seem really proud of me.

On my pillow was a letter from my mother; inside, I found a crisp one-pound note. My parents had come to say goodbye, but Matron couldn't find me and told them I'd left for breakfast.

I am writing this through my tears. Mini has gone, Roxane has deserted me, and I am back to the stuttering, blubbing boy I truly am. I know my parents love me, but I wish they'd taken me home.

> Someone is coming up. I can hear the stairs creaking.
> Time to hide you, my friend.

The door to Robert's dormitory was shut. Malcolm gave a little tap and turned the knob to see the boy, sitting on his bed, weeping.

'Why were you not at breakfast?' Malcolm asked.

Robert looked terrified, clearly in a state of high distress.

'I came to offer my congratulations on your triumphant performance.' The boy leapt up and backed away to the window. 'I want to thank you for coming through after losing your friend, for which I will be forever sorry.' Malcolm opened his arms, almost as an act of submission, to reassure the boy. 'I want you to know that Roxane will live in my heart forever.'

His Roxane ducked under his outstretched arms and darted through the open door. Malcolm called after him and almost chased him down the stairs to the corridor below. 'Robert,' he called again. At the end of the long corridor, he saw the frightened boy hesitate at the top of the stairs that led down to the entrance hall. Almost panting, Malcolm reached out for him, to make him feel safe, but he turned, caught his toe on a raised board and tumbled down the stairs.

Not believing what had just happened, Malcolm stood stock still. Petrified. Someone he cared about, was trying to protect, now lay injured or dead as a direct result of Malcolm's actions. How could he ever forgive himself? Two boys dead at his hands. My God, he was a monster.

Through his tears, a stark horror dawned. The law would not look too kindly on a schoolmaster, already responsible for the death of one young boy, albeit an unavoidable accident, who was ultimately responsible for the accidental death of another. How would a jury regard his actions? Inadvisable at best, murderous at worst.

The boarding house was still empty. There was a chance he could escape scrutiny. Making sure his clothes were all straight and his hair, tidy, he walked down the stairs and looked at the boy. There was no doubt that his neck was broken.

In his head he practised the lie he would tell until his dying breath. *Robert Oakes was not at breakfast and after his wonderful performance in Cyrano de Bergerac, I wanted to congratulate him. When I arrived at the school boarding house, I found him on the floor in the hallway and immediately went to matron's private room to call for an ambulance. I don't know why he fell down the stairs, but I can only assume that he tripped in his haste to get to chapel.*

The boy's English master and the play's director, sank to his knees and wept.

CHAPTER TWENTY

Saturday, December 4, 1965

Lily was sitting at her desk. Her books were open, but her mind was miles away, remembering the day her parents took their children to Camber Sands and she and David had had such fun rolling down the dunes.

'Lily.'

She jumped. Disappointed to have her reverie interrupted until she learned of the reason why.

'This came for you.' Miss Cooper proffered a handwritten envelope.

Lily stood and took it. 'Thank you.'

'The return addressee is Joseph J. Finkelstein, The Jewish Chronicle. Do you know him?'

Lily hesitated a moment. 'I wrote a letter to The Jewish Chronicle and gave it to Reverend Longden to post as I didn't know the address.'

'That is not strictly within the school rules, Lily.'

'But, Reverend Longden is a member of staff. Of all people, I think you and I can trust him to do what is right.'

Sylvia took a deep breath. 'May I know the content of the letter?'

'Of course.' Lily carefully tore open the envelope and unfolded a thin sheet of paper written in longhand.

'Dear Miss Turnbull,' she read. *'Your enquiry with regard to the orphaned refugee, Eva Reimann, has been passed to me. Her story is both rare and common. She survived medical experiments undertaken by Herta Oberheuser, a German Nazi physician at Ravensbrück women's concentration camp. Following the war, in 1946 aged just seven, Eva was sponsored by a British charity who brought her from temporary accommodation in Switzerland and sponsored her care within a Jewish family in Leeds. Part of that care was to pay for her education at your school, Inniscliffe. In 1954, Eva disappeared. I have telephoned associates in Jerusalem, Tel Aviv and New York, but there is no record of her that they can find. I would greatly appreciate it if you would acknowledge receipt of this letter and furnish me with any additional information you may have garnered.*

Yours sincerely, Joseph J. Finkelstein.'

She looked at Sylvia. 'I would like to garner him with more information, if I can. I think we owe it to Eva.'

In truth, Lily did not know what to do next. Instead of studying, which she had always found easy, her mind kept drifting to a time she had witnessed in her nightmares. To add to her sorrow, the Michaelmas term was ending soon, and she was dreading it. Before her mother died, Christmas was the most exciting time of the year. When she was a child, she loved singing Christmas carols, helping to decorate the Christmas tree, making her own Christmas cards, and carefully dividing up her pocket money so that each gift for her mother, father and brother cost exactly the same. If it was even one penny under, she would tape the spare coins to the offending present. How she missed those happy times.

Singing in the school choir gave her pleasure and an opportunity to think about things less depressing than the loss of half her family, the loss of her German lover, the loss of the schoolmaster, and her terrifying visions. She had also volunteered to help dress the Christmas tree standing in the school's main entrance hall and had used her wrapping skills to build a pile of make-believe presents.

Every Christmas, carol concerts were held in the school chapel for anyone from the surrounding villages who wished to attend, with the final concert for parents before they took their daughters home. The choir master was an eccentric but brilliantly talented young musician called Carl Davis who had a mop of black curly hair, an hypnotic accent from the Bronx, and a conductor's baton that all the choristers keenly followed.

At the end of choir practice, Lily saw Reverend Longden sitting in one of the chapel's pews. 'Excuse me, sir. I wonder if I could talk to you if you have a moment?'

'Of course, Lily,' he said as he stood. 'I must say, I have been impressed with your work these last few weeks despite all you've been going through. Your grasp of the Gospels and the Acts of the Apostles is the reason why you are top of the class. You have a clever head on young shoulders and will do well in your divinity exams next summer.'

Lily didn't quite know how to respond and ended up giving the Reverend a little curtsy. 'You're very kind, sir.' She looked over her shoulder at a small group of choristers chatting to the flamboyant choir master. 'Perhaps you and I could go somewhere a little more private?' she asked.

He guided her to a robing room at the back of the chapel. The air was freezing, and she couldn't help but shiver.

'I think we've earned a couple of bars.' William bent down and flicked the switch on an old, round-pin plug socket. Within seconds, the coiled wires in a small electric fire heated up.

'Please sit.' He gestured to a threadbare Parker Knoll armchair, nearest to the fire.

Lily smoothed the back of her skirt and sat down. William pulled up a wooden chair. She handed him the letter from Joseph J. Finkelstein. He took a moment to read the contents. 'It is more information than I expected.' He looked at her and she admired his clear, grey eyes. Up until this moment, his white dog collar had prevented her from truly appreciating just how impressive the young Reverend was. Tall, muscular, a massive brain, and a face that conveyed passion and strength.

'She wants my help.'

'She?'

'Eva. She is haunting me.'

He reached for her hand, and she was surprised by the charge that shot through her.

'Dear Lily, you have suffered two great traumas; deeply tragic personal losses; it is not surprising you are having nightmares.'

She pulled her hand away and intertwined her fingers. 'Would one not expect the nightmares to include my mother, my brother, or even my father?'

'Please, explain.'

She had done everything she could to forget, but each chilling second was impressed on her memory. 'I see what Eva experienced in the camp as a child; I hear her voice begging Doctor Oberheuser; I feel Eva's terror.'

The Reverend took a moment. 'Newsreels recounting the true horror of those times are imprinted on the conscience of all who do not share the hatred and bigotry of the Nazi war machine.'

Lily considered his words. 'Eva is dead. I know it. In the large cave on the beach, caught between rocks, deep in the sand, I felt a human skull.'

'A human skull? Are you sure? Could it be the skull of a seal?'

'Possibly, but I don't believe so.'

Later, in her dorm, she reflected on her conversation with the young Reverend, slightly puzzled by her physiological reaction. She didn't really know what the difference was between a Methodist Minister and a Church of England vicar, but she knew she liked him. She imagined Jesus to be the same kind of man. Someone who stood up to be counted. Who wasn't afraid to speak his mind. And if Jesus really did look like Jeffery Hunter who played Christ in the film, *King of Kings*, then Jesus definitely appealed to her baser senses, as did the Reverend William Longden.

She was still bruised by the deafening silence from the English master and wondered how she could have so misread his interest, his intentions? Regarding her feelings for Rainer, she felt nothing but relief. She had mistaken his lust for love but had no regrets. None at all, *it had been fab!*

'The first time you and a young gentleman make love will be a memory that will last forever,' her mother told her during one of many moments when they were together, away from *the chaps*, as she fondly referred to Lily's father and brother. 'Traditionally, it is on your wedding night, but some couples like to go for a spin before finally tying the knot.'

'In a car?'

Her mother laughed. 'Often, it's the only private place couples can find.'

'Did you and daddy go for a spin?'

Her mother drew a deep breath. 'It's not good for children to know everything about their parents.'

'But did you?'

'Daddy and I were confident when we married that children would quickly follow. But we didn't anticipate twins.'

Lily opened her mouth to ask a question, but her mother put her finger to her lips as they entered The Dutch Tea House, situated above sheer cliffs at North Foreland, on the Isle of Thanet. They were approached by a waitress wearing a curled and pointed Dutch bonnet, a starched white apron over a striped print dress, and a pair of multi-coloured wooden clogs known as *klompen* in Dutch, and *clompers* by those who had to wear them.

They were shown to their favourite table with a view over the English Channel. Happily seated, her mother picked up the menu which was in a leatherette folder. 'I think we deserve a special treat, don't you?'

'Thank you mummy, but I feel bad that David is missing out.'

'Daddy is sure to treat him after his riding lesson and don't forget, each lesson costs ten shillings, a lot more than a knickerbocker glory.'

Lily clapped her hands in anticipation. 'Is that what we're going to have?'

'Or you could have a strawberry fool, or treacle

tart and two scoops of ice cream, or spotted dick and custard. I think I'll have that.'

'What is spotted dick?'

'It's a sort of steamed suet pudding with currants. Delicious!'

'As delicious as it sounds, and you know I love custard, I think I would like to have a knickerbocker glory.'

'Good choice,' her mother said, snapping the menu closed.

How Lily missed those times. Tears always appeared when she thought of her family, now gone forever. She cherished memories of childhood holidays in Margate, far away from the smog of London, when she and her mother would shop together for all manner of things in Bobby & Co. department store; buy shoes in Hoad's where she and her brother would look at the screen as they wiggled their toes in the fluoroscope X-ray machine; and the thrill of going to Dreamland, the greatest amusement park in the world, where Lily and her brother promised they would spend every day when they were grown up.

'Five shillings each,' said their father, as he placed an assortment of silver coins in their eager hands. 'It's important to plan your spending as no amount of pleading will elicit a single penny more.'

'Thank you, daddy,' the twins said.

'Last point,' their mother added. 'Stick together. If one wants a ride and the other doesn't, you must wait by the ride's exit.'

'If, by any chance, you do get separated,' their father interjected, 'go to the entrance of the Scenic Railway, which is where mummy and I will be waiting.' He looked at his watch. 'You have one hour. *Go!*'

Lily and David raced off having preplanned the order of their rides. First, The Tubs, inverted steel thimbles that floated in a channel of flowing water, which took them through scenes in a fairytale cavern. Each circular tub had seating for four, and there was one seat left when Lily and David reached the front of the queue.

'You,' the man at the gate said, pointing to Lily. 'Get in.'

Lily clasped David's hand. 'No,' she said. 'We stay together.'

The next tub arrived, and they clambered in. 'Don't grip the sides,' they both said, echoing their father's words, 'or your fingers will get squished!' They laughed, full of excitement and anticipation as the tub trundled up a conveyor belt and went into freefall as it slid down a slide to splash into dark water. The twins liked the tubs as they flowed silently through caves that sparkled with precious stones and passed dramatic tableaux with scary scenes from fairytales.

'Four shillings left,' they said in unison, as they emerged through the turnstile.

'Candyfloss?' David asked.

'What about a toffee apple?' Lily countered.

Of course it was candyfloss. Their mother made toffee apples every Guy Fawkes Night on November the fifth, but their only experience of candyfloss was at Dreamland. They hurried to the stand where they eagerly watched pink sugar being heated and spun through tiny holes into long threads, then curled around a paper cone to create a great ball of joy that was as bad for their teeth as it was delicious.

David checked his Timex watch. 'Plenty of time,' he said as they strolled to the Bumper Cars, for which they would need both hands and a car each. They found a bin for the paper cones and looked at each other's sticky faces.

At one shilling and sixpence, the bumper cars were a big investment but the thrill of driving their own vehicle was compelling. They contemplated sharing a car and having two goes, but that was nowhere near as good as being wholly in charge. There was a short queue which they didn't join as they had a job to do. They stood on the side and watched holidaymakers race around the rink, sparks flying as the poles fitted to the rear of the cars scraped the electrified metal mesh above. This was important research as some cars were much faster than others.

When it was their turn, Lily and David raced to the same car, and both offered it to the other, but Lily knew how much speed mattered to David. There was one other car, the slowest in the rink but she didn't mind as she knew David would make sure she experienced the full joy of being bumped!

Later, exhilarated and a little bruised, they looked at the coins left in their sticky palms. One shilling spent on the tubs, sixpence for candyfloss, one and six on the bumper cars. Two shillings left. Their final ride had to be the Scenic Railway which was one shilling and sixpence. Rides for tiny tots did cost only sixpence but, aged ten, the twins were not going to sit with toddlers in Cinderella's carriage on a little roundabout.

'I have an idea,' Lily said.

David looked at her expectantly.

'Hold out your hand.'

Puzzled, David did as instructed and Lily placed a sixpence in his palm.

'What are you doing?'

'I want you to go on the Hurricane Jets.'

'What about you?'

'I'll watch. Remember, pull the lever back to go up and push it forward to go down.' Her brother selected an aeroplane and climbed into the cockpit. They waved and enjoyed the wait as other children clambered into different coloured planes, each with stubby wings and flashing lights. The Hurricane Jets moved, slowly at first, but when the speed increased, the pilots were able to climb and descend as they flew round and round.

After, feeling slightly dizzy, David hugged and thanked his sister.

Next, was the big one. They ran to the ticket booth for the Scenic Railway and excitedly handed over their last coins. The man at the turnstile let them through and they selected a car in the middle of the train.

'Why don't we sit right at the front?' David asked.

'I like to see the train as it twists and turns and goes up and down.'

'Me too.'

The man from the turnstile sat in the car behind them and released the brake. Their little fists gripped the security bar as the train trundled forwards along metal rails fitted to the vast wooden structure. First it climbed and climbed and climbed. Lily watched as the cars ahead reached the top and gravity took hold. Suddenly, they were going fast up the track and felt weightless as they reached the apex. The train shot down the far side, twisting left and right, going so fast Lily felt sure they would fly off the track. The man behind pulled the lever and brakes ground against the metal rails. The train slowed for a tight bend, then gathered speed as it swooped down and up and down again roaring past their parents.

Too soon, the brakeman pulled the lever and brought the train to a gradual stop. In their mother's hand was a Kodak Brownie 127 camera, which her parents had given Lily for her birthday. She would take the film to Boots the Chemist to be developed, hoping that all the photos would come out and not be over exposed or blurred.

Where were those black and white prints, delivered in a yellow paper folder together with the negatives?

Boxed-up in a garage with all the other memories her father wanted to forget.

CHAPTER TWENTY-ONE

Annoying as he was, Lily believed that Colonel Craig was a man who fought for Great Britain with honour. In a way, apart from the lovely Reverend, he was the only person within the confines of school she felt she could wholly trust. She saw the colonel in the garden workshop on his knees seemingly trying to fix an old Atco motor mower. 'Problem?' she asked.

He looked up. 'Unless you're here to get dirty, I would rather be left alone to deal with this troublesome beast.'

She looked around the workshop and saw the familiar Hayter ride-on lawnmower. 'What's that weird-looking contraption?' She pointed to a rectangular-shaped piece of orange plastic, with a petrol motor and a long handle.

'That my dear,' Colonel Craig responded, using a familiar term Lily hated, 'is a Flymo lawn mower. It hovers like a hovercraft. Very good for getting around trees.'

'I've not seen one before,' Lily said. 'Although, I am not well-versed in garden machinery.'

'The Flymo has only just come on the market.'

'Clever design.'

'Christopher Cockerell invented the hovercraft. Swedish inventor, Karl Dahlman, saw the idea and thought up the Flymo lawnmower.'

'On the shoulders of others,' observed Lily.

'Yes,' Colonel Craig said. 'Britain habitually invents, and the rest of the world manufactures and profits. Those in charge of this country do not hold boffins in high regard. Our American cousins are not so suspicious of a good idea, hence we are where we are.'

'Where's that?' Lily asked.

'Still struggling twenty years on from the war.' He sucked in air through his tobacco-stained teeth. 'Right, back to this little bugger.'

Lily took a deep breath. 'Colonel Craig, may I ask you a question?'

'Fire away but make it quick. This motor will not heal itself.'

'Is Dr Bircher a German?'

'OW!!' Colonel Craig yelped then swore. 'He got up off his knees and Lily saw blood on his knuckles. He went over to the wall-mounted tap with a green hose attached and turned it on. Water shot from the end of the hose, and he washed the blood and engine oil from his knuckles and hand. Satisfied he turned off the tap, shook off the water and reached into his pocket. 'Would you?' He proffered a handkerchief.

Lily realised she had no choice, much to her annoyance, and set about carefully binding and knotting the pristine handkerchief around the old man's knuckles. Strangely, up close, she found the mix of oil, grass and tobacco odours not as repellent as she had imagined. In fact, she quite liked it and felt herself warming to the old warrior.

Once the handkerchief was secure, she smiled and

turned away.

'To answer your question,' he said. 'Dr Bircher is from Switzerland. Where the Von Trapp Family Singers escaped to when they fled Salzburg, Austria. At least, they did in the film.'

Lily took a moment before responding. 'How do you know?'

'How do I know what?'

'That Dr Bircher is Swiss not German?'

'It's what she told me, and I believe her. What if she is German? The war ended years ago.'

'Do you remember a girl called Eva Reimann? She was a pupil in the early fifties. I believe you were here then.'

'I have no recollection of an Eva Reimann at all.'

'Really? I understand that when she went missing there was a bit of a furore. Police were involved.'

'Do you mean the Jewess who decided our hospitality was not of a sufficient standard and went to live in the State of Israel?'

'No, I mean the young girl who survived Ravensbrück concentration camp and was sponsored by a Jewish charity who paid for her education here.'

The colonel looked at her, all humour gone from his eyes. 'You are remarkably well informed.'

Lily took a breath. 'I think Eva recognised Dr Bircher as someone she remembered from Ravensbrück.'

'Interesting.'

'If Dr Bircher is not who she says she is, we should inform the police.'

Colonel Craig laughed. 'And what do you think they would do?'

'They could question her. See if she is a war criminal.'

Colonel Craig smiled. 'You are very naïve, young lady. If Dr Bircher's documents had been falsified, she would have been called out a long time ago. Forget it. Nobody cares about the war anymore, except for Jews who refuse to accept it was the Nazis and not ordinary Germans who carried out the Holocaust.'

'But was Dr Bircher an ordinary German? I think Eva recognised her from the concentration camp and the doctor got rid of her. The police may not be interested in chasing Nazis but murder on British soil is something else. If you help me prove Dr Bircher is not who she says she is, then the police will be forced to check into what happened to Eva Reimann.'

She waited for the colonel to respond. He was clearly deep in thought. Finally, he looked at her. 'Leave it with me. Keep your suspicions to yourself. If Dr Bircher is guilty of murder and gets wind you're peering under rocks, she could take flight. Let's keep our own counsel and reconvene once I have made some enquiries.'

Lily nodded. 'Good luck with the mower.'

Colonel Craig picked up a spanner. 'One last question. What brought all this on? The young Jew disappeared over ten years ago.'

'I found a textbook with her name inside. She's in several school photos and then she isn't. I asked Miss Cooper about her. She remembers Eva disappearing and there being a bit of a hoo-ha. Funnily enough, she disappeared shortly after Dr Bircher started work as the school doctor.'

Lily sauntered away feeling good, despite being chilled to the bone by the icy air. She had planted a seed in the old army-man's brain and felt sure it would take root. As frightful as he was, he was an upright

Englishman who would see that something had to be done. That Eva deserved justice.

CHAPTER TWENTY-TWO

The train journey from London to Hawksmead was long and tedious. He could not face reading a newspaper and was not interested in the English countryside, vividly green despite the ochre stain of his carriage window.

He dragged in another lungful of his last Rothmans King Size and enjoyed the satisfying hit. Sylvia referred to his cigarettes as coffin nails, but he had more pressing thoughts than the remote possibility that smoking would kill him. More like the KGB or the Stasi would have that pleasure.

He got off the train at Hawksmead and threw his cigarette between the carriage and the platform onto the track. In the station car park, was Sylvia's familiar Sunbeam Alpine and he looked forward to seeing his wife. He opened the passenger door and slipped into the low car.

'We need to talk.' The voice was rich and dark.

Surprised, Rainer stared at the man seated next to him, too long for the little sports car. 'All went well,' he said. 'They have the passports and may have already left.'

'Sadly not. I am told they were arrested at the

border.'

Rainer's insides exploded. The passenger door was barely open before he vomited. His head pounded and his vision was blurred. Great waves crashed into his eyes and within seconds he was sobbing. Slowly, the man next to him was able to calm him down.

'Listen to me, son. The Stasi will retain your mother and sister, but they need to show you they are still alive.'

Rainer gasped as he tried to form a question. 'What can I do?'

The former army colonel fired up the Sunbeam Alpine. 'You could return to East Berlin and hand yourself over to the Stasi. That may free them.'

'I cannot do that. There has to be another way.'

'There is. The school will be breaking up for the Christmas holidays. Miss Turnbull is staying on at her father's request. She will be alone. Accidents happen.'

Rainer could barely breathe. 'What use is her father to the Soviets if both his children are dead? They will have no levers.'

Colonel Craig chuckled. 'You are delightfully naïve. When your countrymen stormed into a village in France, they rounded up half a dozen people - men, women, children, and simply shot them. It ensured that everyone else behaved. The Soviets want to instil fear into our diplomats. If a Russian assassin can kill two children in the heart of rural England, no family of a British diplomat is safe. It converts a loyal subject of Her Majesty's Government to a potential traitor.' He pushed the stubby lever into First and revved the engine.

'Colonel Craig, we must protect Lily at all costs.'

The colonel looked at him. 'At all costs?' he queried.

'The cost of your sister and mother?'

'Are you suggesting that I murder Lily?' Rainer yelled.

'Relax. Calm down. Keep your head. If you were to kill Lily without a proper exit plan, you would be the prime suspect and would probably be hanged for treason and murder.'

'I am utterly confused. I have already made it clear that I will not harm Lily. I love her.'

'Quite right. You will not harm Lily.'

'Perhaps it's my English, but I am at a loss to understand what you are saying.'

'Lily will have an accident, but it has to happen when there is no risk of your being implicated.'

'Are you going to kill her?'

'Perhaps now you understand the true quandary of our situation.'

Rainer was completely spent. He reached for the passenger door handle. 'I will go back to Berlin and hand myself in.'

'Her Majesty's Government will not allow that.'

'Why not?'

'Because the Stasi will insist you spy on the West for the Soviet Union, and will hold your mother and sister to make sure you do. It may be a Cold War, but we are most definitely at war. Britain's interests are paramount. From now on you must follow my orders to the letter. Do I make myself clear?'

'I will not kill Lily.'

'No. If Lily were to die, that would not release your mother and sister and would simply play into the Soviet's hands.'

'Then what are we to do? It's an impossible situation.'

'We must buy a little time.'

'To what end?'

'To enable our people in Berlin to get their ducks in a row.'

'What are you suggesting?'

'We fake Lily's death and smuggle her abroad.'

'How is that possible?'

'Leave it with me.' Colonel Craig released the handbrake and spun the Alpine's rear wheels.

'I have to talk to you.' She was slipping into blissful sleep when she heard the whispered words. She felt a surge through her veins.

'Rainer?'

'I have something to tell you.'

She stroked his hair with the palm of her hand as he knelt by the side of her bed. 'Lie next to me.'

He gripped her wrist gently. 'What I have to say are not sweet nothings. It is important.' He stood. 'Close your eyes. I'll put the light on.'

'No!' Lily sat up. 'If a teacher patrols the corridor, light will be seen under the door.' She lifted her pillow and placed it behind her back. 'Sit on the bed and tell me what's going on. I have double Latin in the morning.' She moved her legs as he sat on the bed.

'I have been in Germany,' he said.

'West Germany?'

'No. My mother and sister are in danger. I tried to get them across the border to West Berlin, but they were stopped.'

Lily felt a hard thump in her chest. She could barely get out the words. 'What will happen to them?'

'Hopefully, nothing at this stage. But, if I do not do as they say, they will be imprisoned, possibly executed.'

She reached for his hand but couldn't find it in the dark. He was silent. Just his breathing and the smell of tobacco. 'What can I do?' she whispered.

'There is something.'

'What? Tell me. You know I'll do anything to help.'

'Would you die for me?'

It was a punch. His words were as shocking as they were crushing. 'I...I...'

'For my mother and sister to be released, you must die. At least, as far as your father is concerned. Once my mother and sister are free, you will miraculously resurrect.'

'I cannot do that to my father. It will kill him.'

'It will only be for a short while, weeks at most. A month or two.'

She pulled back from him, shaking her head in the dark. 'No. Absolutely not.'

A heavy silence. Just their breathing.

He got up from the bed. 'You're right. It's too much to ask. Sleep well.' He opened the door and stepped out into the dimly-lit corridor, shutting the door gently behind him.

She saw nothing but darkness.

CHAPTER TWENTY-THREE

Malcolm Cadwallader had lied to everyone, even to himself. It is said, the road to hell is paved with good intentions and that was all he'd had for little Robert Oakes. He had wanted to put his arm around the shy stutterer, but his intention to congratulate his Roxane had been misinterpreted. Or had it? What had been his true feelings for the boy? He lowered his lean frame until he was sitting on a vast root supporting a mighty oak tree that was one of many that lined the meandering River Hawk.

Perhaps the tipping point, he considered, was when Robert became Roxane and conveyed palpable, innocent appeal. Joining the audience for the final of three performances, Malcolm could see that many fathers were attracted to the beautiful young woman who so beguiled Cyrano de Bergerac. He had wanted to protect Robert, to put his arm around him, to provide support to someone young and vulnerable.

He knew he had to lie when it came to the investigation of the boy's death. He knew that if he told the truth, the police would not believe him, and he could easily be charged with any number of offences. He had to lie, he had no choice, but the falsehood rested heavily on his conscience. He couldn't burden his parents with the truth, or any friends from university. The only person he knew with whom he felt connected, was the young woman at the school across the moor.

'Miss Cooper, I have some news with regard to Lily Turnbull's brother. Would you kindly ask her to give me a call? Perhaps I could give you my parents' telephone number?'

'I don't think that's appropriate, Mr Cadwallader. If you give me the information, I will inform Lily.'

'Please forgive my reticence but I would rather she heard it from me, directly.'

'Then I suggest you write. I will look at the information and if I feel it is appropriate, I will pass it on.'

He hung up without saying goodbye. As much as he wanted a comforting ear, he felt a little disturbed by the headteacher's abrupt tone. Of course, she was right. His interest in Lily was not altruism. He liked her. He liked her the way he had liked Roxane, and he knew his attraction to both pupils was wrong.

The MG 1100, its dented chrome front bumper replaced, responded to Malcolm's heavy right foot as he set off for Inniscliffe School for Girls. The drive across the wild landscape required more concentration than he gave it, and it was only when a sharp bend took him by surprise, that his focus returned to the treacherous tarmac.

Why was he going? He knew he risked strongarm tactics from the former army colonel. Was the desperate wish to unburden his conscience his driving force, or was his desire for the young woman dictating his action? The more he thought about Lily, the more he realised that she was his every dream-woman rolled in one. For her to love him above all others, he would have to be on top of his game. *All's fair in love and war* was a mantra his mother had spouted on many occasions when he seemed backward in coming forwards in his attempts to court the fairer sex. Not this time. Today was the start of a campaign that would end with a wedding, as soon as Lily had completed her education.

It was not just Lily he had to woo. Until she was twenty-one, until she came of age, her father controlled her life. Malcolm would write to him in Moscow and hopefully convey to the bereaved man that Malcolm was the kind of rock, the kind of solid person, from a good background, who he could trust to love and cherish his only remaining child.

The two-tone MG entered the woodland known to locals as the dancing dell. Suddenly, he felt overwhelmed at the loss of the gentleman he had thought himself to be. He tried to shake off the mantle of grief by focusing on devising a plan for when he arrived at the school. He approached the humpback bridge over the River Eyas but was forced to pullover at a passing point on the narrow road when confronted by a stream of cars coming in the opposite direction.

The Christmas holidays had clearly begun. Inniscliffe had broken up a day ahead of Hawksmead College. He was too late. He had missed her. Lead filled his gut as tears filled his eyes. He knew he needed help; that his guilt was skewing his mind. Lily was his only salvation. She would be back at school in early January, and he would fight tooth and claw to see her. Colonel Craig could do his damnedest, and as for the treacherous headmistress who had prevented his correspondence getting through, he would use every trick in his arsenal to twist her arm.

A car stopped and allowed him to manoeuvre a three-point turn and enter the flow of traffic. At a fork in the road, most vehicles took the route south, but he headed back towards his parents' cottage.

How had his good life crashed into the buffers? At the start of the new school year, excited by the prospect of directing Cyrano de Bergerac, he would never have believed that two teenagers would drown in the River Hawk, that he would skid on black ice and kill a young boy, and that his Roxane would trip and tumble down the stairs to his death.

The moor stretched ahead but its rugged beauty brought no comfort. Images of the dead boy on the bridge and the dead boy in the school boarding house blotted out all rational thinking. He was so distracted by their horror, he almost skidded off the narrow road.

Would his death be such a tragedy? Yes, for his parents whom he loved but for everyone else, their memory of him would slip away as if sunk into quicksand. Within a short while, Malcolm Cadwallader would not cross their mind.

Death was the easy way out as his shame would die, too. It was the coward's way. If he had true courage, if he had backbone, he would go to the police and tell the truth as to why Robert Oakes fell down the stairs. It would then be up to a jury to determine the level of his guilt. But whatever happened to him, his parents would be punished by overwhelming shame. He could not do that to them. They deserved better.

He parked outside Mint Cottage and wondered if his feelings of guilt would fade, the way memories did over time. He turned off the engine and pulled out the ignition key. Deep down, he knew the answer ...and sobbed.

CHAPTER TWENTY-FOUR

Lily was the only girl not seeing family over the festive period. The empty school, bereft of pupils and staff, exacerbated her grief, her despair.

Without seeking permission from Sylvia, she decided to abandon her school uniform. According to the rules, any girl staying on at Inniscliffe must wear the school's uniform at all times, unless granted permission by a member of the teaching staff. After turning a blind eye to Lily's shenanigans with Rainer, Sylvia was hardly likely to expel her for wearing her own clothes. Anyway, there was nowhere to expel her to.

Changing into a pair of worsted slacks, thermal vest, plaid shirt and crew-neck jumper, she decided to make a plan for the holidays. Just a few weeks ago, it would have included nightly trysts with Rainer. She missed their lovemaking and had no regrets about him taking her virginity. What an odd phrase, she thought. He didn't *take* her virginity - she willingly gave it up. In fact, the word *virgin* should be replaced with *novice*. People make allowances for inexperience and enjoy youthful exuberance, but when it comes to the elite in all walks of life, whether in the theatre or on the tennis court, most value experience as much as talent. She had no idea whether her only lover would consider her talented, but exuberant most definitely. And, thanks to Rainer, she carried forward a level of experience that would benefit her next lover, whomsoever he may be.

The nearest town that offered the prospect of any fun at all was across the moor in Undermere. She'd heard from a day girl who lived in neighbouring Hawksmead that a new coffee bar had opened called La Cabana and that it was attracting young people. How to get there was the problem. There was a bus, but it would take hours to walk to the bus stop. She could order a taxi, but the cost would use up all the pocket money she had left. She could borrow Sylvia's Alpine, but her provisional driving licence required someone with a full licence to sit beside her. She had also never actually driven, but had observed how drivers pressed the accelerator and clutch pedals and manipulated the gear lever. Colonel Craig was an obvious choice to be her instructor, but to be alone with him in a confined vehicle, was not appealing.

Malcolm, whom she liked, had fallen off a cliff when it came to communication. He would've been ideal but had clearly decided she was not for him. Reverend William she felt confident would help her. But for them to go to La Cabana and drink frothy coffee in a smoky bar with a juke box blaring was an unlikely scenario for a man with a dog collar.

Rainer... for a split second she considered inviting him to come with her, but dismissed the idea as utterly ludicrous as Sylvia would go ballistic.

There was one solution, about as far from ideal as it could be, but she had exhausted all other options.

She looked out of her window across the sward to the lighthouse and shivered, not from the cold but from her feeling of bleak isolation. She needed company and decided to trust that Colonel Craig had not betrayed her confidence.

'What is it girl?'

Lily twisted in her chair, surprised that she had not heard Dr Bircher open her bedroom door. She stood and forced a smile. 'Would you take me to hospital? My head hurts. I think I could have a bleed on the brain.'

'Unlikely, but you may have an underlying problem as a result of concussion. Go to my car.'

'I'd better tell Miss Cooper.'

'I'll tell her.'

'Thank you. It's the Morris, isn't it?'

'Morris Oxford.'

Lily watched Dr Bircher leave then reached for her heavy winter coat hanging on the back of her door. She removed her leather purse from inside her pillowcase and wondered what shoes to wear. She plumped for a pair of wool-lined leather boots her father had bought her last Christmas. She checked her coat pocket for her gloves and woollen hat, cast a quick pan around the room, and closed the door behind her.

It was a pity she couldn't lock it – the school may be remote, but it was far too open. It made sense not having internal locks with all the girls, but often the doors to the rear of the building were left open all night. As she headed for the stairs that led down to the car park, she made a note to check they were all bolted when she got back.

The two-tone Morris Oxford was definitely the vehicle that had nearly run Lily over and had obliterated the young girl. The front passenger door was unlocked but she decided to wait by the car and formulate a plan of escape once they arrived at the hospital. A few moments later, the stout doctor emerged from the school building and placed her medical bag in the boot of the car.

'Get in.'

Lily opened the front passenger door and was immediately overcome by the intense smell of old red-leather, repellent and appealing in equal measure. Dr Bircher landed on the padded bench seat and Lily almost slid down into her. Without a word, Dr Bircher started the engine, depressed the clutch, pushed the gear lever into first, released the handbrake and drove off at a surprising speed.

Lily wasn't sure whether she should make conversation or not, and decided to stay quiet, but when they reached the brow of a hill and they were presented with the wild expanse of Hawksmoor, with its meandering serpent and jagged ridges lit by the winter sun, she gasped.

Dr Bircher smiled and turned to look at her. 'Yes, it is Ehrfurcht einflößend.'

Lily had no idea what the doctor had just said and looked away from the dangerous landscape. Images of her brother fighting for his life flooded her mind.

'Problem?' asked the gruff voice.

Tears came which Lily tried to wipe away. 'Please take me back to school.'

'After examination at hospital.'

They came to a fork in the road and Dr Bircher followed a weathered sign pointing to Undermere. The tarmac was a warren of potholes, many hidden under pools of water. It was a relief when the surface improved and civilisation beckoned. Lily spotted Malcolm's car parked outside a row of little cottages. 'Stop. Please stop.'

Distracted, Dr Bircher applied the brakes and the heavy car almost skidded. 'What's the problem, girl?'

'I have to collect something.' She reached for the door handle as the car accelerated. 'I want to get out,' she yelled.

'After examination,' the doctor replied, her tone calm.

Accepting her fate, Lily observed the route from where Malcolm's car was parked to their arrival at a grand, double-fronted, Georgian house, served by a semi-circular drive with a separate entrance and exit. Off to one side was a garage, its green wooden doors partly open.

'Come,' the doctor ordered.

Lily looked at the impressive façade. 'Where are we?'

'My house.'

'Really?'

'It was my late husband's. The Bircher family were landed gentry. All gone now apart from this house. When I go, some developer will probably tear out its guts and turn it into flats for the proletariat.'

'People have to live somewhere.'

'Come. Time is of the essence. I have patients due in half an hour.'

'How will I get to hospital?'

'I will examine you here, first. My surgery is well equipped.'

'It was just a headache. I'm feeling much better.'

'There are health risks associated with concussion. I have to be sure.'

'They can examine me at hospital.'

'I am more thorough.'

Lily's car door opened, and Colonel Craig smiled down at her.

'Dear Colonel,' Dr Bircher said. 'The girl's not feeling well. Would you kindly help?'

His sinewy fingers gripped her arm.

'I don't want an examination,' Lily almost wailed.

'Doctor knows best,' he said, and hauled her out of the car.

'Please take me back to school,' she pleaded. 'I'm feeling much better.'

'We have to be sure,' Dr Bircher said, as she closed the car door.

Firmly held, Lily was almost frogmarched to the grand entrance. Dr Bircher reached for the bellpull with its ceramic head and gave it a tug. There was an answering tinkle. They waited.

'Die faule Alte mußte schon nach Hause gegangen sein,' she snarled.

'You need a housekeeper prepared to put in the hours,' the colonel responded.

Dr Bircher laughed. 'Tell me where to find one in England,' she said as she produced a key from her coat pocket.

Colonel Craig helped Lily over the threshold. 'I want to go back to school,' she shouted as she tried to break free of his grip.

Off the cavernous entrance hall, Dr Bircher opened a door.

'Please, let me go,' Lily begged.

The examination room was like no doctor's surgery she had ever seen. Devoid of colour, it was cold, clinical, almost brutal in its lack of any comforting factors. By the window, was a large, mahogany desk, inlaid with faded red leather; and a swivel chair in front. To one side was an upright wooden chair clearly selected for its lack of comfort.

On a metal trolley were kidney-shaped steel dishes containing scalpels, scissors with strange, bent ends, and a truly terrifying array of syringes with needles. Partly obscured by a modesty screen on castors, was a leather-covered table with long straps and metal stirrups. Above, was a rectangular light unit with three neon strips.

Lily had never felt so scared in her entire life.

'Kommen Sie auf den Tisch.' The command from Dr Bircher was so stark, so authoritarian, she felt her knees give and her bladder release. Through her tears, she saw a little girl with dark hair, no older than five, strapped to the table, naked. Green eyes pleaded for help from her malnourished face. The room spun, black sheets flapped, and Lily spiralled backwards down a long tunnel.

CHAPTER TWENTY-FIVE

Malcolm parked his car in Hawksmead High Street and turned off the engine. A few weary-looking people were walking home after an early shift at the textile mill. Perhaps he should take a job there? Working on the looms was hard labour, but would it mete out sufficient punishment?

He needed help. He had been wrong to want to dump his pain on Lily and seek salvation from a young woman who was suffering herself. And yet, he knew, that if he could be with her, she would be some kind of panacea. He doubted he would ever get over the guilt, the remorse he felt for actions that were misguided, but were never meant to cause harm.

Angry, frustrated, bereft, he flung open the driver's door and was blasted by a horn as a car roared past. He checked the road was clear and got out. He could end his pain now. All he needed, was to throw himself off the humpback bridge into the fast-flowing River Hawk and hope that drowning was not too painful.

Tears flooded his eyes as his soles crunched the gravel path that led to a plain church. He reached double-oak doors and turned a knob that had been handled by worshippers for over a hundred years.

He half-hoped the door would be locked but it gave immediately, and he found himself standing in a small vestibule. Ahead were two more doors, with leaded lights that offered a distorted view of the interior. He pushed a door open, and a musty smell of old hymn books, old oak, and dust motes filled his nostrils.

Cloudy daylight flooded the cavernous interior through plain, high-level windows. On three sides was a gallery with further seating for additional worshippers, probably no longer needed in the modern era of the *Swingin' Sixties*. As he stepped inside, he asked himself why he'd chosen Hawksmead Methodist Church as opposed to St Michael's down the road. Perhaps he needed the austerity offered by the redbrick Victorian edifice; the unadulterated simplicity of the stark interior, with its plain leaded lights, hard wooden pews, and icy draughts through the floor grilles. Roman Catholics could unburden their sins in confessional booths. Malcolm, a member of the Church of England, preferred the hairshirt approach of the Methodists.

He sat on an unyielding pew with a thin felt covering that offered little comfort. Hanging on a brass hook was a kneeling pad with a hymn book and prayer book on the shelf above. He looked towards the front of the church and admired the pulpit's solid carved wood and the vast metal pipes that towered above an impressive organ with numerous stops, three rows of keyboards and multiple foot bars.

He held his breath and listened to absolute silence, interrupted by the faintest noise of traffic. He slowly breathed out. If he could slip away to blessed oblivion now, he would happily take it. Tears came easily these days. Without distractions, the pain of regret and guilt was overwhelming.

He fell to his knees, not cushioned by the kneepad, and buried his face in his hands. How could he, someone considered at the top of his class when it came to grey matter, make such a dog's breakfast of his life? And who was he weeping for? Himself, or the boys who would never go home? His parents would be so ashamed if they knew the truth. He would rather they grieved his death than bear his guilt.

A large presence blocked out the light. 'I'm sorry,' Malcolm said as he reached for his handkerchief and slid back onto the pew.

'Would you mind if I joined you?' the young man asked.

Slightly flummoxed, Malcolm slid along the pew to make room for the stranger.

'My name is William. May I know yours?'

Malcolm sniffed and cleared his throat. He glanced at the man seated next to him. He was wearing a dark grey worsted suit, a black shirt and a smooth, white collar. 'It's Malcolm. I apologise for the intrusion.'

'No apology necessary. The Lord's house is open to all at all times. I'm a visitor, too. I thought I would pop in on a dear old friend and seek his counsel.'

'You seem young for a minister.'

'I started early.' William picked up a prayer book. 'Sometimes, when I cannot marshal my thoughts, I seek words of wisdom from those who have gone before. Their view of life and its many complications can be truly enlightening, even an emollient when shared with a stranger.'

Malcolm stood. 'Thank you. Please excuse me, but I must go.'

William got to his feet but didn't let Malcolm pass. 'Why don't you and I join Reverend Manson for a cup of coffee? I understand he has saved a bag of ground Colombian donated for the Harvest Festival. And he always has a good supply of custard creams.' The tall man, perhaps a few years older than Malcolm, had a strong face with the profile of a young Sir John Gielgud, an actor Malcolm greatly admired for his Shakespearean prowess.

He allowed himself to be guided by the Good Samaritan through a door at the rear of the church into a small study and on to a little kitchen, somewhat embarrassed to be receiving hospitality from a total stranger. Leaded lights above a stained ceramic sink distorted images of weathered gravestones, some at an angle and some with faded bouquets of flowers.

He watched the young minister pour roasted coffee beans into a compact grinder. 'Stand clear,' William said. 'It makes a terrible noise. Enough to wake the dead.' He placed the lid on the grinder and Malcolm's ears were consumed by hideous grinding. Mercifully, his suffering was swift, and the screeching noise stopped.

William turned to him. 'Come and smell the ground coffee. It's the best part.'

Malcolm leaned forward and was infused by the magical aroma of the Colombian roast. 'Wonderful,' he said, stepping back.

William carefully transferred the ground coffee into a steel pot. He reached for an electric kettle and poured in the near-boiling water. 'A true treat for the day,' he said. 'I'm so pleased you could join me. A pleasure shared is more than a pleasure doubled.'

'What about the minister for this church?'

'He'll be along in a few minutes. He knows we're here. The coffee grinder is louder than our lonely church bell.' William pulled open a drawer and removed a dessert spoon. 'Quick stir, let it settle, and then the dunking can begin.' He glanced up. 'What is your biscuit of choice?'

Malcolm smiled. The young Reverend was giving him a masterclass on how to break the conversational ice. 'If it's tea,' he replied, 'there is only one choice and that's McVitie's Rich Tea. Coffee, on the other hand, offers scope for adventure and can be the perfect complement to digestives, custard creams, and even Scottish shortbread.'

William picked up a metal biscuit barrel with assorted images of biscuits on the side and opened the lid. 'We have Garibaldi, also known as squashed flies, classic Huntley and Palmers gingernuts and, king of them all, chocolate bourbons.' He picked out a few biscuits and placed them on a plate. 'Hope you don't mind the hand of God!'

Malcolm chuckled, liking the young minister more every second. He watched William retrieve a couple of ceramic mugs from the drainer and a new bottle of milk with a gold cap from the fridge. The cream had risen to the top and looked a satisfying yellow compared to the white milk in the rest of the bottle. William poured two mugs of coffee and Malcolm relished the aroma. 'We have a choice,' William said. 'You and I can share the cream at the top of the milk bottle, or we can be noble and shake it.'

'Is the good Lord watching?' Malcolm asked.

William carefully removed the foil cap and poured the cream equally between each mug. He replaced the cap loosely on top and put the bottle back in the fridge door. 'Sugar?' he asked.

'Thank you, no. I have weaned myself off sugar for the sake of my teeth, in order that I may enjoy a ginger nut long into the future.'

William laughed. 'I knew you and I had a lot in common.' He carried the mugs of coffee and placed them on a Formica table, together with the plate of biscuits. 'Please sit.' He gestured to a chair with a circular padded seat and splayed metal legs. 'Not the most comfortable seating,' William said. 'It ensures that morning elevenses do not go past noon.'

The two, tall men sat at the table and sipped the creamy coffee. 'Do you smoke?' William asked. 'I know the minister always keeps a reserve pack behind a tin of Campbell's Scotch Broth.'

'I've always regarded cigarettes as an unnecessary expense,' Malcolm said, 'although they can be good for the vocal cords, I believe.'

William gestured to the plate of biscuits. 'Please, avail yourself.'

Malcolm picked up a chocolate bourbon and carefully dunked it in his coffee.

'As a man of the cloth and soon to be a Methodist Missionary,' William continued, 'good, vocal projection is an essential tool. I am of the firm belief that smoking cigarettes will not help.'

'I'm sure you're right,' Malcolm responded as he munched. 'My mother doesn't mince her words. In her eyes it's a filthy habit.'

'I'm inclined to agree,' William said, and they both laughed. There was a pause whilst almost in unison they took a sip of coffee. 'What's troubling you, Malcolm? What brought you here today?'

Malcolm was desperate to unburden himself but

knew he mustn't. The shabby kitchen was no confessional with a vow of secrecy. The dear Reverend may feel compelled to inform the police. But Malcolm needed a sympathetic ear. He needed a friend who was not a friend. 'I killed a boy,' he said. 'There was black ice. My car skidded. He died instantly.' His eyes, once again, filled with tears.

'I read about the accident in the Chronicle. Were you speeding?'

Malcolm shook his head.

'Are you responsible for the construction of the narrow stone bridge?'

Malcolm shook his head, again.

'Could you have predicted that rain would freeze when it landed on the tarmac, turning the water into transparent ice?'

Malcolm took a deep breath. 'The weather was arctic. Perhaps I should've thought it was a possibility.'

'How long have you lived here?'

'All my life. I went to Hawksmead College.'

'And in that time have you ever experienced black ice on the humpback bridge?'

'No. Not until that morning.'

William picked up a Garibaldi. 'The glaze on this biscuit prevents proper absorption and requires longer dunking. But dunk it for too long, and it breaks in two. We assume that our intelligence prevents us from tripping up and yet, frequently, I fail to judge the additional dunking time needed for my Garibaldi and more often than not, as I have now, end up with squashed flies floating in my coffee.' He looked keenly at Malcolm. 'Do good with your life. Don't waste it.'

Lily had no idea what time it was when she awoke. She was lying in a mahogany bed, with pristine white sheets and pillowcases. Across the room were three sets of sliding sash windows, partly obscured by net curtains and framed with full height drapes restrained by rope ties. The walls were papered with a traditional fleurs-de-lys design on Wedgwood blue, peppered with portraits in oil and Constable-style country scenes. The wooden floorboards were partly obscured by a Persian silk rug, its geometric patterns in once vivid colours, now faded by sunlight.

The door opened and Dr Bircher entered carrying a tray. 'Good. You're awake. I've brought you a restorative cup of tea and a slice of Colonel Craig's Victoria sponge cake to help your low sugar.' She placed the tray on a circular table and smiled at Lily. 'Your clothes will be dry soon.'

Involuntarily, Lily lifted the sheet and blanket and saw that she was wearing a cotton nightdress and nothing else. 'What happened?'

'You fainted. Colonel Craig carried you upstairs and helped me get you out of your wet clothes. Nothing to be embarrassed about. You were in shock.'

Lily pushed herself onto her elbows. 'It was your examination room.'

Dr Bircher smiled. 'I try to make it as welcoming as possible, but it can look daunting.' She carried the cup of tea with saucer and spoon and placed it on a bedside table. 'You must try the cake. Colonel Craig told me he learned to bake when in India during the last days of the British Raj.' She placed a fine porcelain plate with a tiny cake fork and a generous slice of jam sponge topped with icing by the cup of tea. 'I've spoken to your headmistress and told her that you will be staying with me tonight, so that I can keep you under observation.'

Lily's mouth went dry.

'Have some tea. It will help settle you.' Dr Bircher left the room, leaving the door ajar.

Lily looked at the tea and cake and wondered if they were drugged, or poisoned but, realised, that if Dr Bircher wished her harm, she could have done so whilst Lily was unconscious. She picked up the fine china cup and took a sip. A bit too sweet, but delicious. She tried the cake and from a tentative nibble to devouring the last crumbs took no more than a couple of minutes.

The bed she was in was a large-sized double, with a beautiful counterpane depicting scarlet red tunics worn by riders gathering for a hunt. The image of a fox, hiding behind a tree, its bright red brush poised for flight made her smile in sympathy.

She threw back the covers and enjoyed the feel of the silk rug below her bare feet. Almost on tiptoe, she walked tentatively across the room and peered between the net curtains out of the window at the semicircular drive below. The winter sun was already setting. She turned back to the room and surmised that it must be the master suite. In the adjoining bathroom were a few personal toiletries belonging to the good doctor. Was she planning on sharing a bed with Lily? She looked down at her cotton nightdress and knew she had to escape. Her bare feet poked out, feeling cold on the vinyl. Shoes were another question. Where were her boots?

She peered around the bedroom door into a galleried landing and for a moment marvelled at the Georgian interior architecture, replete with original features complemented by wall lights with yellowing shades. Carefully avoiding bare floorboards, Lily stepped onto a carpet runner and walked towards an ornate oak staircase. The wooden treads were burnished brown and worn from years of wear and she wished they were carpeted. Taking care, and trying to imagine herself as a feather, she eased her way down the stairs with its two half-landings and right-angled turns. As she approached the bottom, she was amazed to see five people, whom she realised must be patients, sitting in the hallway on upright wooden chairs. As one, they turned to look at her. Instinctively, she put a forefinger to her lips. On a hall table she saw a telephone with a circular steel dial. She tiptoed across to it and picked up the heavy receiver, relieved to hear the dialling tone. The question was, could she remember the five-digit number? She put her finger in a round hole and turned the dial. After the fifth number she heard the comforting sound of ringing.

A friendly voice, answered. 'Hawksmead College.'

'Hello. My name is Lily Turnbull,' she whispered. 'I'm David Turnbull's sister. I am desperately trying to contact Malcolm Cadwallader, but I don't have his home number.'

'One moment.'

Lily was expecting a negative response as she had experienced last time when Old Ma Barry's sister-in-law answered.

'It's Undermere five, three, eight, six, seven.'

'Thank you. That is so kind.'

'Any time I can help, Lily, please let me know. My name is Sandra.'

'Thank you so much.' Lily pressed the chrome buttons on the phone's cradle. As soon as she heard the dialling tone, she dialled the number she had memorised. A man answered, his voice late middle age.

'May I speak to Malcolm, please?'

'If you would care to hold on, I will see if he can come to the phone. He's just got home.'

'Thank you.'

'Shall I say who is calling?'

'Please tell him it's Lily. I need his help. Urgently.' She heard the man place the receiver on a table and waited anxiously. Everyone seated in the hall was staring at her. The door to Dr Bircher's surgery opened and an elderly woman strode out.

'Next,' she said as she headed for the front door.

Lily waited, holding the receiver, hoping the good doctor would not emerge. She was relieved to see a man get up from his chair and hobble across to the open door, closing it firmly behind him.

'Lily?' It was wonderful to hear Malcolm's comforting voice.

'Can you come and get me?' she asked. 'I'm in a house somewhere in Undermere.'

A woman spoke up. 'It's The Old Vicarage, dear, Pratt's Hollow Lane.'

'I heard that, Lily. What's the problem?'

'Please bring a coat, and shoes. And please hurry.' She put the phone back on its cradle and stared at the enquiring faces.

An old man got to his feet, as gnarled as his walking stick. 'What's this place coming to? A lunatic asylum?' He stared at the waiting patients, challenging them to comment. 'This scrap of a girl is clearly unhinged and I'm not going to wait here for her to escape and run amok.'

A pregnant woman spoke. 'It's not our business.'

'I'm making it mine.' The man tottered to the surgery door, knocked and entered.

'Get out, Mr Pierce. Now!' They all heard Dr Bircher's gruff voice. The man shuffled backwards and closed the door.

He looked pointedly at Lily. 'You're not going anywhere, young lady.' His voice was a mixture of British army and north country.

She returned his glare, willing Malcolm to arrive.

'I command you to sit down on that chair.' He pointed with his stick to an available seat. Patients, waiting to see the doctor, collectively held their breath. 'Are you disobeying me?'

Lily, feeling vulnerable in her nightdress, was not sure how best to react.

'Do as I say.' The man puffed out his chest.

She would have made a run for it but without shoes, she had to stand her ground, which seemed to enrage the old man.

'If I were ten years younger, I'd put you over my knee and give you a damned good hiding.' Spittle flew from his mean mouth.

The front doorbell tinkled, and the pregnant woman almost leapt up from her chair.

'Sit down, young lady,' commanded Mr Pierce.

'It's not meant to be locked during surgery hours,' she said as she reached for the catch. 'It could be a patient needing help.' She pulled open the door and Lily was thrilled to see Malcolm, with a coat over his arm and a pair of shoes gripped between thumb and fingers.

Mr Pierce moved surprisingly quickly and stood between Lily and Malcolm. 'You're not going anywhere unless Dr Bircher says so.'

At that moment the surgery door opened and to Lily's dismay, Dr Bircher stepped out. 'What's going on?'

She tried to retain her cool. 'Mr Cadwallader is driving me back to school.'

Dr Bircher looked at Malcolm. 'Come in young man. It's cold out.' She walked up to Lily. 'Your clothes should be dry. Follow me.' She spoke to the old man. 'Get back to your seat, Mr Pierce.'

Malcolm stepped across the threshold and closed the door. 'I'll wait here,' he said to Lily. 'You go and get dressed.'

She followed the doctor to the rear of the house and entered a dark room. Dr Bircher switched on the light and as the neon tube flickered into life, Lily saw an emaciated girl lying on a rack above her head.

She gasped.

'Yes?' demanded the doctor.

Lily could barely breathe. She summoned the courage to look up again and saw her clothes draped over the wooden slats of an airer hanging from the ceiling via a pair of pulleys.

What was happening to her?

Dr Bircher untied the rope securing the airer to a wall-mounted cleat, and lowered it. Lily's coat was hanging on a hook and her boots were on the floor below.

'I presume you intend to leave with that man?' Dr Bircher asked, as she handed Lily her clothes.

'He's a friend.'

'I see.'

The two women stared at each other.

Dr Bircher broke the impasse. 'I will not pretend to like you, Lily, but you are in my care. I shall give you a bottle of Codeine tablets which should knock your headache on the head.'

The doctor laughed at her own joke as she walked back down the hall.

Malcolm felt many pairs of eyes on him as he waited for Lily to return. He watched the doctor approach, her steely eyes fixed on him. He took a breath, expecting confrontation and was relieved when, without comment, she turned into her surgery. A few moments later, he saw Lily appear and although her clothes looked creased and her hair dishevelled, he wondered whether he had ever seen a more beautiful sight. He opened the front door, not wanting to delay their departure.

'Take this, girl.'

Malcolm spun round in time to see Dr Bircher give Lily a small bottle. 'Thank you,' she said.

'I shall call your headmistress and inform her that you are on your way back to school.'

Lily did not respond and walked with purpose into the cold twilight. Malcolm closed the heavy front door and guided her to his car. He opened the passenger door and made sure she was safely in before gently closing it. He hurried around the rear, placed the coat and shoes he'd brought in the boot, and slipped into the driver's seat.

'Thank you,' Lily barely said.

'Would you care to join my parents and me for dinner, before I take you back to school?'

'I'm not going back.' She turned to him, and he saw her eyes reflected in a streetlight. 'Can I stay with you? I won't cause any trouble.'

Malcolm was conflicted. Aged only eighteen, Lily was still a minor and in the charge of her school's headmistress. 'We'll talk about it over dinner. I'm sure you're hungry.'

She turned away as he fired up the engine and they travelled in silence to the home he still shared with his parents. They arrived at a row of English cottages.

Malcolm pushed open a wooden gate and ushered Lily under an arch and up a stone path, towards the glow of an exterior light. To one side, was a rose garden, pruned for winter. He fiddled with the keys and unlocked the latch. Warmth emanated from a small hallway, lit by a hanging ceiling light with a maroon card shade. On the walls Lily observed a mix of paintings, in an array of gilt frames. Malcolm hung his mother's coat on a mahogany hat stand and placed her shoes on the floor.

'Let me help you,' he said, as she took off her coat.

A rotund man in his fifties entered the hallway from the kitchen, wearing a blue-striped apron.

'Lily,' Malcolm said. 'I would like to introduce you to my father.'

She offered her hand. 'How do you do Mr Cadwallader.' He was shorter than his son but with an equally good head of hair and an open, friendly demeanour.

'Lily, welcome. Please call me Wilbur.'

'I'm sorry to impose,' she said, 'and looking such a crumpled mess.'

'I can assure you, my dear, your youth more than trumps a few creases and hair tangles.'

Lily couldn't help lifting her hand to her head.

'Malcolm's mother, Marion, will be down in a moment,' Wilbur said. 'She finds it painful watching me cook. I hope you will agree that the quality of my shepherd's pie compensates for the copious washing up.'

Lily laughed. 'I'm sure it does, and I shall be more than happy to don the rubber gloves.'

'And who is this extraordinary young lady gracing our hallway?'

Lily looked up at the creamy features of a slim woman, wearing a tweed skirt, ivory-coloured blouse, a red-beaded necklace and with eyes that almost popped out of her softly beautiful face.

'I'm sorry to interrupt your evening, Mrs Cadwallader. My name is Lily. Your son heroically rescued me from an awkward situation.'

'I'm so pleased Malcolm was able to be of service in your hour of need.' She took Lily's hand. 'My name is Marion. Come through and let me pour you a restorative drink.' She led Lily into a lovely reception room, with glowing logs in the grate of a stone fireplace, bordered by bricks each side and topped with a dark-wood mantelpiece. To the front was a bow window adorned with porcelain figurines depicting milkmaids, shepherds, and various animals. To the rear, an archway framed a fine-looking dining room with French windows leading into what Lily presumed was a little garden, although it was too dark to see.

'Take a seat.' Marion gestured to a two-seater sofa in a faded floral design. 'I suggest a comforting sherry, or would you prefer a G & T?'

Lily glanced at Malcolm who smiled encouragingly. She swallowed. 'A sherry would be very welcome, Mrs Cadwallader. Thank you.'

'It's Marion and it's my pleasure.' Lily watched as Marion extracted a large sherry glass from a drinks cabinet and proceeded to fill it with a dark brown liquid. She placed it on a side table, ensuring that a circular coaster protected the varnished surface. 'Drink up. A schooner of Bristol Cream has remarkable restorative qualities.' She looked at her son. 'Malcolm?'

'No thank you, Mummy. I'll go and see if Dad needs a hand.' He walked by Lily, gave a little wink, then entered the kitchen via the dining room.

Marion poured herself a generous gin, using metal tongs to drop in two large lumps of ice from a crystal bucket, followed by a slice of lemon and half a bottle of Schweppes Indian Tonic Water. 'Dear Lily,' she said as she sat down in a worn armchair. 'Malcolm has told us much of your family's great loss. I want you to know that you are always welcome here.'

'Thank you.'

Marion smiled and lifted her glass. 'Chin, chin. Drink up.'

Lily reached for her sherry. 'Your good health. Prost.' The German word for cheers popped out before she could stop it.

Colonel Craig slowed to a halt behind the two-tone MG and turned off his lights. He pushed in the cigarette lighter and reached into an inside pocket for a battered silver case. Within seconds the car was full of unfiltered fumes. He smoked and watched as his eyes adjusted to the dark. Happily, gas streetlighting had never reached the little row of cottages. When the burning tip was too hot for his lips, he pushed open his car door and flicked the glowing stub onto the slicked tarmac.

He reached into the passenger glovebox, removed a Swiss army knife and eased out of the car. Careful to make no noise, he closed the door and ambled over to the MG. The night was the kind of black that reminded him of wartime, and he smiled as he squatted down and stabbed a tyre wall. He pushed the blade in until there was a satisfying hiss. He looked across at Malcolm's cottage - a chink of light shone through a gap in the front-room curtains. He crabbed across on his haunches and stabbed another tyre and relished the audible hiss as if it were a symphony by Beethoven.

Sabotage mission complete, he strode back to his car and started the engine. Gently revving, he slipped the gear lever into reverse. It wasn't easy driving backwards in the dark without lights, but he kept on until he could only just see an outline of the MG.

He lit another cigarette, relaxed, and enjoyed the smoke. Waiting and watching was something he was used to. During the war, he was parachuted into England by the Abwehr, Germany's intelligence unit. He was fortunate to speak English as an Englishman having attended a minor public school in the 1930s when his father was a diplomat working from the German Embassy in London. The risk of being caught and hanged or shot as a spy still filled him with dread. During the latter stages of the war, he worked for counterespionage in Berlin and was responsible for the capture and interrogation of Soviet agents. When Germany surrendered, he handed himself over to the British authorities. His knowledge of Soviet Union espionage techniques at the start of the Cold War, shielded him from prosecution by the war-crimes unit. In 1949, he received a new identity and the army pension of a retired colonel with twenty-six years' service.

Friedrich Schellenberg, or Colonel Edward Craig as he was now used to, knew he could not attend any army reunions, hence his decision to seek employment far away from inquisitive veterans. Working in a remote boarding school was the perfect solution for him and his German lover, a doctor he had protected during the postwar years in Berlin, for whom he secured a new identity. Life was sweet for the former Nazis until a young East German washed up on the shore and was rescued by Sylvia. Colonel Craig was contacted by Military Intelligence and ordered to keep an eye on the former Stasi officer. After so many years, he thought he'd been forgotten by the British authorities but some over-enthusiastic agent working for MI5 must have dusted off his file. Now there was a real risk that his true identity would be exposed to the public. He was convinced the Soviet Union was not behind the drowning of Lily's brother but was utilising the fatal accident as an opportunity to pressure her father into handing over secret documents. If he failed to comply, an example would be made to ensure that those in positions of trust within the British establishment understood the full power of the Soviet Union.

Colonel Craig should have informed MI5 about the direct threat to Lily's life and had Rainer deported. But he felt no loyalty to Britain and regarded the letter from Rainer's fictitious aunt as fortuitous. If Rainer, in order to spare his mother and sister from a life of hell, was encouraged to dispose of Lily, then the overcurious schoolgirl would no longer pose a threat to the woman he admired and loved. Of course, Rainer had no idea that it was Colonel Craig who betrayed Rainer's mother and sister to the Stasi in East Berlin, hence their arrest trying to cross the border.

'She's pregnant,' Gretchen told him after closing the

front door on her last patient.

'You're sure?'

'I don't need to inject a rabbit with her urine. I know.'

'A German baby,' he mused.

'We must act before she is expelled and talks to her father about Eva,' Gretchen stated, emphatically. 'Our life here, in England, is too good to put at risk.'

Christmas was coming. First, he had to clip the turkey's wings to keep her confined to school, the way ravens were clipped to prevent them leaving the Tower of London.

Shadows emerged from the cottage. Timing was key if his plan was not to look too convenient. He watched the young man open the MG's passenger door and the girl get in. As expected, her escort hesitated and looked at the nearside of the car. Clearly puzzled he walked around to the off-side and Colonel Craig could tell by his exasperated gestures, that he'd detected the double punctures. He waited; he needed to see what decision the young man came to. After a few moments, he watched him walk back to the passenger door and open it.

Colonel Craig started his engine without revving and put on his side lights. He eased the lever into first gear and gently got up to speed before flicking on his headlights.

'Lily, you asked if you could stay, well this is the perfect excuse,' Malcolm said, feeling the intense warmth of the young woman standing by him in the chilly night. 'I'll call your headmistress and tell her what's happened. I'll explain that you will be perfectly safe with my parents and that I'll be sleeping on the sofa downstairs.' In truth, he could've driven her back to school in his parents' car.

A toot of a horn interrupted Malcolm's reverie and both he and Lily looked at the Vauxhall Victor Estate as it came to a halt in front of the MG. The driver's door opened, and Colonel Craig stepped out. 'Puncture?'

'Two, I'm afraid.'

'Bad luck old chap. It's these roads. Shards everywhere.' His gaze turned to Lily. 'Hop in young lady. I'm heading your way.'

Malcolm sensed Lily stiffen. She turned and whispered, 'I don't want to go with him.'

He whispered back in her ear, 'I fear you must, or we'll have the police at our door. Telephone me when you're safely returned and away from him. I shall wait up.'

'Thank you for this evening.' Her lips touched his cheek, and he knew he was in love. 'Colonel Craig, excellent timing,' she said, and he watched her walk up to the passenger door, which the colonel made no move to open. Before slipping into the car, she spoke again to Malcolm. 'I'll give you a tinkle, later.'

He waited until he could neither see nor hear the car before shivering and hurrying back inside his parents' cosy cottage.

'Bloody puncture. Unfortunately, Inniscliffe's dodgy handyman was passing and insisted on giving her a lift.'

'You're rather smitten, aren't you?' his mother asked, standing in the doorway to the living room.

'I am, but I'm not sure I deserve her.'

'Why do you say that?'

'Death seems to follow me.'

'Her brother drowned. It was a tragic accident that

had nothing to do with you.'

'And the boy on the bridge?'

'It was not your fault.' She touched his arm. 'You're a good man.'

His chin dropped and he gave his head a little shake, desperate to erase the image of Robert's broken body lying at the bottom of the stairs. 'I'm not worthy of her, mummy. She deserves so much more than I can give.'

'Malcolm, your father and I could not be more proud of you. Shrug off your misguided guilt. Don't let another's misfortune destroy a lifetime's happiness.'

Lily stared at the narrow strip of road, lit by the headlights. She hadn't dared look at her driver. She still felt shocked by the hallucination in Dr Bircher's surgery. Perhaps her twin brother's death disturbed her mind more than she realised, although her hallucinations started before he drowned.

'Warm enough?' Colonel Craig suddenly asked.

'Er, yes, thank you.'

He twisted a knob, turning down the car's fan. 'Fully recovered?' he asked.

'Yes.' She watched him drive for a few seconds.

'Shocking road,' he said. 'Even a Panzer tank would have a problem. I came across a few of those in the war. Our tank shells bounced right off 'em.'

Lily did not know how to respond. The war seemed so long ago, and yet old people never hesitated to mention it.

'My father was in Burma,' she said. 'He still hates the Japanese.'

'Hiroshima and Nagasaki probably saved his bacon.'

'When they heard about the atom bombs, he said all the men cheered and got ready to go home.'

'After Victory in Europe day, those fighting the Japs were pretty much forgotten.' The Colonel navigated a pothole. 'Where did your parents meet?'

'India, Calcutta. My mother was the daughter of an Adjutant to Field Marshal Sir Claude Auchinleck. I think he was a bigwig.'

'He most certainly was. Pretty much one down from Lord Mountbatten. Not that they got on. Auk was not in favour of India's partition.' He glanced at Lily. 'Did your parents marry in Calcutta?'

'No, in London. My brother and I were born in Trevor Square, Knightsbridge, where my parents rented a house.'

There was a pause. Colonel Craig dipped a hand into an inside pocket and produced a silver cigarette case. He offered it to Lily. 'I wonder if you would do me the honours?'

'Of course.' She opened the case and removed one of his untipped cigarettes and placed it between her lips.

He handed her a flip-top steel lighter. 'From my army days. Push open the lid and roll the wheel.'

Lily did as instructed and was surprised by the height of the flame. 'Whoa. That's big.'

He chuckled. 'Just filled it.'

She dipped the cigarette tip into the flame and coughed. It went out. Colonel Craig laughed, and she handed the lighter back.

'Take a puff,' he said, 'but not too deep.'

Lily drew in the smoke and immediately blew it out. 'Not for me.'

He took the cigarette and inhaled a lungful. 'No greater satisfaction.'

She had her own thought on what gave her the greatest satisfaction but kept it to herself.

Colonel Craig parked in his usual place and Lily shivered as she climbed out. An easterly wind rocked the car accompanied by a sharp howl as the gale whipped through the Victorian buildings. 'Thank you for the lift.'

Colonel Craig walked around the nose of the car and stood too close to her. She could see the car park's yellow lighting reflected in his pale eyes.

'Take care, Lily. That man is not for you.' He leaned forward and kissed her on the cheek. 'Goodnight.'

Her heart pounded. She had a question. Perhaps too dangerous to ask, alone, at night, but she was going to ask it anyway.

'Why were you at Dr Bircher's. Is she your doctor?' She had trusted him but now realised that was probably misplaced.

There was a moment. Almost a chasm whilst she waited for his response. 'Dr Bircher is a friend of long standing. During the war, I suffered an injury that causes me problems every now and then. My own doctor, though a skilled practitioner, does not have Dr Bircher's expertise that she accrued during the war.'

'But she was in Switzerland.'

'Yes, at a specialist clinic where she developed certain techniques for particular types of injuries, especially those in the nether regions.'

Another uncomfortable pause.

'I could show you my war wounds, if you'd care to see them.'

Now she felt sick. 'Goodnight, Colonel. Thank you for the lift.' Any warm feelings she may have developed for the colonel during the journey froze in the night air.

She hurried away and entered the school through

a rear entrance, bolted the door, and made her way along the dimly lit corridors until she came to Sylvia's office. She hoped it wouldn't be locked. Usually, during term time, it was, but the door opened with its customary creak. Her fingers sought the light switch and a bulb within a faded, floral shade with missing tassels lit the way to Sylvia's old fashioned Bakelite phone with its frayed braided flex, metal rotary dial and numbers one to zero. She picked up the receiver and listened for the dialling tone. Malcolm's number was etched in her mind, but she pulled out the little drawer at the base of the phone to check the area code on the laminated card. She rotated the dial ten times, worried that at any moment she would be interrupted.

'Lily?' His voice sounded young and excited.

'I'm back, safely.' A pause. She waited.

'My parents and I were wondering whether you would care to spend Christmas Day with us. Just a quiet affair with turkey and all my father's delicious trimmings.'

Her heart skipped. 'I would love to.'

CHAPTER TWENTY-SIX

'Absolutely not.' Sylvia's terse response surprised and shocked Lily who was sitting at the scrubbed pine table in Sylvia's private kitchen the following morning. Rainer studiously avoided looking at her as Sylvia, wooden spoon in one hand and saucepan in another, stood over. At the end of the table, Colonel Craig ate porridge whilst reading a skilfully-folded Daily Telegraph.

'Why not?' Lily asked, trying to contain the defiance she felt.

'Your father has asked me to take care of you. I do not know the young man's family and so it would be a dereliction of your father's trust for you to be so far away on such an important day.' Sylvia plonked a mound of porridge in a bowl in front of Lily. 'Help yourself to brown sugar and milk,' she added, and banged the saucepan back on the range.

A heavy blanket of silence descended.

Sylvia bent down and spoke to her dog lying under the table by Lily's feet. 'Come on Bella. Walkies.'

Rainer suddenly stirred. 'I can take her.'

'I need fresh air.' Sylvia reached for a leather dog lead hanging on a hook and clicked it onto Bella's collar. 'I'll see you later.'

'May I come with you?' Lily asked.

Sylvia stopped. 'Another time. Finish your porridge.'

'Please. It's important.'

A pause. A sigh. 'Get your coat. I'll wait for you in the quad.'

Lily wasted no time with niceties and hurried out of the kitchen, leaving the mound of porridge, untouched. She ran up the stairs, down the corridors and was almost panting when she reached her bedroom. Heart pumping, she pushed open the door. Weak December daylight through partly drawn curtains made her reach for the light switch, and then her hand froze. On the rumpled white sheet of her unmade bed was an object she had never seen before but instantly recognised. Her head spun, her world uptilted, and she sank to the floor.

From the depths of an ocean Lily felt herself surfacing. A long tongue licked her cheeks and eyes as she struggled to push herself up.

Sylvia pulled Bella back and cradled Lily's head. 'I've called Dr Bircher. She'll be here soon.'

'No. I'm fine,' Lily croaked.

'You're as far from fine as it's possible to be.'

'On my bed. Is it still there?'

'There's nothing on your bed.'

Lily struggled to get up off the floor and looked at her jumble of sheets and blankets. 'I saw a shoe. I did not imagine it.'

'This shoe?' Sylvia asked. 'Bella, drop.' She picked up a sea-ravaged leather shoe, sticky with the dog's saliva. 'Bella found this on the beach, yesterday, and must've given it to you as a present. God knows how many years it's been tossed in the surf.'

'It's Eva's.'

'Eva?' Sylvia looked closely at the shoe. 'I suppose it's the right size for a teenage girl, but not very likely.' She threw the shoe into the corridor and Bella scampered to retrieve it.

Lily sat on the side of her bed and put her face in her hands.

Sylvia stood and looked down at her. 'From now on, Lily, you are confined to school. No sneaky phone calls, here or down the drive. I shall keep your purse and the money your father sent, safe, until the start of the new term.'

Lily soon discovered she meant it. Sylvia's study door was kept locked preventing Lily from using the phone. She went to the bursar's office and the staff room, to find both doors, also locked. She snuck into Sylvia's private lounge and was thrilled to see a telephone sitting on a side table. To her disappointment, a steel cylinder lock prevented the rotary dial from turning. She opened a couple of drawers in a rosewood sideboard, hoping to find the key, but Sylvia was clearly too wily.

One route of escape from the confines was to take Bella for long walks but without money, she couldn't even use the phone box and talk to Malcolm. If she'd had a stamp, she would have written. School post was usually delivered by a member of staff to the sub-post mistress in Crowford, three miles away. Outside, was a red post box, set within a stone wall, but without a stamp or return address on the envelope, the Royal Mail would have opened her letter, read the contents, and probably guessed it was written by a pupil at Inniscliffe, which would have got her into even more hot water.

The school library had a limited number of books that she regarded worthy of her attention. She had read most of the novels by Charles Dickens before she arrived at the school. In the recent summer holidays, she had watched the film Doctor Zhivago with her brother, and had wanted to read the novel, but the only book set in Russia she could find was War & Peace by Tolstoy, and it didn't appeal.

Fortunately, television wasn't rationed by Sylvia, and Lily spent hours in the prefects' lounge watching whatever was on, in black and white. The aerial on top of the set had to be adjusted for each of the two main channels. She ignored the overtly cerebral BBC Two, but to get a decent picture on the commercial channel which, for inexplicable reasons and always in the most exciting parts, would often start flickering, she had to fiddle with the vertical and horizontal-control knobs, until the picture settled again, by which time the end credits were usually rolling.

Some of the programmes for very young children she found quite amusing, especially The Woodentops, about a family of string puppets that worked on a farm. She also laughed at The Flowerpot Men who spoke in silly voices and were friends with a female flower called Little Weed.

Once the sun had set, she would settle down to watch programmes for older children and especially enjoyed those that featured horses. *My Friend Flicka* was a favourite as she had read the novel when she was young. Flicka, Swedish for little girl, was a wild filly, which was how Lily saw herself.

After dinner and after offering to wash up, she would never miss *Ready Steady Go!* and *Top of the Pops*;

two must-see music programmes for young people. She didn't love all the groups featured, but hearing the latest chart toppers from the Hit Parade, connected her to what was happening in the outside world.

Before heading off to read in her bedroom, she would always watch a TV drama. Her favourite was Doctor Kildare with the dishy Richard Chamberlain. School work didn't feature within her busy schedule as she knew, once the girls were back, it would be nothing but studying. Until then, she was determined to fill her mind with pink bubblegum... *if only she could get some*.

When her family was whole, Lily used to relish Christmas more than her shared birthday. She loved choosing gifts and took a great deal of time before making a decision. Her brother was always top of her list, but not this Christmas, not any future Christmas. Her mother was never easy to buy for and once, desperate, she bought her a book token. Her mother's ill-disguised expression told her it was a terrible choice. For her mother's birthday, Lily was determined not to make the same horrible mistake again and took forever choosing a lipstick from Elizabeth Arden. When her mother twisted the base and a bright red stick emerged, she was thrilled and relieved to see the delight on her mother's face. It was one of her happiest and saddest memories as that birthday turned out to be her mother's last.

For her father, she would buy Old Spice aftershave which she knew he liked as he said it gave a real zing to his skin. She'd seen advertisements for a new aftershave called Brut which came in an attractive green bottle. She would like to buy it for Rainer but knew it would inflame her fractious relationship with his wife.

'Will you take me shopping?' Lily asked Sylvia at breakfast.

'What do you need?'

'I want to buy some Christmas presents. It's only a few days away.'

Sylvia placed a pan with solid porridge back on the stove's hot plate. 'Nobody expects you to buy a present.'

'But I want to give a little something. Christmas isn't Christmas without unwrapping presents. Would you mind driving me to Undermere?'

She watched Sylvia as she digested the question. 'I will go shopping with you. I will hold your purse, and you must give me your word of honour that you won't run away.'

'Where would I run away to?'

'You promise?'

Lily shrugged, dismissively. 'I won't run away.'

'We'll go this morning.' She turned back to her porridge. 'Damn. It's burned.'

It was a bumpy ride across the moor in the Sunbeam Alpine and conversation was limited, partly because Lily didn't want Sylvia to take her eyes off the narrow road. She thought about Christmas and yearned to be with Malcolm and his parents. Why hadn't he been in touch? Weren't they developing a strong friendship? Why invite her for Christmas if that weren't the case? Could something have happened to him? Her mother once told her that the woman was the flower and the man the bee who had the freedom to choose which flower to pollenate in exchange for nectar. Lily didn't understand what her mother meant at the time but to be a flower, waiting for a bee, was not her idea of an emancipated woman.

Undermere town centre thronged with Christmas shoppers. She decided they should first visit Timothy Whites, a chemist and homewares shop in the High Street, which offered a good range of personal grooming items. She would buy a selection of aftershave and Cologne and decide later who to give them to. If, by some miracle, she got to see Malcolm again, she wanted to make sure she had a gift without revealing it to Sylvia.

'Three bottles of Brut? Are you sure?' Sylvia asked, in front of a smiling sales assistant, much to Lily's embarrassment.

An idea suddenly took hold. 'Miss Cooper. How can I buy you a present with you by my side?'

Sylvia smiled. 'It's a sweet thought, Lily, but it's not going to work. As headmistress, I have come across every trick in the book.'

'I want to buy you a surprise for the big day.'

'That's very kind of you. I suggest you choose a little something and give it to this sales assistant. I will then use your money to pay for it.'

'You'll know how much it costs!'

'I promise not to look at the change.'

Outmanoeuvred, Lily wondered what to buy. Timothy Whites had its own little bookstore, and she decided to see what was on offer. Her eyes alighted upon *Lady Chatterley's Lover* by D.H. Lawrence. Perfect, she thought, for an older woman married to a younger man. A marriage of the body if not of the mind.

That evening Lily was back alone in the prefects' lounge watching The Saint. During the drama, Simon Templar answered the phone in his flat.

'This is the operator here,' spoke a distorted voice.

'We have a Miss Jones requesting to make a reverse charge call. Will you accept the charge?'

The sun was just rising over the North Sea when Lily donned her woollen pom-pom hat, wrapped a tartan woollen scarf around her neck and slipped on her duffel coat. She looked at her feet and wished she had hiking boots, but her wool-lined boots would have to do. She didn't dare wear her school shoes, in case they got dirty and gave away where she'd been. She checked the time on her mother's watch. If she hurried, she could be there and back before breakfast.

She decided to give Sylvia's private quarters a wide berth by going through the empty school refectory and kitchen, and exiting through the tradesmen's entrance, which was beyond the line of sight to where Colonel Craig stored the lawnmowers. The weather was definitely closing in with dark clouds threatening sleet or snow. She pulled on her mother's fur-lined gloves as she hurried across the open area in front of the school and strode out down the long, lonely drive. The forest of trees on each side of the narrow, twisting sliver of tarmac offered some respite from the biting wind, but their stark branches with bony fingers, and the impenetrable shadows made her shiver more than just with the cold.

The pale light within the red telephone box was a beacon that gave her comfort, and she felt immense relief when she pulled open the heavy door. She lifted the black receiver and dialled 100.

'Operator. How may I direct your call.' The voice was clear, precise, perfect diction, and made Lily nervous.

'Hello. I would like to make a reverse-charge call. Is that possible?'

'If the charge is accepted by the respondent, I will

connect you.'

'Thank you.'

'What is your name and the number you wish to call?'

'My name is Lily Turnbull, and the number is Undermere 53867.'

Lily heard the number being dialled and within a few rings the phone was answered.

'Cadwallader.' Lily recognised Malcolm's father's voice.

'Hello, this is the operator here with a request from Lily Turnbull to make a reverse-charge call. Will you accept the charge?'

'Absolutely. Please put her through.'

'Miss Turnbull, I am connecting you now.' Lily heard a couple of clicks, and the operator had gone.

'Lily?'

'Mr Cadwallader, thank you for accepting my call. I promise to pay you back.'

'I wouldn't hear of it. Hang on, I'll just go and rouse Malcolm.' She heard him place the handset by the telephone base. 'Malcolm,' he called. 'It's Lily. She wants a word.' A few seconds later, there were heavy footsteps on the stairs and a rather breathless voice.

'Lily?'

'I'm sorry to call you so early,' she rattled out. 'I was hoping we might meet again but I know you've been busy.'

'I wanted to see you, very much, but as you didn't reply I concluded I was out of favour.'

'Reply?'

'To my letters. I've written quite a few rather long missives. Perhaps they got caught up in the Christmas post?'

Lily felt the heat of ice cold rage. 'They were caught up somewhere as your missives never reached me.'

'Did your headmistress mention that I had telephoned?'

'No, she did not. I've been a prisoner up at the school without means of making contact, and no money to catch a bus or make a phone call or buy a stamp.' She could hear him breathing as he digested the information. 'Hello?'

'Yes, I'm here,' he said.

'May I come and visit you?'

'Lily, you are always welcome.'

'I'll start walking. I'm calling from the phone box at the end of my school drive.'

'You wish to visit, now?'

'Yes. Unless you're too busy.'

'I'll get dressed and jump in the car.'

'What about the punctures?'

'They weren't punctures. The tyres were slashed. My father insisted on buying me four new boots.'

Lily had no doubt as to who had slashed Malcolm's tyres. 'Look out for me on the road,' she said.

'Why not go back to school and I'll pick you up from there?'

'I might not be able to get away again.'

Malcolm appeared to hesitate, then said, 'I'll be with you in half an hour. When the road does a sharp left, make sure you take the turn for Hawksmead and Undermere or you'll end up in Crowford.'

'Thank you. See you soon,' but the line had already disconnected. She replaced the receiver on its cradle, smiled and pushed open the door.

'I thought it was you,' spoke a guttural voice.

Lily gasped.

'Jump in,' Dr Bircher said. 'I'll give you a lift back to school.'

'Thank you. I'd like to walk.'

'Nonsense. The air is almost freezing.' She clamped her hand on Lily's upper arm.

Lily forced a smile. 'Thank you for the kind offer, but I would rather walk.' She shrugged off the doctor's grip. There was a momentary stand-off as the two women stared into each other's eyes.

Eventually, Dr Bircher sniffed and said, 'I'm glad you feel better.' She strode back to her car and started the engine. Cogs ground together as she sought first gear. Her rear wheels spun on the icy surface and the heavy car roared away. Soon it was lost from view, but Lily knew she would return with re-enforcements.

She took a deep breath and felt the cold air penetrate her lungs as she marched to freedom and Malcolm's arms. Even the satanic branches of swaying trees did not affect her mood. She came to the stone bridge over the River Eyas and as she climbed the humpback, she knew she was, in effect, crossing the Rubicon. Halfway, she looked down at the fast-flowing tributary to the River Hawk and thought about the evil serpent that had taken the life of her dear brother. 'Come on Malcolm. Please hurry.' She shivered, desperate to feel safe in the warm confines of his car.

Rainer was in his private space. On the desk was a Christmas card from his aunt. The message of goodwill to all men was as clear as the bell in the school's clocktower. The hot war may have ended in 1945, but the Cold War was bubbling over. He thought about his mother and sister and what he'd done to them by escaping to the West. They did not deserve to be punished for his impromptu action. He picked up the Christmas card and read the delightful message. It was clear and unequivocal. He dropped the card on his desk. After so much time, he thought he'd escaped the Soviet bear, but its claws were deeply entrenched. His mother and sister were already suffering, and he knew they would be deported to the frozen wasteland of a Siberian gulag, or its modern equivalent, until he complied.

What about Lily's father? He'd lost his wife to cancer, his son to a boating accident. Could Rainer deprive him of his daughter as well?

The windows in his turret room rattled as the bitter nor' easterly whipped the solid edifice, home to a thousand biting draughts and one terrifying thought.

Malcolm pressed the accelerator and had to use all his youthful driving skill to avoid the potholes and the crumbling edge of tarmac. The winter sun had melted most of the frost but following his tragic experience with black ice, his focus was at maximum. The last thing he needed on his way to the love of his life, was to skid and slide into a bog. As the nippy MG 1100 reached the crest of yet another hill, he saw her lone figure in the distance and, to his consternation, a car draw up alongside her. There seemed to be a stand-off and then the road dropped down.

He accelerated as hard as he dared and weaved around a rocky outcrop that would stop his car dead. He kept his foot on the accelerator, only releasing the pedal to change to third. From the scream of his pistons, he knew the revs were too high, but he had confidence in the little motor and was relieved to see Lily walking alone when he reached the top of the next ridge. He lost sight of her as he rounded a steep escarpment, to face, head on, the smooth lines of a green sports car heading straight for him.

There was no room. He slammed on his brakes. In that split moment he had a choice. Collide or swerve off the road onto the moor. In summer, it would be a spongy surface, but after the freezing temperatures since the end of October, he knew the ground would be unyielding. He flew off the edge of the road and slid, only coming to a sudden halt when his car's nose burrowed into a mossy mound.

His chest slammed against the steering wheel; he felt intense pain …and then nothing. Oblivion.

CHAPTER TWENTY-SEVEN

'Wake up,' ordered a harsh voice. Malcolm opened his eyes, but he was blinded by hot blood. Every part of him hurt though his head pounded the most.

'I'll help you out,' the voice said. Strong hands gripped him and by pushing with his legs, Malcolm was able to flop out of the car onto the frozen ground.

His head swam as he tried to gather his thoughts. 'What happened?' he gasped.

'You were driving too fast and lost control. It was a good thing I came along when I did.'

'I don't remember.'

'You must go to hospital. I will drive you. But, first, we have to get you to my car.'

With his arm wrapped around the young foreigner, Malcolm staggered and slipped up the steep incline back to the strip of tarmac. He leaned on the bonnet of the sports car and saw his blood drip onto the green paint.

'Get in,' demanded the foreign voice.

Malcolm's head was spinning. He knew he was quite seriously injured. His ribs hurt so much he could barely breathe. 'Who are you?' he gasped.

'My name is Rainer. I teach German at Inniscliffe.'

'I know that name.'

'Get in the car. You need urgent medical help.'

It took a lot of courage for Malcolm to ease his long frame into the sports car. The pounding pain in his head was matched by the stabbing pain in his ribs. Once seated, he closed his eyes.

Lily was furious. Rainer thought he could order her to get in Sylvia's car. She should never have started a relationship with him. He had betrayed the woman who had saved his life and thought he could also treat Lily with the same lack of respect. He must've read Malcolm's letters that Sylvia had kept from her because he guessed that was who she planned to meet.

Where was Malcolm? She strained her eyes and ears for sight of his two-tone car, but the wind was blowing in the wrong direction for her to hear his engine, and the road kept disappearing.

Why was he taking so long? Had Rainer used Sylvia's car to block the road? His behaviour was outrageous and to her dying breath she would regret the feelings she once had for him.

She looked at her watch. It had been over forty-five minutes since she'd spoken to Malcolm and would jolly well walk all the way to his cottage if he didn't show up soon.

The biting wind cut through her coat but not her determination. She thought about her brother and tried to get warm by remembering a very happy summer holiday they'd had with their parents in north Devon, staying in a hotel overlooking Saunton Sands. They'd had such fun on the beach, which stretched for three miles, playing in the surf and all working together to build an amazing sandcastle with its own moat. Their hotel had a lovely white art deco exterior, brilliantly lit each evening by the setting sun. She had felt so grown-up eating with her parents and brother in the dining room. The twins were always on best behaviour; although she often fell asleep at the table, exhausted by the fun of the day.

Lily was jolted out of her reverie. Malcolm's MG was at least forty yards off the road with its nose rammed into an earthy mound. She could see what had happened from the skid marks on the tarmac. Rainer had clearly been driving much too fast and, to avoid a head-on collision, Malcolm had taken evasive action.

Her stomach in knots, she hurried over the mossy ground slipping and sliding down to the car. The driver's door was open, and Malcolm was gone. She saw the windscreen was cracked and there was blood spattered over the dashboard.

For a moment she was in shock, and fearful that Malcolm was fatally injured. Rattling pistons straining on an incline attracted her attention. She climbed as fast as she could over the treacherous moss and rocks back to the road, but her sole slipped, and she fell to her hands and knees. She pushed herself up and saw a green bus trundle past on its way to Hawksmead and Undermere. She scrambled to the road and jumped and waved, hoping the driver would see her in his rearview mirror, but her heart sank as the bus disappeared over the brow of the next hill.

A large spot of rain landed on her nose. Dark, bulbous clouds gathered above, and more spots splashed her face. She pulled up the hood on her duffel coat as the deluge began.

The rain came in sheets; she looked about her desperately, willing the arrival of a car, and yet fearful of who may be driving. There was no shelter, no tree, no shepherd's hut; she had no choice but to press on, getting more and more soaked with every stride. The road was awash, and she feared falling over, but she kept going, kept running until hailstones hammered her head and she was forced to stop and curl up in a ball like a hedgehog.

The hail subsided and the rain reduced from torrential to heavy. Soaked to the skin and colder than she'd ever been, she knew she had to keep moving. Moments later, pain shot up from her shinbone like a stabbing knife and she stumbled and screamed. The rain continued to lash her as she hopped and limped and whimpered, unable to put any weight on her leg. Overwhelmed by agony, she sank to her knees into rivulets of water as rain pelted down, driving icy arrows through to her bones.

The pain in her shin, which had snapped like a twig in Austria when she was ten, gradually subsided and she was able to gather her thoughts. She looked around and realised she was slumped in the middle of the road. Gritting her teeth, she pushed herself to her feet and looked through the sheets of rain at the soft hues of the terrifying moor.

Had she ever been more alone or more vulnerable? She had no choice but to keep going. Sparks of pain shot up her shin, but she was able to limp along. Downhill hurt more but was easier on her muscles. Uphill was just a slog but less painful. Feeling hopeless and exhausted, she was tempted to seek solace on the mossy moor and let sleep overtake her. To rest for some time, the way Captain Oates explained his departure from the tent to Scott of the Antarctic on the way back from the South Pole. He had demonstrated great courage and fortitude. So must she, Lily thought, so must she, and she limped on, through the unrelenting rain until she was rewarded by the twinkling lights of The Rorty Crankle Inn. The sight renewed her resolve but, like a mirage, it never seemed to get closer. She walked, her pain numbed by the bitter cold, until she staggered into the saloon bar in a drenched and wretched state.

The warmth hit her like a wall, and it took a few moments, dripping onto the oak floorboards, before she could adjust to her surroundings. Asleep in a worn armchair she spotted an elderly man, a briar pipe loosely held in his hand. Blazing logs in a massive inglenook fireplace drew her like a moth to its flames. Her soaked coat steamed as she convulsed and shivered, standing almost within the spitting and crackling grate. She rubbed her white hands together as she tried to get blood to circulate within her numb fingers.

'Here. Drink this.' A balloon glass swilling with a golden brown liquid was thrust under her nose. She reached for it and cupped the balloon in the palms of both hands.

'My name's Jim.' She looked at the swarthy barman. 'I remember you had lunch here with a young chap.'

Lily's lips were so cold she could not form any words.

'Have a sip,' he said. 'It'll work wonders. It's my finest cognac.'

Lily relished the warm glow that spread through her body. 'Thank you,' she shivered through immobile lips. 'My friend has had an accident, and I need to go to him. May I use your phone?'

'Of course, but tell me what's happened, first.'

'He was on his way to meet me when a vehicle in the

opposite direction forced him off the road. By the time I got to his car, I could see from the footprints he'd been taken by the other driver. I presume to hospital. At least, that's what I hope. There was an awful lot of blood.'

'Drink up. I would take you to the hospital myself, but I've got a few regulars coming for a pre-Christmas lunch.'

Lily took another sip and followed Jim to the phone at the back of the bar. 'Do you have a telephone directory?' she asked.

Reverend William Longden was surprised to receive a phone call from Lily. When she rang, he was writing his sermon for the Christmas service and was a little annoyed by the interruption; but as soon as he heard her voice, all annoyance evaporated and he reached for his trilby, winter raincoat, lined-leather gloves, and put on heavy shoes he reserved for long walks.

The rain had turned to hail as he hurried from the dilapidated Methodist manse in Crowford to his equally dilapidated Austin. He felt truly battered by the elements when he closed the car door and hoped and prayed that the battery still had its charge. Relief flooded through him when the engine started. He put his foot on the brake pedal, depressed the clutch, shifted the gear lever into first and released the handbrake.

The little motor responded well to the terrible driving conditions and soon he was passing through the dancing dell. Bare branches, silhouetted by menacing clouds, looked particularly satanic. This was not a place he relished breaking down.

He emerged onto the open road that traversed Hawksmoor and through his ineffective wiper blades he marvelled at its bleak green, brown and purple hues. He kept his speed low, fearful of what he may meet on the lonely road with its ups and downs, lefts and rights.

Until he received the telephone call from Lily, he had not dared to imagine that he could appeal to a woman as beautiful and kind as her. If he were a priest in the Roman Catholic Abbey that once stood on the moor by Hawksmead College, he would be begging God to forgive his wanton thoughts. Fortunately, for his heart and soul, he was a Methodist Minister who was at liberty to seek the love of a good woman.

He knew that Lily's waywardness was part of why he found her so attractive, although he believed her troubled soul was probably a result of her great personal grief. Underlying her rebellious nature, William detected a wholesome girl who was open to the teachings of the Holy Bible and who seemed ready to devote her life to Jesus. At least, that's what he told himself as he navigated the meandering strip of rain-slicked tarmacadam.

Lily stared at the pub's double inner doors, with their engraved glass panels, and waited, willing them to open. She knew her exhaustion was partly due to the stress of everything that had happened. She was also worried for another reason; her period was late, very late. If she were pregnant, there was no mystery as to the father. Unmarried teenage girls were not treated well by the British establishment, despite it being the *Swingin' Sixties*. Often illegitimate babies were forcibly taken from teenage mothers and put into care. She had read in a newspaper, that some babies were deported to Australia, such was the shame. She shivered at the thought of such a cruel act. One teenage mother had described how she was treated with disdain by the midwife, offered no pain relief, and despite requiring stitching after being cut, she was left with her legs in the stirrups for over an hour while her baby was removed and bundled-up for forced adoption.

Tears came to Lily's eyes. She knew her father would do everything he could to protect her, but he would also be keen to avoid a scandal that could affect his career as a representative of Her Majesty's Government. She could try and get rid of the baby, but the thought of visiting some backstreet abortionist filled her with terror. Dr Bircher was a last resort, but whether she would agree to breaking the law and abort the foetus was another matter.

What was she thinking?

The idea of that vile woman poking around inside her, filled her with abject repulsion. She willed her period to start.

'Lily?'

Startled, she looked up. William was a big man. Handsome in a Charlton Heston, Ben Hur sort of way, rather than the good looks of Richard Chamberlain.

'Are you all right? You're not hurt?'

'It's my friend Malcolm. He's had a crash, and I think Rainer has taken him to hospital. He was meant to pick me up.'

'Rainer was?'

'No. Mr Cadwallader, Malcolm. I'm worried about him. Perhaps we could drive to the hospital?'

'We're not family. I doubt they will tell us anything.'

'They'll tell you.' She looked at his grey frontispiece topped off by his white dog collar. 'You're a man of the cloth.'

William smiled. 'True. God can be persuasive. Doesn't Mr Cadwallader have a family?'

'Yes, he lives with his parents.'

'Do you know their telephone number?'

'Malcolm could be seriously injured. It's the kind of news I feel I should convey in person.'

He reached for her elbow and helped her up out of the chair.

CHAPTER TWENTY-EIGHT

'Mr Cadwallader,' Malcolm heard a man say. 'Your son is receiving anaesthetic drugs to slow the flow of blood to his brain and thereby decrease its activity. He received quite a knock on the head and by reducing the level of oxygen, his brain will take a rest and rebalance the chemicals in his nerve cells.'

'Are you saying, he's in a coma?' Malcolm recognised his father's voice, usually jovial but now devoid of all humour.

'In effect, yes,' came the reply.

'How soon will he come out of it?'

'We will bring him round in two to three days. He'll be here over Christmas.'

'What about his other injuries?' Malcolm heard his mother ask.

'Broken ribs, and stitches to his head, above his hairline so the cat-gut sutures won't spoil your son's good looks.' The doctor chuckled at his own inappropriate joke.

Malcolm wished he could speak, but he couldn't move. In fact, the only sensation he had was hearing. Unfortunately, the reduced oxygen flow didn't stop his brain from whirring. He had been driving to meet

Lily and remembered a car coming much too fast in the opposite direction, and that was it. He presumed he was in Undermere General Hospital but had no idea how he had got there.

'You're absolutely sure there is no brain injury?' he heard his mother ask.

'We cannot be absolutely sure until we carry out cognitive tests,' the doctor answered. 'But your son is young and, with a following wind, should make a full recovery.'

And that was it. He heard a few more murmurings and then nothing. He assumed that he must be in a private room or intensive care facility rather than a general ward with loads of bustle. He tried to calm his thoughts and focus on opening his eyes, but it was as though his mind was completely encased in steel. Could he be dying? He'd heard that hearing is the last sensation to go before the spirit leaves its host body.

He thought about Lily and pictured her beautiful face. She was blessed with thick blonde hair that most girls bought bottles of bleach to emulate, lovely wide grey eyes, the sweetest nose and the most kissable mouth he'd ever seen. She was the perfect embodiment of womanhood, and he loved her more than he could contain in his heart.

Her voice echoed through his head, but her words were not what he expected to hear. 'Malcolm knew my brother. Perhaps, through him, David and I will always be together.' He did not feel the tears that rolled from the corners of his eyes.

Another voice, that of the man in whom Malcolm had confided, and whose words that day in the Methodist Church, gave him a reason to live.

This time, he felt his tears.

Christmas alone with Mater and Pater was not what Malcolm had hoped. He was lucky to be released from hospital on Christmas Eve. They attended St Mary's Church in Undermere and, thanks to his partly shaved head and large Elastoplast covering his wound, he was the centre of much attention. The morning service was traditional with many of his favourite Christmas carols, but his heart lay elsewhere. During his time partly comatose, all he could do was think and sleep and dream about Lily. She and the Reverend had visited often when he was sedated, and also when he was awake and recovering. What disturbed him most, was that their friendship was clearly growing, despite the constant presence of Lily's headmistress cum chaperone. Of course, the clergyman may just be offering a steadying arm as Lily had suffered so much following her brother's death. In truth, he feared the Hand of God was at work and that Lily was being seduced, not by the Reverend, a giant of a man who he believed to be of the highest integrity, but by the comfort and strength she seemed to be gaining from his company.

Should he fight for her? In his current bashed-up state Malcolm looked more like Quasimodo than Romeo. He had no choice but to bide his time and hope that once school restarted in January, Lily would be more focused on her exams than romance with the Reverend who was, after all, her school chaplain and divinity master.

CHAPTER TWENTY-NINE

'What a feast,' proclaimed Dr Bircher, who looked genuinely excited at the prospect of such delicious fare. Lily had tried her best to sit as far away from the Swiss-German doctor as possible, but it meant being next to Colonel Craig who was pouring red wine. To her left, was the lovely Reverend William Longden who had given such an inspiring sermon in Crowford Methodist Church, which had been packed with villagers. On his left, was Reginald R. Sterck, the lighthouse keeper who was well into his eighties. At the far end of the table stood Rainer who was skilfully carving a large turkey, that looked and smelt delicious.

'Since Mrs Sterck's passing, I have not enjoyed a roast.'

'Mr Sterck,' Sylvia said. 'You must eat with us more often, especially during term time in the refectory.'

'Am not I a bit old to pass off as a pupil?'

They all laughed.

'In truth, I think I'm also a bit too old to pass off as a member of staff.'

'It's a sincere offer, Mr Sterck,' said Sylvia.

He looked up at her as she stood by the table. 'I cannot drive anymore. My distant vision is still good, but I've given my old jalopy to Daphne's nephew. It was just gathering rust.'

'I hope you're not going to give up the lighthouse, too?' Sylvia asked.

'I'll stay until it's finally automated. Hopefully, I'll be ready for my box by then.'

'What drew you to the lonely light?' Rainer asked.

'Peace. After the Great War, and being pounded by the Hun, no offence Mr Rainer, I wanted solitude and silence. I expected a monastic existence, reading, observing, being part of nature, maintaining the light. And then Daphne came along. She was a shepherdess who had lost her sheep.' He laughed. 'It's why I called her Bo-Peep.'

'Did she find them?' Sylvia asked.

'All bar one. Her favourite ram had chased a seagull and fallen over the cliff. The carcass was still fresh, so I suggested we make mutton stew. As I watched her skin the animal, I fell in love and shared nigh on forty happy years.'

Colonel Craig stood and raised his glass. 'I would like to propose two toasts. The first to Sylvia, our amazing chef, who has given us this delicious feast to relish on our Lord's birthday.'

Lily picked up her wine glass and smiled at Sylvia. 'Thank you,' she said, but before she could take a sip the colonel spoke again.

'My second toast is to Gretchen, who has bestowed on me the greatest honour of agreeing to be my wife.'

Rainer stopped carving. Sylvia stopped transferring Brussels sprouts into a dish, and Bella stopped pacing around the table, panting for morsels.

Dr Gretchen Bircher laughed. 'My car was broken down in Undermere. It was the only way I could get him to go and fix it.'

Sylvia was dismayed. Eleven years ago, when she was Head Girl, she had fallen for the war hero and had loved tracing the tips of her fingers over his battle-scarred, lean body. She thought they were in love, despite the vast age difference. She treasured the memory of their first kiss, in the former stables where he stored school equipment including the chalking machine for marking up the lacrosse pitch. The mix of earthy smells she found intoxicating and had determined that this heroic man should be the person to change her from a girl to a woman.

'Do you want to explore the lighthouse?' she had asked him one day.

Colonel Craig put down his spanner and appraised the schoolgirl. 'Now?'

'It's the longest day and I've finished all my exams.'

'You're leaving?

'Of course.'

'What will you do?'

'I would like to go to drama school, but my father told me I have to attend secretarial college. He said it's important to have real skills such as typing and shorthand.'

'Can you not do both? I thought your performance in the Persian Princess was remarkable.'

'Thank you.' Sylvia did a mock curtsy and dropped the tartan blanket she'd been holding under her arm.

He picked it up and handed it to her. 'Won't the keeper be in the lighthouse?'

'It's a beautiful day. Clear skies and a calm sea. Mr Sterck'll be in his cottage with his feet up sleeping-off his wife's Sunday roast.'

Colonel Craig contemplated her response. 'I'll wash

my hands.'

She followed him out of the workshop into the school car park. Attached to the side of a row of brick garages was a brass tap. Colonel Craig turned it on and rubbed his hands under the flow of water. He turned off the tap and waved his hands in the air. 'I'm looking forward to this. I've wanted to go in the lighthouse, but I thought it was forbidden.'

They walked together, side by side, across the sward. She was desperate to take his arm or hold his hand but if they were seen being familiar it could result in senior members of staff clamouring for her to be expelled. She was confident her Godmother would not take such drastic action, especially as it was so near the end of the summer term, when she would be leaving anyway. At the time, her juvenile brain didn't worry about Colonel Craig and the risk that he may lose his job for canoodling with a pupil.

They strolled, relishing each other's company, enjoying the warm summer breeze and the wildflowers that brought a rainbow of colours to the grassy plane that led to the sheer cliffs. Ahead was the white, rendered edifice of the lighthouse. Beyond, barely visible behind a high privet hedge, was the lighthouse keeper's cottage.

'How do we get in?' Colonel Craig asked. 'Won't it be locked?'

'I chose the lighthouse and its keeper for a humanities project last year. I know where a spare key is kept.'

'Sylvia, you do surprise me, although I know I shouldn't be. You are a remarkable young woman.'

She glowed with pride and excitement as they approached the lighthouse with its stone steps leading to a small, steel door.

'Up close, it's size is pretty impressive,' said the colonel.

'It's eighty-five feet tall and the light is one hundred and eighty-seven feet above high water. The beam was electrified in 1920, and it can be seen, on a clear night, nineteen nautical miles away.'

'And when it's foggy,' Colonel Craig said, 'the foghorn keeps us all awake.' They both laughed. 'So, where is the key?'

'Guess.'

'Under a rock?'

She slipped her hand into the pocket of her plaid skirt and displayed a brass key in her palm. 'Mr Sterck lent it to me and I never got round to returning it.' She climbed the few steps and slipped the key into the lock and opened the door.

Colonel Craig chuckled. 'You are truly a remarkable woman.'

They entered the cylindrical enclosure. Ahead was a stone spiral staircase, dimly lit by small windows emitting sunlight through thick, salty panes. Each time one or other said a word, their voice strangely echoed within the circular brick walls.

They clip-clopped up the stairs until they reached the service room and were presented with a giant motor that rotated the lantern above.

'When it was driven by paraffin,' Sylvia said, 'there had to be an effective ventilation system but, now it's all electric, the airflow has been closed off.'

'Impressive.'

'Did you know that lighthouses have flash codes?

'You mean like Morse code?'

'Exactly. That way a ship knows which lighthouse it

is. It's the same with the foghorn.'

'Shall we go up to the top' he asked, 'and enjoy the view?'

'Better not. We could damage the reflectors or magnifiers just by brushing our clothes against them.'

'There's a walkway outside.'

'But then we can be seen from miles away and reported.'

'To whom?'

'I dread to think. You'll be okay. They can't lay a finger on you. But my Godmother has quite an arm. As for Old Ma Barry, her belt leaves welts that last for weeks.'

'Okay.' He looked around the circular room with its sparse furnishings including a chair, a table with an assortment of cleaning cloths and chemicals, and an antique-looking telephone.

'That's not a normal phone,' Sylvia said. 'The cable goes underground to the coastguard in Reculver. If there's an emergency, a lifeboat can be launched with a crew in just a few minutes.'

'You really are a mine of information.'

Sylvia laid out the rug on the steel floor.

'Not much of a view from this room,' Colonel Craig said. 'Why don't we go and sit near the top of the cliff?'

She took his hand in hers. 'For what I have planned, this is perfect.' She knelt on the rug and laid down on her back.

He didn't move. 'Have you done this before?' he asked.

'Never. Have you?'

'Of course!'

'That's what I hoped.'

'I don't have anything with me. You could get

pregnant.'

'Not if you pull out at the last moment.'

He smiled and knelt beside her. 'I'll do my best.'

It was a sad day when her schooldays came to an end, and she had to say a fond farewell to her colonel.

'I'm keeping the key for the lighthouse,' she said, 'as a memento of a very happy time.'

He smiled. 'My pleasure, I can assure you.' He gripped her arms, and his pale eyes looked squarely into her face. 'One piece of advice.'

She waited, anxious to hear what he was about to say.

'If your father will not permit you to become an actress, then you must go to university. I know it's rare for girls to seek higher education, but you are an utter brainbox and will be accepted wherever you apply.'

Nine years later, when Sylvia took over the reins having inherited Inniscliffe from her Godmother, she was surprised and pleased to see that her colonel still worked at the school. He, on the other hand, kept their relationship formal and never referred to that amazing summer in '54. She often wondered why. Now she knew.

'Congratulations,' Sylvia forced herself to say. 'Wonderful news. I hope you will be married in the school chapel.' She placed the dish with the sprouts on the table.

William stood. 'If you would permit me, I would deem it the greatest honour to join you in Holy Matrimony.'

Lily was in shock. She had confided in Colonel Craig her deepest fears regarding Dr Bircher's wartime past, and now he had declared his love for her. And Rainer, a fellow German, had run Malcolm off the road and nearly killed him. As she looked around the Christmas table a deep seated fear set in. The only person she knew she could trust was Reverend William. She thought about the scrap of life inside her and wondered what kind of person her half-German child would become. Strong and resolute like The Reverend, or tainted by a murderous ideology? She took a sip of wine and decided that nurture would win the day. Her child would never know about its Teutonic heritage.

Despite all her misgivings and fears, Lily enjoyed the meal and found herself greatly warming to William's engaging mind and colossal intellect. He was a linguist, with Latin at his tongue tip, together with another half-dozen modern languages.

'Reverend, what are your plans for 1966?' Colonel Craig asked as Lily and Sylvia cleared away the plates.

The Reverend dabbed his lips with his napkin. 'I have been asked to administer the Methodist Church in Hawksmead.'

'We shall miss you, here,' Colonel Craig responded.

'However,' William continued, 'I shall decline.'

There was a momentary pause. Dr Bircher spoke. 'Hawksmead has a much bigger church than the piddling one in Crowford. Why would you turn it down?'

Everyone looked at the Reverend. 'I have plans that must be fulfilled, first.'

'Plans?' Rainer asked. 'What are they?'

'To be frank,' William said, 'they are still on the drawing board.'

Sylvia struck a match and waved it near a brandy-soaked Christmas pudding which flared up and glowed with dancing blue flames. 'Rainer,' she said. 'Would you kindly get the brandy cream from the fridge? It's in the white jug.'

He opened the door to the large refrigerator as everyone watched the flames die away, having filled their senses with an enticing aroma.

'Christmas pudding,' Dr Bircher said. 'What exactly is it? I've always gone for sherry trifle.'

'I considered the trifle route,' Sylvia responded, 'but as it's so chilly out, I thought we all needed a solid base.'

Everyone laughed and, almost as one, rested a hand on their full stomachs. Lily stood and collected some bowls from a pine Welsh dresser and placed them on the table.

'It smells delicious,' William said.

'What are the secret ingredients,' Dr Bircher asked, 'apart from fine Cognac?'

Sylvia cut into the pudding. 'I am no Fanny Cradock, but I did follow her recipe. Fundamentally, it's a mix of self-raising flour, spices, eggs, dried fruit, orange peel, sultanas, butter, almonds, walnuts, cinnamon, and grated nutmeg. Did I mention brandy?'

Everyone laughed. Lily wondered whether eating Christmas pudding with all the strong liquor would hurt her foetus; she didn't need a doctor to tell her she was pregnant. Her mother once told her that when she was expecting, she enjoyed a nightly gin and tonic with ice and lemon, accompanied by the occasional cigarette. But, owing to post-war rationing, and the cost of her favourite brand, Senior Service, she was only ever a social smoker. Lily was not interested in smoking but quite liked watching men going through the process of lighting a cigarette and blowing smoke rings.

'I think it's time for a Capstan.' Lily watched Colonel

Craig fish in his inside pocket and produce his silver cigarette case. 'Anyone care to join me?' he asked.

'I will,' answered Rainer. Colonel Craig lit his own cigarette with his flip top lighter, then passed the silver case and lighter to Lily for handing on to Rainer.

'Many doctors recommend cigarettes for calming patients,' said Dr Bircher, 'but I have seen evidence that babies born of mothers who smoke heavily during pregnancy, can be born smaller than the average and are sometimes malformed. There was a study in Germany that linked smoking to cleft palates in infants.'

Lily wanted to comment on Dr Bircher's knowledge of the German study, but decided not to rock the boat.

Dr Bircher looked at Sylvia. 'I would very much like to try your pudding. In Switzerland my family tradition was Christollen; a type of bread filled with nuts, dried fruits and spices. My mother was a very good baker.'

'When did she die?' Lily asked, not sure what she expected her question to reveal.

'In 1929 she contracted tuberculosis,' Dr Bircher answered, her tone almost challenging. 'It was called the white death, owing to the anaemic pallor of those infected. Without antibiotics, she had little hope. The cough is incredibly painful. There are sweats, horrendous bowel emissions, and a wasting away until little more than skin and bone. She died alone, quarantined in a nursing home.'

There was a painful pause and then William stood. 'Miss Cooper, Sylvia. Thank you for inviting me to share your table. I am greatly honoured but must now take my leave to officiate at Evensong. There won't be many there, I grant you, but I will conduct the service even if Our Lord is the only one to hear.'

'I'll walk you to your car,' Lily said, her voice almost hushed.

William nodded. 'If your headmistress approves.' He looked at Sylvia.

'Of course.'

Lily stole a glance at Rainer who seemed focused on his glass of brandy; ash from his cigarette hung precariously. She forced a smile as she looked at Dr Bircher. 'Many congratulations on your engagement. I hope you and the colonel will be very happy.'

Colonel Craig stood, and William shook his hand. 'Congratulations Colonel. Perhaps we could discuss the content of your marriage service next week?'

'Thank you, Reverend,' Colonel Craig said. 'Something simple and joyous, would suit us both fine.'

William adjusted his waistcoat and reached for his jacket which was hanging on a row of hooks to one side of the kitchen. 'Thank you, again, Miss Cooper,' he said. 'We have a usual Sunday service in the Methodist Church, tomorrow, if you'd care to attend.'

Lily jumped in. 'Excellent idea. The walk will do us all good.'

'It's three miles, Lily.' Rainer spoke for the first time in a while.

'I don't blame anyone for wanting a lie in on Boxing Day,' William said, 'especially our wonderful chef.'

Feeble daylight quickly gave way to night as Lily walked William along the corridors and down the back stairs to the exit for the staff car park. They approached his Austin. 'I didn't expect to enjoy the Christmas festivities quite as much,' he said

She looked up at the tall man. 'Nor I, despite the

presence of Dr Bircher.'

'She is a bit of a one-off. To be frank, I cannot make her out. She is part of the healing profession and yet I sense a dark heart.'

'I do too. Perhaps it's her German heritage.'

'As a Swiss-German, the atrocities committed by her Germanic cousins cannot be blamed on her.'

'She was a new doctor at the school when Eva disappeared.'

'Is your mind still occupied with the young girl?'

'I spoke to the colonel about my suspicions regarding Dr Bircher's past, and he said he would look into it. Next, he announces, they're getting married.'

'I've not been here long and have paid scant attention to Colonel Craig, and even less to Dr Bircher, as I have my own physician, but I was also a little surprised by their engagement.'

'I don't trust either of them.'

'Sadly, there is little we can do except honour Eva, and pray that her fighting spirit helped her escape to the Promised Land.'

Lily shook her head. 'No. She never left. I have no idea what she wants from me, but she is here.' Lily stared into his grey eyes. 'They say, the first sign of madness is hearing voices. Do you think I'm mad?'

'I hear the voice of Our Lord all the time. I like to feel, on balance, that I am sane.'

She laughed. 'You are wonderfully sane.' Her words came out in a rush. There was a momentary pause.

'1966 beckons,' he said. 'Perhaps, with a following wind, it will be a kind year for us all.'

'1965 could not have been worse.'

'No, Lily, it could not.'

'My father telephoned this morning. For the first

time, ever, we had nothing to say.'

'Silence can speak volumes.' His eyes seemed to swallow her up. 'It's cold out here,' he observed, 'and you don't have a coat.'

She stood on tiptoe and kissed him on the cheek. 'Thank you for all you've done.'

'It's at least a week until school returns so come and see me, anytime. I live in a large, leaking manse and it needs the warmth of company.'

She felt something stir within. It wasn't the longing she had felt for Rainer, nor the affection she had for Malcolm. It was different, more spiritual. 'I would like that. I would like that very much. Thank you.'

'God Bless. I'll wait here until you go back in.'

'Tomorrow,' she blurted. 'May I come tomorrow?'

He opened the driver's door. 'Give me a ring and I'll jump in the motor.'

'I don't have any money left.'

'Money?'

'I need fourpence for the phone box.'

He fished around in his pockets. 'No change, I'm afraid.' He held the tops of her arms in his big hands. 'After morning service, I will drive over, assuming Miss Cooper does not object.'

Lily grunted. 'Hopefully, she'll be too tired to care.'

'I'll say a little prayer,' he said, and she felt his eyes embrace her. 'Now, go inside, or you'll catch your death.'

She nodded. 'I'll be waiting.'

For a few moments Lily felt true, complete happiness; and then she remembered the baby and her feet were as heavy as her heart. She entered the school and wanted to crawl into bed, but her conscience dictated that she should help Sylvia with the washing up.

Her conscience? Why did she not feel guilty about carrying Rainer's baby? Sylvia would find out soon enough, and when she did, Lily would be rightfully expelled. She would not take her final-year exams. She would not go to university. She would be a fallen woman incarcerated in a nursing home until her baby was taken away.

Her head spun as dreadful thoughts crowded her brain. Feelings of nausea spread from her full stomach as she ambled along the dimly-lit corridor, touching the wall for support, not paying attention to her surroundings. The floor uptilted and she fell back, enveloped by a stench that was overwhelming. Her lungs filled with dense, acrid smoke and her body burned from within.

A hand gripped hers and with eyes streaming, she allowed herself to be led blindly, deafened by horrendous cries of pain and loss. She wanted to scream, but every sense was subsumed by overwhelming terror.

Voices… harsh, brutal, shouting. Words she didn't understand. A figure took shape, not old, not young, but solid and strong.

'Was machst du da, Mädchen?'

Lily felt the hand slip from hers. 'Don't go,' she cried. Another hand, large, calloused, gripped her wrist and dragged her forward. Her face rubbed against heavy serge cloth as screaming and wailing intensified. She couldn't see, she couldn't speak, and she couldn't break free. Darkness closed in and she gave up the fight.

Icy water splashed onto her face. The floor in the washroom was cold. She looked up from her prone position and saw Dr Bircher standing over her, her legs astride. In her hand was a dripping toothbrush mug.

'I was on my way to my car when I heard yelling and screaming,' Dr Bircher said, stepping away.

Lily used the edge of a basin to pull herself up. She lurched over to the towel on the roller and mopped her face. Shaken, frightened, she summoned her courage. 'What did you do in the war, Dr Bircher? Which side were you on?'

'Switzerland is a neutral country. We don't take sides.'

'But Switzerland was Hitler's Banker, and you did take stolen gold'.

'We have made amends for that oversight.' She looked at her watch. 'As you've recovered your equilibrium I'll be on my way. Frohe Weihnachten.' She reached for the door's brass handle.

'Dr Bircher.'

She turned and stared at Lily.

'You haven't answered my question. What did you do during the war?'

'I was a doctor in Bern. Once hostilities were over, I decided to seek a new life here.'

'Why Britain?'

She paused for a moment. 'I had fallen in love, and now we are to be married.'

'If you were in love with Colonel Craig, why did you marry Mr Bircher?'

She smiled at Lily. 'Financial expediency, Meine Süße. Gute Nacht.' She opened the door and let it swing shut behind her.

Rainer entered Sylvia's private kitchen from their lounge and looked at his wife who had artfully piled dishes from the Christmas lunch high on the drainer. 'Bella needs a walk. She hasn't been out all day.'

Sylvia replied without looking round. 'The wind has picked up. Don't let her off the lead.'

'She won't pee or poop on the lead. I have to let her off.'

'Just walk her in the school grounds. The sward is too dangerous.'

He grabbed the leather lead from a clothes hook and Bella rushed up to him. He clicked it onto her collar. 'I'll see you later.'

'You'll find me watching The Black and White Minstrel Show with my eyes closed.'

He chuckled and sang in German, 'Mama, wie ich dich liebe, wie ich dich liebe, meine liebe alte Mama.'

'Al Jolson will be rolling in his grave!'

'I don't blame him. I'll see you later.'

Parked alongside her Morris Oxford, Colonel Craig's Vauxhall felt warm and smoky when Gretchen opened the front passenger door and slipped in beside her husband-to-be.

'You smoke too much,' she said.

'I promise to give up once you make a good man of me.'

She laughed and leaned across and kissed him. 'You've always been a good man.'

He chuckled.

'So, do you think the little tart will fall for his plan?'

'It is *my* plan.'

Gretchen laughed. 'Viele entschuldigungen.'

Colonel Craig took a long drag. 'Rainer fell for the plan hook, line and sinker, but she is perceptive.' He looked at Gretchen. 'Best you get in the back so she has no choice but to sit in the front.'

Dr Bircher did as suggested and sat next to her medical bag on the rear seat. 'Open your window when you want me to do it,' she said. 'The cold draught will stop her smelling the chloroform until it's too late.'

There was a brief knock on her door and Lily looked up from where she felt warm and safe, under her bed covers. Silhouetted in the doorway was the man she had once loved and deeply desired, but since meeting Malcolm and getting to know William, his allure had distinctly faded. By his side, Bella panted excitedly.

'We could use your company,' he said. 'It's a bit dark and scary out there.'

'I think I'll stay where I am, but thank you for the invitation.'

'Bella is desperate or else I would join you,' Rainer said.

Lily didn't know how to answer. There was a part of her that despised him, and another part that wanted him more than ever.

He continued, his voice noticeably softer. 'You know how much I love you, liebling.' He switched on the light.

Her resolve ebbed and she threw back the covers. 'Okay, I'll come,' she said, taking delight in showing off a matching pair of knickers and suspenders she'd bought mail order from Freemans Catalogue; and pleased she'd decided to wear stockings on Christmas Day, rather than very unsexy tights. 'I think I'll put on a pair of slacks as it's so cold out,' she mused, taking her time choosing which ones to wear, relishing the knowledge that Rainer was ogling her figure, not yet showing but imbued with hormones, especially her breasts.

Why was she worried about his thoughts? He would know soon enough about the baby and even though it was his, he would never be the child's father.

She zipped up her slacks and pulled on a thick, polo-neck sweater.

'You look absolutely beautiful,' he said.

For a moment she was almost tempted to tell him about the baby, just to see his reaction. Would he still find her desirable? Would he leave Sylvia and marry Lily? She reached for her duffel coat hanging on the back of the bedroom door.

Bella barked. 'Ready?' Rainer urged.

No, marriage to Rainer was not what she wanted. Standing in front of her wardrobe mirror, she took her time buttoning up her coat and adjusting her woollen pom-pom hat.

Bella barked, again.

She slipped on her mother's leather gloves and smiled at Rainer. 'Torch?' she asked.

'No need. There's a bright moon and the lighthouse beam will be circling overhead. That's enough. Come on. Bella is crossing her legs; she needs a pee.'

Lily pulled open her bedside drawer and retrieved a heavy torch. She switched it on. 'It's running out of batteries but it's better than nothing.' She strode out of her room and grabbed Bella's lead from Rainer. 'Come on girl, walkies.'

A gust wrenched the school's front door out of her gloved hand and Rainer caught it as it swung back. Icy air blasted her cheeks. 'Why don't we just let Bella run around the quadrangle?' Lily asked. 'The wind has really picked up.'

Rainer ushered Lily and Bella out and used both hands to pull the front door closed. They stood, buffeted by swirling gusts. The front circular area was lit by a few exterior lights, but the sky looked impenetrably black.

She took Rainer's arm, and they walked head on into the gale, partly shielded by the Victorian edifice. Beyond the protection of the school buildings, the onshore wind slammed into them hard, and both were bent over as they crossed the sward towards the cliff steps. Without the faint circle of light from Lily's torch, it would have been impossible to stay on the trampled path.

Rainer bent down and unclipped Bella's collar and she immediately ran off. 'Why did you do that?' Lily shouted.

'She'll be fine. She's been cooped up all day. She needs a run.

'If she goes over the cliff, you're telling Sylvia.'

'She won't go over. She's way too smart.' He reached for Lily's hand, and she let him take it. She wanted to feel his skin against hers, but it was too cold to take off her mother's glove. They walked, occasionally stumbled towards the cliff edge. The powerful beam sweeping above picked out white specks. She shivered, fearful of the North Sea's ferocity and the great rollers she knew would be pounding the cliff below.

'Come on,' Rainer said. 'Let's go down the steps to the tunnel. It will be exciting. Dramatic.'

'No. It's too dark and the steps will be slippery.' She looked about her for the dog. 'Bella!' she called, although the wind snatched the words from her mouth.

'Did you hear her bark?' Rainer asked.

Lily whipped round. 'No. Where is she?'

'I heard an echo. I think she's gone down the steps.'

Lily pushed past Rainer and hurried to the top of the cliff steps. She shone her torch, and the faint yellow beam picked out green slime. 'Bella,' she called. 'Bella.' She listened, but the constant buffeting of the *beast from the east* drowned out all sound. She breathed in and took a tentative step, determined not to slip. Rainer was right behind her as she gripped the rusted iron rail with her gloved hand. Beautiful, soft leather was about to be ruined. She made her way down the steps and reached the first turn. Out of the buffeting wind, she could now hear the flow of seawater rushing through the cave and sucking at the lower steps.

'Keep going,' Rainer said over her shoulder. She pressed on, now surrounded by wet rock and a roaring cacophony from below. She came to another turn and called for the dog.

'Don't stop,' Rainer said, breathing down her neck. Without the torch they would have been totally blind as the blackness that enveloped them was crushing. She came to the final turn and saw glowing phosphorus in swirling white water.

'Bella's not here. Go back up.' She tried to turn but Rainer gripped her shoulders from behind.

'Listen to me,' he said. 'My sister and mother are in grave danger in East Berlin. If I fail to do what is asked of me, they will disappear forever. I will never see them again.'

'We can talk about it later. My feet are getting wet.'

'Lily, your father is an important man, but he is not playing ball with the Soviets. They are going to make an example of him.'

This time she was able to turn and look up into his face, which she couldn't see. 'What do you mean, make an example of him?'

'I have to kill you.'

She felt a dread like she'd never felt before. Horror

squeezed her lungs so she couldn't speak.

'But I love you, Lily,' he continued, 'so I can't. But I also love my mother and sister. I cannot let them suffer more than they are. By escaping to the West, I have endangered them.'

Lily could feel the strength of his muscles. A strength she had lusted after, but now instilled a level of fear she had never known before.

'I have a plan,' he said, 'which you must follow to the letter. Colonel Craig will drive you to the railway station in Derby where you will take the train for London. From there you must travel to South Kensington and take the coach to Heathrow Airport. A ticket in the name of Catherine Westlake will be waiting for you at the Lufthansa desk. You will fly to Hamburg where a friend of mine will meet you. You will be looked after until I can come and collect you. It is vitally important that you speak to no one, most of all your father. Everyone must believe that you fell from the cliff and drowned. Now take off your coat and shoes. Colonel Craig has new clothes for you in a suitcase in his car.'

She took a few seconds to digest his words. 'Without a British passport in the name of Catherine Westlake I cannot travel.'

She felt Rainer release her shoulder and slip a hand in his pocket. 'I have a British passport with your photo and a new identity.'

'How is that possible?'

'It's what I do. I forge documents. I am good. Colonel Craig delivers them for me.'

'No.'

'No what?'

'No. I am not going to Germany. I am not going to

live in hiding. I am not going to make my father suffer the loss of a daughter as well as a son.'

'But he won't. In a few months, a year at the most you can tell him the truth.'

'By then he may be dead from grief. I will not hurt him that way.'

He did not respond.

'Anyway,' she said. 'It's Christmas Day, there are no trains.'

'There's a train first thing tomorrow morning. Derby is a busy city station, no one will remember you. That's important. Colonel Craig has a brown wig for you to wear until you get to Heathrow.'

'Do you trust Colonel Craig?'

'Yes, I do.'

'I don't.' She waited for him to respond. He didn't. She pressed on. 'Unless you're going to kill me,' she said, 'I'm going to find Bella and go back to Sylvia.'

She pushed past him, and he offered no resistance. The batteries in her torch had finally expired and she was forced to use the iron handrail to guide her back up the steps. At the top, the rotating beam of the lighthouse brought her a little comfort as it swept overhead. Bella rubbed against her, and she felt for her collar, clipping the lead back on. 'Home girl. Take us home.'

She stumbled over tufts of grass as she tried to keep pace with the dog, her mind a jumble of terrifying thoughts. She didn't believe that Rainer would ever kill her, but desperate people do desperate things. More than anything, she needed to call her father, and she needed to get away from the school.

Colonel Craig observed Lily hurrying with Bella across the car park. 'She's still got her coat. Clearly, Rainer lacked persuasion.'

'Let's finish it now.'

'When Eva went missing,' Colonel Craig said, looking at Gretchen in his rearview mirror, 'the finger of suspicion could easily have pointed at you or me. But it didn't, because of planning. In order for us to escape the long arm of British justice, Rainer must be full square in the frame.'

Gretchen nodded. 'Ja. But we must act before school starts again.'

'Our chance will be tomorrow. I have an idea.'

'Tell me on the way home. We'll go in my car.'

'Now we're officially engaged,' he said, 'I think it is perfectly respectable for you to stay over in my billet.'

She leaned forward and wrapped her arms around his neck. 'Why did we wait so long?'

'A war hero marrying a wealthy widow with your accent, would have attracted the attention of the Hawksmead Chronicle, and reporters can be very nosy.'

'And now? Are they not still nosy?'

'They'll be much more interested in the Soviet spy I uncovered, who killed his schoolgirl lover and then fled.'

Rainer entered the kitchen, now cleared of all signs of Christmas. Bella was dozing in her bed. He crossed to their private lounge and saw his wife asleep on the sofa. Her eyes opened.

'I think I'll make coffee,' he said. 'Would you like a cup?'

She yawned. 'Normally, I would say no at this time, but it's Christmas, so yes please.'

'If either of you went outside it would be extremely dangerous,' spoke a man's voice from the TV.

'I didn't know you liked Doctor Who,' Rainer said.

'I was waiting for Max Bygraves.' She got up from the sofa and turned off the set. He followed her back into the kitchen. 'I'm surprised Lily's not been down,' Sylvia commented as she warmed herself against the range.

Rainer was not sure what to say but decided a partial truth was preferable to a complete lie. 'She was on her way here after a nap when I invited her to clear the cobwebs with Bella and me. She's back in her room. I doubt we'll see her 'til morning.' He part-filled the electric kettle.

'What did you talk about? I trust you didn't encourage her in any way?'

'Of course not. It's over. I gave you my word.' He opened a door to a walk-in pantry, picked up a tin from a shelf, and closed the pantry door. He used the end of a teaspoon to prise open the lid and then used the spoon to transfer ground coffee beans into a pot. He poured in the boiling water, stirred the mixture, and placed a heat-resistant mat on the table.

'Smells good,' Sylvia said as she sat down. 'I was thinking about our lunch guests. What a diverse bunch we were.'

'And very surprising.'

'Yes indeed.'

Rainer placed the coffee pot on the mat and complemented it with a small jug of milk and a bowl of sugar crystals.

'I hope Lily enjoyed it,' Sylvia continued. 'Christmas is very important to young people.'

'I think she did. We all tried hard to make it a special occasion, especially you.' He rested a steel strainer on a cup and poured the coffee. 'I'll let you do the milk.' He filled a second cup and sat down at the table, reached for the sugar bowl and tipped in two large mounds of brown crystals.

'That amount of sugar will destroy your teeth,' Sylvia said.

'Pepsodent will save them.' He took a sip.

'Do you find Gretchen attractive?' she asked.

'Nein!' he spluttered. 'No! I could never.'

'Why not? She's a handsome woman. Stout in girth, I grant you, but not without allure.'

'Sylvia, I wish to make it clear as a bell, I have never seen Dr Bircher as anything other than a capable person with a stethoscope. The only image that comes to mind, is her in a white coat brandishing a syringe. And that is not one of my fantasies.'

They laughed, then both looked at Lily who stood in the doorway.

Sylvia smiled. 'Lily, come and join us for coffee. You were brave to go out and risk such a buffeting.'

Rainer stood and reached for a cup and saucer.

Lily sat down.

Sylvia poured the coffee and Rainer slid across the jug of milk. Lily used a small silver spoon to stir it in. 'I didn't realise how brave I'd have to be,' she said. 'Bella, as usual, was a great comfort.'

The black and white collie pricked up her ears but did not move.

Lily looked pointedly at Sylvia. 'Thank you for a lovely Christmas lunch.'

'I'm so pleased you enjoyed it.'

'I did.' She cast a glance at Rainer. 'I think we all did.' She sipped her coffee. 'Mmm nice. Rainer?' she asked. 'Have you told Sylvia about your plan for me?'

'What plan?' Sylvia demanded of Rainer.

'To kill me,' Lily added. 'Or to make you, the police and my father think I'd had a fatal accident.'

There was a leaden pause.

'What is going on, Rainer?' Sylvia's voice was quiet but steely.

He jerked a cigarette out from his almost empty soft pack and flicked his late father's lighter. He took a deep drag and exhaled smoke as he replied. 'The Soviets want to send a message to British diplomats working in the Eastern Bloc.'

'What message?' Sylvia asked.

'That their families are vulnerable, even in the heart of the English countryside.'

Sylvia did not immediately respond as she absorbed the magnitude of what Rainer was saying. She turned to Lily. 'I promised your father that I would keep you safe.' She looked back at Rainer. 'Nothing must happen to Lily. Do I make myself clear?'

He took another deep drag. 'My mother and sister will suffer for the rest of their lives if I don't do as ordered.'

'How did they find you?' Lily asked. 'I presume Rainer Herrnstadt is not your real name?'

Sylvia looked sharply at her husband. 'Have you been lying to me?'

'Rainer Herrnstadt is the only name I have. I left who I was, behind the wall in East Berlin.'

'And yet they found you,' Lily stated.

'Yes.' His reply was muted.

'How?' Sylvia asked.

Rainer shrugged. 'Soviet agents are everywhere.'

Lily looked at her late-mother's watch. 'May I use your phone? I want to speak to my father. I'll reverse the charges.'

'Lily,' Sylvia said, her tone, pleading. 'I promise you are safe. Rainer would never hurt you.'

'How can you be sure?' Lily asked, angrily.

'Sylvia is sure, liebling, because she knows how much I love you.'

Lily locked eyes with him. 'But not as much as your mother and sister.'

There was an ugly pause.

Sylvia reached across the table for Lily's hand. 'If you call your father tonight, he won't sleep. Try in the morning, although the lines are bound to be busy.' She turned to Rainer. 'Please unlock the phone dial.'

'Where's the key?' he demanded.

'It's under the telephone.'

CHAPTER THIRTY

Lily woke early, freezing cold. Her feet felt for her slippers. She wrapped her dressing gown tightly around her as she crossed to the window to pull back the curtains. Through frosted panes, she could see the sun's weak rays poking above the grey North Sea. The sward, usually verdant, was white with frost. She was pleased not to see snow, unlike Boxing Day in 1962 when it snowed and snowed, much to the delight of England's children. Though even they were glad to finally see the back of it the following March.

Lily contemplated having a shower but decided it was too damned bitter. The air outside was icy and still, unlike the wind of the night before. She stood by the window transfixed by the sun's slow appearance, and the beauty of the light refracted in the frosted crystals. By the edge of the cliff, a mist was rising above the deep void, its tiny particles diffusing the sun's rays. Almost like white water, the mist rolled inward across the glistening grass. She shivered. A howling wind was scary, but the silence of the thickening sea fret was almost scarier.

Was someone standing in the mist? She turned away from the window to clear her mind. Since the death of her brother her thought processes were as erratic as a pinball, ricocheting left and right, up and down. She knew her visions were pictures in her mind. There were no ghosts, no such entity as a spectral presence and yet her father had once said that first thoughts, initial instincts, invariably prove to be right. He explained that the subconscious brain does so much more than the conscious mind can comprehend; if it sends the whisper of a message, it is often worth acknowledging.

What was the message her brain was relaying to her this morning? That she should have acted sooner and that she hadn't out of fear? That was the stark truth. Her cowardice had prevented her going back to the cave and digging up what she had felt buried in the sand when Bella was trapped.

She switched on the centre light and dressed in her warmest clothes, slipping on many layers as her mother had always advised. She pulled open her bedside drawer and reached for her torch, then remembered to her dismay that it needed new batteries.

What about the tide? Last evening, when she was with Rainer at the bottom of the cliff steps, it was high tide. Fifteen hours later it should be going out. She checked her mother's watch. It was already 8.30 despite being barely light. How she hated the long, cold nights of winter. Once she had completed her A-levels, she would head south and never be cold again. And then she remembered ...her baby.

Fully dressed, she switched off the light and went back to the window. The waxing gibbous moon looked brighter than the rising sun, adding to the haunting quality of the sea fret as it gently swirled over the frozen grass. She couldn't see any figure in the mist, but the message was clear. If she wanted to know the truth, she had to go now, when no one was about.

She checked her watch again, barely able to see its face in the drab light and grabbed her duffel coat. She opened the door and stuck her head into the soulless corridor. An empty silence. She walked as fast as she dared, not wanting to convey any sense of urgency were she to bump into Rainer or Sylvia. Most of all, she feared coming across Colonel Craig who she regarded as more threatening than the evil doctor, now she knew they were to be married.

By the time she reached the sward, the mist was clearing and it was easy to follow the path of trampled and worn grass to the top of the steps. She wished she had Bella for company. In the pale, morning light, the worn steps looked dark, slippery, and forbidding. She told herself that in just a few minutes she would be back up top and on her way to a cup of tea; she just had to do this. Through the leather of her glove, she gripped the pocked and rusting metal handrail and carefully stepped down the first flight. At the turn, she looked into the black void and felt her stomach churn. She really needed her torch. At the next turn, she heard the sound of waves. Tense but determined, she continued down the slimy steps until she reached the gate. It was locked. It took considerable effort to turn the rusting key within the old mechanism, and was relieved when she heard it clunk. She put the key in her coat pocket and pulled the gate open.

She emerged from the manmade cave and was pleased to see the tide was low and going out. At least she thought it was as the rock pools were full. Anyway, she wasn't going to linger. She picked her way along the shore towards the dense blackness of the large cave, accompanied by the kee-yaaa call of herring gulls circling above. On the one hand, she hoped she was wrong about her suspicions, but on the other hand she wanted to see the German doctor's expression when faced with the truth.

Darkness within the cave was suffocating as she walked on the wet sand to where she had rescued Bella, wishing she had a spade. She knelt and took off her gloves, stuffing them in her coat pocket. Already feeling cold, and fearful of what she was about to discover, she dug with her hands into the sand.

Her fingertips felt it. It was smooth and there was no jawbone, but she could feel the eye sockets, and where the nose would have been, and the roundness of the skull. She tried to twist it free from between the rocks but was scared to break it. Perhaps it was best if the police came and dug it up themselves. Somehow, she would have to persuade them.

She stood up and brushed the sand off her wet slacks, took a few deep breaths and was about to head back to the steps when a bright torch beam blinded her, and she was forced to shield her eyes.

'What are you doing, girl?' The tone was refined, terrifying, and it echoed around the cave.

'I... I... was just out having an early walk to clear my head after yesterday's festivities and thought I saw a seal trapped between these two rocks.'

'Was it?'

'No. Just a weird shadow.'

He walked into the cave 'What were you digging for?'

'I've lost my crucifix. It was outside my sweater, and I caught it with my hand.'

'Found it?'

'No.'

Colonel Craig approached her and the feeling of being trapped and totally vulnerable was overwhelming. 'I... I think it's lost for good. It wasn't expensive.'

'Let me look. You say you dropped it by these rocks?'

'I'm not sure exactly where. I just noticed it was gone. It's not important.' She faked a smile. 'Having Jesus in one's heart is what matters, not a trinket.' She shivered. 'I'm frozen.' She pulled out her gloves and slipped them on.

Her explanation seemed to satisfy the colonel. 'I'll walk you back,' he said.

They emerged from the cave and covered their eyes from the sun, now firmly risen.

'Have you made any plans for your wedding?' Lily asked, determined to get the colonel's mind off what she may have been doing in the cave.

'Not as yet. We both want a simple affair.'

He ushered her ahead of him along the manmade tunnel.

'I didn't see a key in the gate,' he said.

'It was open when I arrived.' She would come back later and lock the gate to prevent Colonel Craig returning to the cave.

Up on the sward, they walked in silence back to the almost deserted school. With every step, she fought the desire to run.

In her room, she changed out of her wet and sandy slacks, pulled on a pair of thick, woollen tights, and wrapped around a tartan kilt. She ran her fingers through her hair, which was sticky from the salt air. In the freezing washroom, she washed her face and brushed her teeth. Checking in the mirror, the end result was not Hollywood glamour, but good enough for breakfast.

On her way to Sylvia's private kitchen, she pondered her next move. If she called the police, they would dismiss her claims as schoolgirl fantasies. The only person they may possibly listen to, was The Reverend William Longden.

Colonel Craig stopped his car by the public phone box at the end of the school's long drive. He opened the heavy door, grabbed the receiver and gave it several hard tugs. He fed four pennies into the box and listened for the dialling tone. Silence. He pressed button B and scooped the pennies out of the steel cup. For good measure, he gave the receiver another hard tug.

Confident no calls could be made he returned to his car and drove until he saw a small mound of rocks on the side of the road. He stopped and performed a three-point turn so that he was pointing in the direction of school. He located a rope he had previously secured to the bough of a sycamore tree and attached it to a steel tow loop under the rear of his car. He got back in behind the wheel, started the engine and engaged first gear. He felt the rope tense as he eased the car forward and kept going until he heard a satisfying pistol shot. He accelerated then brought the car to a gentle stop.

In the glove box he retrieved a knife with a protective leather sheath; ideal for scouts, camping, and cutting rope. He walked to the rear of the car and examined his handiwork. The branch had torn away from the tree's trunk and pulled down the telephone wires he knew led directly to the school and the village of Crowford. He took care cutting the rope free, convinced that, to the casual eye, it would look like the branch had simply come down in the wind. He coiled the rope, threw it into the boot of his car and got back in, happy with his vandalism. As he drove past the phone box, he mused that damaging the cable to the handset was probably overkill but overkill was how he had survived during the war ...and after.

'Porridge? Or would you like a fry-up?'

Lily was sitting at the kitchen table, nursing a mug of tea. 'After yesterday, I don't want to put you to any trouble.'

'You're not. It's been lovely for me to have you around.'

Lily smiled, slightly embarrassed. 'My period is late.'

Sylvia paused by the open fridge door. 'How late?'

'Very late.'

Sylvia slammed the door shut. 'I'll ask Dr Bircher to examine you.'

'Dr Bircher is never coming near me again.'

Sylvia picked up a small spoon, tipped a large mound of instant coffee granules into a mug and poured in boiled water. 'I presume it's Rainer's? Does he know?'

Lily shook her head. 'Please don't tell him.'

Sylvia splashed in some milk and took a sip. 'Well done, Lily. You've completely mucked up your future. You'll be an unmarried mother without qualifications, shunned by everyone with a shred of decency.'

Lily was shocked by her outburst but didn't blame her for being wounded, hurt. 'I am sorry. I am very sorry.'

Sylvia sighed and sat down at the end of the table. 'No, I'm the one to blame. I'm the one married to

Rainer. I should have kept him on a much tighter leash.'

Lily pondered what to say next, not appreciating how much Sylvia wanted a baby.

'I thought I knew him,' Sylvia said, 'but I realise, since your little liaison, I don't know him at all.'

'How well do you know Dr Bircher?'

Sylvia knitted her manicured brows. 'I know she's a competent, albeit expensive doctor, who's here to stay, thanks to the announcement of her marriage to Colonel Craig.'

'I think she's a Nazi War Criminal who murdered Eva Reimann.'

Sylvia sat back in her chair, looking truly shocked. 'Lily, that is pure fantasy. Conjecture.'

'I don't think so. I have enough evidence for there to be an enquiry.'

'What evidence?'

'If I tell you, it could put you in danger, but Reverend William and I plan to go to the police.'

Silence. Both women stared at each other.

'Well,' Sylvia said, 'that is quite a revelation for Boxing Day.' She looked pointedly at Lily. 'Anything else you wish to tell me?' She sipped her coffee.

'Do not trust Colonel Craig. He does not have your best interests at heart. His loyalty is only to Dr Bircher.'

Sylvia banged her mug down, splashing coffee onto the table. Lily was surprised by the reaction, unaware that Sylvia and Colonel Craig had once been lovers.

Sylvia took several deep breaths, then spoke calmly. 'I want you to pack your things and go. Get the hell out of my school. You're nothing but trouble.'

'Don't you care about what happened to Eva?' Lily

asked, truly shocked. 'Or is she just another statistic to add to the six million?' She pushed her chair back and stood.

Sylvia looked up at Lily, her eyes blazing. 'You are expelled. Pack your things, what you can carry, and leave. You're not staying here one more night.'

Lily felt her heart race as she took in the enormity of her situation. 'I cannot leave without the money my father gave you.'

'I'll write a cheque.'

'I need cash!'

'I'll see what's in my purse.'

Lily ran to her room. She stuffed her most important possessions and mementoes into a leather holdall, pulled on her woollen hat and duffle coat, and checked her mother's gloves were in her coat pocket. She felt the gate key. It was too risky to go back and lock the gate at the bottom of the cliff steps. If Colonel Craig saw her, he would know for certain she had lied. She hid the key under her mattress and rushed to Sylvia's office. She needed to call William before his Sunday service. The door was open. She strode across to the large desk and lifted the black telephone receiver. No dialling tone. She tapped the buttons at the top of the cradle. Nothing. Dead. It was clearly out of order. She ran full tilt to the bursar's office, and then the staff room – both doors were still locked. Where else was there a phone? She thought the refectory kitchen had one. She grabbed her holdall, hurried across the entrance hall and down the corridor that led out to the inner quad. She ran across the centre but the door on the far side was bolted. She would have to go the long way around.

Breathless, she arrived in the school kitchen and

hurried to the wall-mounted phone. The stained receiver felt sticky in her hand. She put it to her ear and dialled. It took two rotations before she realised, the line was completely dead.

As she slowly retraced her steps, she recapped her thoughts. Thanks to Bella getting stuck in the cave, she had found a human skull trapped in rocks. A skull that had been covered and uncovered by the North Sea twice a day for many years. She doubted it was possible for it to be confirmed as Eva's, but the police would investigate its origin and perhaps look more closely at Dr Bircher. The odds seemed overwhelming, especially as Lily had just been expelled by her headmistress, but she was not prepared to give up yet.

When she and Colonel Craig had walked together back to school he didn't talk and was probably formulating a plan. The chances were, he would return to the cave before the next high tide and dig around the rocks until he found the skull, which he would no doubt destroy. She entered the main entrance hall still carrying her bag but decided to jettison it in a broom cupboard.

No worker would fix the phone line on Boxing Day. Her only choice was to call William from the public telephone at the end of the drive and reverse the charges. By the front door, she lifted the large iron key off its hook and slotted it into the heavy lock. It turned easily and thanks to her height, she was able to pull down the top bolt and pullup the bottom. She opened the large door just enough to slip through, and made sure it didn't bang shut.

She shivered. The sun had made little impact on the bitter temperature. Hoping nobody would see her, she hurried across the turning circle to the start of the drive, her heart pounding. She hated the prospect of being encased within the grip of bony trees, with their dense shadows accompanied by an orchestra of distressed animals screaming their last. Twenty minutes, she told herself. Twenty minutes. Faster if she ran.

She hadn't got far down the drive when she heard heavy breathing behind her. She kept up her steady pace, hoping to exhaust the person following. It could only be Colonel Craig or Rainer – both smokers.

The breathing got louder. She was tempted to turn around and challenge whichever one it was, but she could then be grabbed. She increased her speed, determined to get to the phone box and dial nine nine nine before the person caught up. She would tell the call handler who it was chasing her, hoping that would stay the hand of her predator.

She ran, and ran, praying that the broken road would not trip her up. She was fit, athletic, blessed with a lean frame and long limbs, but it was a good half mile to the phone box and the panting behind her was getting closer.

A painful stitch in her side and shooting pains from her shinbone had slowed her pace when the word TELEPHONE, backlit below the Royal Tudor Crown, came into view, spurring her to run faster. Any moment she expected the panting breather to grab her, but did not expect the thick fur of an animal to press against her running legs.

Gasping with exhaustion and relief she stuttered to a halt and squatted down to cuddle Bella whose lolling tongue dripped viscous saliva. Together, they walked to the red phone box with its little panes of thick glass.

She pulled open the heavy door and let Bella in

before easing it closed and picking up the receiver. She listened for the dialling tone. Nothing. She clicked the buttons. She tried dialling the operator. Still nothing. She dialled nine nine nine. Dead.

'Okay, Bella... let's go find William.' The happy dog, barked with excitement. She pushed open the door and, feeling weary, walked along the country lane, comforted by Bella, and hoping no car would come from the school. Within a few minutes, she came across a tree branch lying in the road and broken telephone wires. For a moment she stared at the mess of wood and cable then examined where the branch had torn away from the trunk of the tree. The wood was full of sap. She looked around and saw that no other branches had broken off in the wind. This was foul play and only one person sprang to mind.

The leathery veteran of Montgomery's war in North Africa was the likely culprit and she realised, for the first time, that she was in very real danger. 'Come on Bella,' she said, and watched the dog scamper ahead. She strode out, too tired to run but keen to get as far away from the school as possible.

She reached the fork in the road and saw the sign pointing to Hawksmead and Undermere. For a moment, she thought about Malcolm and his lovely parents in their sweet cottage. The sign to the left was marked Crowford in faded letters, one and a half miles away. 'Bella, we've got to find William.' She started jogging, determined to maintain a steady pace although she knew that it would be impossible up the steep incline that led to Crowford village at the top of Beacon Hill. Despite the frosty air, Lily was soon hot and very thirsty and feeling distinctly weary. In a car, it was so easy to underestimate the pull of gravity when going up even a gentle incline. Bella kept pace with her, but even she, with her panting and lolling pink tongue, looked as though she needed a drink.

A lightning bolt shot up Lily's shin and she wilted at the sharpness of the pain. She staggered for a few paces then sank to her hands and knees as she tried to rise above the stabbing that sent her leg muscles into a spasm. As the pain subsided the sound of an approaching motorcar, coming at speed, revs racing, sent a chill down her spine. She pushed herself up onto her feet and looked back along the road. She could tell by the shape of the nose, that it was Colonel Craig's Vauxhall glinting in the winter sun.

The car whizzed past her and Bella, whose collar she was holding, and skidded to a halt. Both front doors opened, and Colonel Craig emerged followed by Dr Bircher.

'Where are you going, Lily?' he asked.

'I'm visiting Reverend William.'

'Jump in. We'll drop you off. We're going that way.'

They both came up to her. Colonel Craig gripped her arm and Dr Bircher grabbed Bella's collar. She dragged the yelping dog to the back of the car, opened the boot and almost threw her in, and slammed the lid down.

Lily could hear Bella's screaming barks. 'What are you doing?' she shouted, horrified by how cruelly the doctor had handled the collie.

'She annoys me,' Dr Bircher said. 'It's time she got too close to the edge of the cliff.'

'No!' Lily was beyond shocked. 'How could you even think of doing such a thing?'

'Or you can do as you're told,' Colonel Craig said, 'and get in the car.'

Lily realised she had no choice. 'I will on condition

you let Bella out of the boot.'

Dr Bircher looked at Colonel Craig, who nodded. She opened the boot and Bella leapt out. She ran off as though her tail was on fire.

'We must go after her.' Lily demanded. 'She could get run over.'

Colonel Craig glanced at Dr Bircher. 'You're right, Lily. Sit in the front. We'll go after her.'

Concerned about her dear friend, Lily sat in the front passenger seat. When all three were in the car, Colonel Craig started the engine and drove in the direction of Crowford. They found Bella about half a mile later, lying on the verge, exhausted. Lily jumped out of the car and, with a little difficulty, picked her up.

Dr Bircher opened a rear passenger door. 'She can lie in the back with me.' Lily placed Bella on the car's leather seat and carefully closed the door. She got in the front. 'Colonel Craig, please take me to William's. It's not far from here.'

'All right Miss Turnbull, I will do as you request.'

Relieved, she sat back in her seat, closed her eyes, and tried to relax.

Gauze laced with chloroform covered her mouth and nose. She struggled to escape Dr Bircher's grip, but the chemical was too strong, and she slipped into nothingness.

CHAPTER THIRTY-ONE

Rainer looked up from his desk at the front sight of a Luger P08. He knew the gun well. It had a 10 centimetre barrel and an effective firing range of 50 metres. There was no way the gnarled hand of the British Colonel could miss at almost point-blank range.

'A Luger, Colonel Craig. You do surprise me. I expected you to have a Webley or a Browning, not the favoured weapon of the Waffen-SS.'

'Gather whatever passport you have forged that will get you out of the country.' Colonel Craig threw a wad of used five-pound notes on Rainer's desk. 'You have five minutes.'

'Well, well, well. What has brought this on?'

'Lily is dead, and suspicion is about to fall on you.'

He was shocked. Grief for the beautiful girl would come later. He fought to control his reaction. 'Why will I be suspected?'

'She is carrying your baby.'

Rainer was positively dumbfounded. 'I don't believe you.'

'If her body is found, they will do an autopsy and discover the foetus. As her lover, and a foreigner, you will be charged with murder and hanged.'

'The Death Penalty has been suspended in England.'

'For the British, not for an East-German spy.'

Rainer felt sick. 'I am not a spy. You know full well my work has been for the British Government.'

'Has it?'

Defeated, his head slumped. 'There is no point running. Interpol will catch up with me.'

'Not in East Berlin.'

Rainer's mouth went dry. 'I... I cannot go back there.'

'Take my car and use what skills you possess to leave Britain.' He threw his ignition key on the desk. 'If you don't go within ten minutes, I will kill Sylvia and then you... in self-defence, of course. This is your Luger.'

'Who are you?'

'I am *Standartenführer* Friedrich Schellenberg.'

Rainer laughed. 'You look remarkably well for an executed man.'

'They hanged an innocent German, if there was such a thing.'

'I always thought your accent was a little too British.'

Colonel Craig looked at his watch. 'I suggest you hurry. If you have not left by the time the bell in the clocktower strikes noon, I will shoot Sylvia.'

'One last question,' Rainer asked, 'seeing as you are being so honest.'

'What?'

'Who is Dr Bircher?'

The old Nazi smiled. 'There was a Jewess here, called Eva. She recognised Gretchen as the doctor in her camp. Your girlfriend should have let sleeping dogs lie.' He checked his watch again. 'Nine minutes. My car is at the front.' He clicked his heels and was gone.

Rainer looked at the money on the table and knew he had no choice but to leave.

Colonel Craig opened the passenger door to Dr Bircher's car and climbed in beside her.

'In a few minutes, Rainer will make his escape.'

'You think so?'

'There is no other option. He knows Lily is dead and that I will kill Sylvia to protect you.'

'How do we know Lily is dead? Did you bash her with a rock?'

'The tide my dear.'

'You should have made sure.' She looked at him. 'Why didn't you? The chloroform will only keep her unconscious for a limited time.'

'If she were found with her head stove-in, who knows what secrets may be uncovered in the ensuing enquiry. Far better for it to look like the possible suicide of a desperate young woman expecting the baby of her Soviet lover. It will be easy for the police to dismiss, and they won't also consider you and me, or Sylvia as suspects.'

'One possible problem,' she said. 'The lighthouse keeper. He may have seen us carrying Lily to the steps.'

Her comment gave Colonel Craig pause. His answer was slow and deliberate. 'That is a problem. His eyes are not good enough to drive, but if Reg did see me, we'll convince him it was Rainer.'

'Rainer carrying Lily accompanied by a woman, Sylvia?'

'I take your point.' He sat back in his seat. 'It's unfortunate, Lily forced our hand to act in daylight.' He removed the Luger from his coat pocket. 'New story. Rainer must have discovered the girl was pregnant and left her in the cave to drown. He shot the lighthouse keeper as he saw him carrying Lily to the steps.'

'If he shot the only witness, why steal your car and run? It makes him look guilty.'

'Another very good point, liebling. I heard a gunshot, went to see what was happening. Rainer aimed his pistol at me, it jammed, I tried to apprehend him, but he escaped in my car.'

'Sehr gut.'

He proffered the Luger.

'The lighthouse keeper may have already called the police,' Dr Bircher said.

Colonel craig smiled. 'Unfortunately, the line is down.'

She took the gun and felt the weight in her hand. 'We were far smarter getting rid of the Jew.'

'Tie up this loose end and we're completely in the clear.' He leaned across and kissed her. 'If there's no response from the lighthouse, Reg will be in his cottage.'

'Will you wait for me here?'

'Go to the woods and dispose of the gun. I'll pick you up in the drive once I am sure Rainer has left. I'll flash the headlights in an S.O.S. sequence, so you know it's me.'

'Then what?'

'We drive to your place and report Rainer to the police.' He looked intently at her and smiled. 'Just like the old days, Gretchen.'

She opened the driver's door as the bell in the clocktower chimed the hour.

CHAPTER THIRTY-TWO

William swerved to avoid Colonel Craig's Vauxhall driven at speed and vocalised an expletive for which he apologised to the Good Lord.

Feverishly scratching the imposing front door was Sylvia's collie. He stopped the car and ran over to the dog whose fur was matted with sand and bits of seaweed. His heart sunk. Fortunately, the front door to the school was unlocked, and he hurried to Sylvia's study, the dog following. He knocked and entered.

She looked up from behind her desk. 'Back so soon, William?'

'I would like to see Lily. I promised I would take her out today after morning service.'

'All you had to do was ring, and I would have driven her over.'

'The lines are down. Nobody can call out from Crowford.'

Sylvia frowned and picked up her phone. 'You're right. That's odd.'

'Where is she?' he asked. 'Have you seen her?'

'No, I haven't, but I've not seen my dog, either. The two will be out together.'

Bella pushed past him.

'I found your dog in a distressed state outside. Look at her. She's covered in sand. Something has happened.'

Sylvia laughed. 'Fear not, Reverend, all is well. Bella often plays in the surf when out for a walk.' She got up from her desk. 'I'll see where Lily is.'

'I'm worried about her.'

She looked pointedly at William. 'I think you worry a bit too much.'

He knew she was right. His feelings for Lily went far beyond pastoral. He followed Sylvia's confident stride through the hallway, up the stairs and down, what seemed to him, never-ending corridors at a painfully slow walking pace. They reached Lily's room and Sylvia knocked. When there was no reply, she opened the door. Daylight streamed through the far window into the lifeless room. 'She's probably taking a shower,' Sylvia said. 'Are you going to follow me there too?'

'Yes,' William responded.

She sighed and marched off with William trying to jiffy her along. They reached the washroom. Sylvia pushed open the door and called out. No response. She checked all the cubicles and turned to William.

'I have a confession. I lost my rag with Lily this morning and told her to pack her bags.'

'What had she done to raise your ire?'

'Slept with my husband and fallen pregnant.'

He saw the pain of betrayal in her eyes. 'Take your car,' he said, 'and get help, or that baby will never be born. I'm going to the beach.' William wasted no time saying goodbye. He stretched his long limbs as he ran down corridors and stairs trying to find the quickest way out of the school building. With relief, he entered the car park and was surprised to see Colonel Craig smoking a cigarette. 'I think Lily may be trapped on the beach. I've asked Sylvia to drive for help, but it will be quicker if you go. The phone lines are down.'

'Rainer's taken my car.'

'Where's he going?'

'I don't know.' Colonel Craig approached William. 'He threatened me with a gun. He's not all that he says he is.'

William looked from Sylvia's Sunbeam to Dr Bircher's car. 'Does it work?'

'As far as I know.'

'Drive to Reculver and alert the coastguard.'

'Will do.'

'Please hurry.'

Lily felt terrible. Her mouth was bone dry and yet her feet were cold and wet. She sat up on her elbows and looked around the dark cave. She was alone. In the sand she could detect numerous frenzied paw prints. A wave washed over her legs.

'Bella,' she croaked through dry vocal cords. She pushed herself up and tried to remember what happened. With the crash of another wave, it all came back, and she feverishly dug around with her hands amongst the rocks. The skull was gone. Eva's last hope for justice, destroyed. Lily would still talk to the police, but she didn't expect them to believe her. She trudged towards the mouth of the cave as a great wave blotted out the weak winter sun and propelled her to the back.

High tide was coming, and she was trapped. She got to her feet and, slightly wobbly, followed the retreating water to the mouth and saw to her dismay, mighty rollers pounding the base of the cliff.

She had a choice. Enter the icy water and try to swim for the passage that led to the cliff steps or wait and drown in the cave. Either way, she was doomed. The cave had been Eva's last resting place. It would be Lily's, too. She smiled. She would see her mother and brother again. How her heart yearned to be enveloped by their love.

Colonel Craig had waited until William was out of sight, then went into his workshop. He opened a toolbox and ferreted around. Happy with his find he crouched down beside Sylvia's Sunbeam Alpine and pushed a nail into a tyre.

'Colonel Craig,' he heard call.

He stood and watched Sylvia hurrying across the car park towards him. 'Have you seen Lily?' she panted.

'The Reverend said he was going to look for her on the beach.'

'We need to alert the coastguard, in case she's in trouble.'

'That trollop has caused nothing but trouble.'

'Whatever we think of her louche behaviour, she is still a minor in my care.' She opened her car door.

'What are you doing?' he asked.

'The phone lines are down. I'm going to drive to the box at the end of the drive.'

'Not with that flat.' Colonel Craig indicated Sylvia's deflated tyre.

She slammed the door. 'Where's your car?

'Rainer took it. I don't know what's got into that boy. I heard what I thought was a gunshot and went to have a look. Rainer came running towards me waving a Luger. Fortunately, it jammed. I tried to apprehend him, but he managed to escape in my car. I'm quite shaken up. It's twenty years since I last fought a German.'

Sylvia looked puzzled. 'I don't understand.'

'I think there's a lot we don't understand about your Rainer. Was he really escaping to the West, or is he a Soviet agent?'

She reached for the colonel's cigarette and inhaled deeply. 'Lily's carrying his child.' She took another drag.

'Now it all makes sense,' Colonel Craig said. 'Rainer found out Lily was pregnant and arranged an accident. Someone saw him and he had no choice but to shoot the witness. Unfortunately for Rainer, I caught him in the act, so he ran.'

Sylvia stubbed out the cigarette with her shoe. 'Last night he talked about faking Lily's death to protect his mother and sister. Perhaps that's what he's done.'

Colonel Craig looked at her intently. 'Sylvia, Rainer tried to kill me. There's your answer.'

She shook her head. 'I know Rainer, he's not a killer. Something's happened out of his control.' She looked up at him. 'We must alert the coastguard. William could also be at risk.'

'I'll go.'

She followed Colonel Craig to Dr Bircher's car. 'I'll come with you,' she said.

'No. It's best if you wait here and hold the fort.'

'Where's Gretchen?'

'I ran her home last night. She didn't want to drive on her own.'

Sylvia gripped his arm. 'If the phone box isn't working, go straight to Reculver. Impress upon them that it's an emergency.'

He slid in the car, adjusted the bench seat position, and wound down the window. 'Sylvia, you mean a great deal to me, I hope you know that.'

William had hesitated at the top of the steps that led down to the shore. He knew being associated with a pregnant teenager may not help his mission within the Methodist Church, but his deep affection for the tragic young woman trumped all consideration for his ministry. He had gripped the pocked-iron handrail and took care going down the slippery steps. The cold metal truly bit into his palm and the cutting air almost hurt his lungs. At the entrance to the passage, he saw the gate was open and didn't know whether to be relieved or sorry. A wave rushed in, and the iciness of the water shocked him. In truth, he could not be sure whether Lily was trapped on the beach or not. If she were, and he hadn't checked, he would never forgive himself. He undid the laces on his brogues and slipped out of his jacket. Fortunately tall, he felt confident he could wade to the mouth of the short passage. He waited for a wave to recede and hurried as fast as the swirling water allowed. Before he reached the mouth, another wave surged in, and he was washed back to the open gate. Now completely soaked and hypothermic, he knew he only had minutes. He dug his fingertips between the bricks to gain purchase, determined to combat the force.

He reached the mouth of the passage and stood head and shoulders above the grey, swirling water. He looked over to the cave where Lily had described finding the skull. There was now a vast expanse of white water, flowing and ebbing to the base of the cliff, with the largest waves crashing down onto the rocks creating an admirable spray. Despite his size and strength, he knew the rollers would overpower and exhaust him. A wave gathered and a hard object hit the back of his head as he was subsumed by the forceful mass. Fearful, his feet found the bottom again and he cleared his eyes, shocked to see a lace-up shoe, too small to be a man's, spinning in the riptide. His inner voice demanded he escape the bitter cold and save himself, but his heart ordered him to put his trust, his life in the hands of the Almighty. If he failed to act, he could not in all conscience continue his mission to spread The Word.

He launched himself into the oncoming waves and used every ounce of muscle to swim away from the shore. Once he reached calmer waters he paddled until he was opposite the diminishing mouth of the large cave. If she were still alive, that was the only place she could be. Choosing his moment, he allowed the water to take him until it spat him out onto rocks partly buried in the sand, far into the depths of the cave. He staggered to his feet as the sea swirled about him.

Sylvia warmed her hands on the range in her kitchen. She had loved Rainer despite his infidelities. Was everything he told her a lie? That he was here, in England, at the behest of his Soviet masters, not escaping from them?

Colonel Craig was her rock. She would always cherish the memory of their time together in the lighthouse.

The lighthouse!

There was a dedicated phone line between the lighthouse and the coastguard. It would save valuable minutes for her to call than wait for her colonel to raise the alarm. But on such a clear afternoon, there was no requirement for the light or foghorn. Mr Sterck could be enjoying a Boxing Day walk along the coastal path.

The key she'd kept as a memento was at the bottom

of her jewellery box.

The cavernous interior was dark and menacing. He tried to call her name, but his voice stuck in his waterlogged lungs. Another wave came and the force of the surf nearly knocked him off his feet. He waded deeper into the cave and realised that at its furthest reaches, it climbed to a point almost like the cone of a winkle sea snail.

Was that Lily? He thought he saw a shape and rushed as fast as the swirling water allowed. 'Lily,' he called, this time with the force of voice he reserved for preaching. 'Lily.' He touched her inert body and despite the cacophony of noise within the cave he was sure he heard her moan. He shook her vigorously and she struggled to sit up.

'You came for me?' she exclaimed.

'Yes, my dearest.'

'They killed her.'

'We'll talk about it, later.' He did his best to get his arm around her, but she pulled away.

'Leave me.'

'Lily, you have to concentrate. Time is against us.'

'I have sinned. I am a wanton hussy bearing another man's child.'

'And we will care and nurture your baby, together.' He saw the puzzled expression on her face.

'You know?'

'Yes.'

'And you still came for me?'

'Of course. Now, please, my dear. Let us go.' He pulled her to her feet and hugged her to him. Together, they walked through the sucking and swirling water. He tried to gain purchase on the limpet shells that were almost part of the rocks, but a wave crashed in knocking them off their feet and propelling them to the rear of the cave, scraping their limbs on rocks that stood proud from the cave bed.

He dragged her back onto her feet. He knew it was now or never. He waited for the wave to recede and, hurrying as fast as the water allowed, lurched to the mouth and daylight. He grabbed hold of a rock and hung on for their dear lives, exercising every sinew as another wave crashed over them, pulling and tugging at their sodden clothes. As soon as he felt the water receding, he dragged Lily out of the mouth of the cave and looked along the base of the cliff towards the narrow passage that led to the steps and safety. Only a miracle could save them. But he was with Lily, and he had joy in his heart.

He turned to her. 'Come my sweet. We must swim.' She was limp in his arms, and he was already exhausted. The great William Longden, proud captain of rugby football, knew he was spent.

'Do not give up, William.' Her lips touched his ear. 'We swim together.'

'Yes, my darling. We swim together.' He released her from his grip, and she dived under the next incoming roller. William followed her, fighting the force of the tide. Free of her weight, he felt his strength renewed and he swam as hard and as long as his lungs would allow. When he broke the surface and rose in the swell, he saw a dark blue and white lifeboat rolling in the waves, and men in yellow oils with white peaked caps and lifejackets.

He watched as Lily was hauled out of the water as though she weighed nothing. He saw her fighting their grip and pointing in his direction. He tried to lift his hand in acknowledgement, but was swamped by a breaking wave, the great roller spinning him as though in a tumble dryer. He crashed into the base of the cliff and all strength, all courage, all resolve was gone.

Sylvia stood on the gallery circling the lighthouse lamp and saw a lifeboat slip from view below the cliffs. She had no idea whether she had wasted their time or not, but there was no doubt a terrible crime had been committed. She had let herself in and was shocked on opening the door to see the lighthouse keeper's inert body on the floor, a great pool of blood growing around him.

What had happened? Did Rainer shoot him? When her shaking hand picked up the old phone, she had feared the line would be dead.

'Coastguard,' crackled a voice, and relief flooded through her.

William was drowning. He had heard it was painless, but his chest hurt like hell. Since he was a boy, he had wanted to meet Jesus. To be in the presence of the Son of God and to bask in His glory. To feel His love, for his sins to be vanquished, and to live in a state of bliss, without sorrow.

The bow of the lifeboat swung away from the towering cliff; the helmsman ignoring Lily's pleading, her face awash with sea spray and tears, her voice barely discernible above the roar. The first of multiple waves almost submerged the voluntary crew, each tethered to the craft including Lily who mustered all her strength to beg them to turn back.

'I'm the duty sergeant at Undermere Police Station. I understand you wish to report a murder.'

'Yes, that's correct.'

'Name.'

'Reginald Sterck.'

'*Your* name, madam.'

'Sylvia Cooper. I'm the headmistress at Inniscliffe School for Girls, near Crowford.'

'And the deceased?'

'Reginald Sterck. He's the lighthouse keeper.'

'You are quite certain he is dead?'

'Yes. He's been shot.'

'By you?'

'Me? No, not by me.'

'Did you see who shot him?'

'Er no, but I have an idea who may be the guilty party.' She thought about what Lily had said at breakfast. *Do not trust Colonel Craig. He does not have your best interests at heart.*

'Where is Mr Sterck now?'

'In the lighthouse.'

'And where are you, madam?'

'In the lighthouse. The phone line from the school is out of order. I'm speaking to you via the coastguard.'

'You are aware that it is an offence to waste police time?'

Sylvia took a very deep breath before replying. 'Mr Sterck has been murdered. His body is in the lighthouse.'

'Do you believe yourself to be in immediate danger?'

'No. I believe the culprit has gone and is getting away as we peak.'

'One moment...' She could hear him talking on what she assumed was a police radio. 'I have dispatched a patrol car. Wait where you are for my officers to arrive.'

'I shall do no such thing. It's freezing in the lighthouse. Tell your men to ring the school bell at the main entrance and I shall attend. Goodbye.' She replaced the phone on its cradle and steeled herself to walk past Mr Sterck's body. So much for Christmas cheer.

Hands grabbed him, his arms were lifted, and a hard ring slipped over his head. 'Hold on,' yelled a gruff voice in his ear. 'You're in for a bumpy ride.' The rope tightened and, sandwiched between two brave men, the three were dragged through the surf. By the time they reached calmer waters, William was completely numb and was sure he had drunk half the North Sea. He was pulled and tugged and dragged over the side and into the bobbing lifeboat. His stomach heaved and he vomited. The pain in his lungs was acute and he feared he would still drown. Strong hands rolled him onto his back and turned his head to the side. A heavy weight compressed his chest and water shot out of his mouth. His rescuers repeated the process again and again until he begged them to stop.

He lay on his side and convulsions overtook him. His whole body shivered. He knew it was from a combination of shock and biting cold, but the knowledge didn't help. A blanket was wrapped around him, and it gave him a little comfort as he slipped unconscious.

CHAPTER THIRTY-THREE

Lily opened her eyes. She was lying in bed, in a hospital ward, buzzing with nurses walking purposefully, tending patients and serving white-coated doctors. She had no memory of being taken to hospital. Her last recollection was being lifted aboard the lifeboat.

William. Where was William? She threw back the sheet and blanket and was surprised to see she was wearing a nightdress. Her feet touched the cold floor and, taking it slowly, she padded over to a nurse who was sitting at a desk. 'Where am I?' she asked.

'You're in Undermere General Hospital, and you're doing very well.'

'My friend. How is he?'

'He'll be in the male ward. I'll see if I can get you some news. What's his name?'

'William. William Longden. The Reverend William Longden. He saved my life.'

'Go back to bed, and I'll come over in a few minutes.'

Lily did as she was told. As soon as she was under the covers, a bigwig approached her bed and lifted a chart that was hanging on the base. 'Lily Turnbull,' he said. 'How are you feeling, my dear?'

'I'm anxious.'

'Nothing to be anxious about. You'll soon be going home.' He replaced the chart. 'But we want to keep you in for observation for a few days owing to your inhaling chloroform. I'll talk in more detail to your parents. Now you lie back and relax. No need to worry that pretty head of yours.'

Lily did not lie back. 'I need to speak to the police,' she said. 'Urgently.'

His head pounded. He had taken aspirin, but the maximum dose wasn't helping. 'I think I should visit a doctor,' Malcolm said to his mother who was in the kitchen making a pot of tea.

'At the hospital?' she replied, concern creasing her chocolate-box beauty.

'I've telephoned the surgery but there's no reply from Dr Jeffery.'

'Not surprised, after all it is Boxing Day.'

'I thought I may as well see if Dr Bircher's home.'

'Dr Bircher? Didn't you steal Lily away from her?'

He smiled. 'I'm hoping her innate empathy will override any resentment she may harbour, and my head is really pounding.'

'I'll drive you.'

'What about dad?'

'He has a bet on some nag running in the King George the Sixth steeplechase.

'Arkle?'

'The odds are too short on Arkle, whatever that means. He's betting on Dunkirk.'

'Dunkirk? A small boat?'

His mother laughed. 'Let's hope the horse goes a bit faster.'

It was dark when Marion turned into the circular drive

in front of Dr Bircher's impressive Georgian house. 'No car,' she observed.

'There's a garage around the side. It's probably in there. Wait here.'

'I'm coming with you.'

'Mum, I'm not a child. Keep the engine running and stay warm. If she's in, I'll only be a few minutes.'

'And if she's not, I'm taking you to the hospital.'

Malcolm opened his door.

Colonel Craig heard a car door slam and switched off a table lamp. He peered through heavy bedroom drapes and looked down at the turning circle, dimly lit by a streetlamp.

'What is it?' Gretchen asked. She was lying in bed, relaxed, happy, and engaged to the man she loved.

'It's the schoolmaster.'

'Schoolmaster?'

'The one who absconded with Lily Turnbull.'

'What do you think he wants?'

'He's probably looking for her. On the other hand, he may be looking for you. He appears to have a bandage on his head. A bit hard to see.'

'I'd better get dressed.'

Colonel Craig watched his wife-to-be get out of bed and walk naked across the dark room up to him. 'Du bist ein großartiger Liebhaber,' she said, and kissed him gently on the lips.

They were interrupted by the sound of more cars arriving.

Colonel Craig turned to the window and saw the driveway entrance was blocked. 'Ford Zephyrs, I believe.'

'Was sind sie?'

'Police.' Lit by headlights, they observed uniformed

officers swarm around the schoolmaster's car and drag out a woman. Her arms were twisted behind her back, and she was marched to one of the police cars, protesting vociferously. The young schoolmaster was ordered to place his hands on his head and kneel on the ground. Metal handcuffs were clicked onto his wrists, and he was unceremoniously shoved into another police car.

'I told you to make sure the girl was dead,' Dr Bircher said, her voice full of recrimination. 'How long have we got before they realise their mistake and come looking for us?'

'An hour at most.'

CHAPTER THIRTY-FOUR

Colonel Craig had first prepared their escape in case of emergency shortly after Military Intelligence initiated contact, following years of silence, and requested that he be the conduit between the British authorities and the former Stasi agent. He always feared that Rainer was a ticking time bomb who would one day discover that Dr Gretchen Bircher was not whom she purported to be. Ironically, it wasn't the East German who lifted the lid on Gretchen's wartime past, or how they dealt with the little Jewess who recognised her, but a wretched schoolgirl. Consequently, Gretchen's Morris Oxford was now the proud owner of fake licence plates, and an Esso tiger tail flapping from the petrol cap. Hardened fugitives would not deliberately draw attention to an oil company's *put a tiger in your tank* advertising campaign.

As they drove south, that Boxing Day evening, the car's full beams lighting the dark country road, he smiled at Gretchen who was sitting as far away as possible on the bench seat. 'Cheer up. We prepared well for this. We have a choice of passports, we have cash, and we have friends in Germany who still honour the Führer's memory.'

She dabbed her nose. 'I am not prepared at all. I like my life in England. I like my home. I even like being a doctor. I am not prepared to give it all up. I don't want to leave.'

'Well, my liebling, we have no choice.' He chuckled. 'I'm surprised we lasted as long as we did.'

'She must have survived somehow. You tried to be too clever. Now they will hang me for advancing medical science in the camp.'

'Relax. You will be safely tucked up in Bavaria.'

'What will I do?'

'You will be a doctor, of course. I instructed Rainer to forge letters of recommendation, certificates, everything you could possibly need. He had no idea it was for you until it came to forging a new passport. By then, he was under my full control.' Colonel Craig took a deep drag on his cigarette and looked at the empty road ahead. He glanced at the car's clock. 'Shall we hear the news?' He turned on the radio and they listened to Big Ben clanging six times in St Stephen's Tower.

'Good evening. This is the BBC Home Service. Here is the news read by Bryan Martin.' The vowels of the presenter were perfectly rounded and his consonants, precisely clipped. 'Britain's first gas drilling platform, located in the North Sea off the coast of England, has capsized killing four men. Waves are reported to have been fifteen to twenty feet high; hazardous conditions for air-sea rescue.'

'No amount of money would get me working on a gas rig,' Colonel Craig commented.

'It could be a good place to hide,' Dr Bircher responded.

'Until it capsizes.' He took another pull on his

cigarette.

The news reader continued. 'The James Bond film, Thunderball, the fourth in the series, had its London premiere tonight. Starring Sean Connery as the fictional MI6 agent, and produced by EON Productions, the glamorous event was attended by many Hollywood film stars.'

'I'm a more realistic secret agent than James Bond.' He laughed at his boast.

'And just as lethal,' she added.

'The Home Office has issued a description of two people wanted for questioning with regard to the murder of a lighthouse keeper.' Colonel Craig and Dr Bircher listened attentively, almost holding their breath. 'The fugitives are described as a well-spoken military man in his fifties, trim moustache; and a German woman...'

'Swiss-German,' interrupted Dr Bircher.

'I don't think it matters now,' Colonel Craig responded, dryly.

'If anyone sees them,' continued the newsreader, 'members of the public are urged not to approach, as they may be armed, but to call the police by dialling nine, nine, nine.'

'Preparation is the key to our successful getaway,' Colonel Craig said. 'We look like a typical couple going on holiday. We have suitcases packed with all the right type of clothes. I do not have a moustache, nor in my passport photo, and you have a blonde wig that matches yours.'

Dr Bircher looked at him. 'You seem pretty pleased with yourself.'

He wound down his window and tossed out his cigarette butt, not realising that the glowing stub landed on the bonnet and rolled towards the windscreen of a black Wolseley 6/110 MK II Saloon, following closely behind.

Colonel Craig smiled at the woman he loved. 'You know, my darling, if I appear smug it's simply that I am confident.'

'We should have kept the gun,' she almost growled.

'It was damning evidence. If discovered, it would've hanged us both.'

She grunted. 'If we're caught, we're finished, anyway.'

Colonel Craig looked at her. 'From now on, you and I must call each other by our new given names. Let's practice our history and dates. Where did Tom and Hildebrand meet?'

Before she could answer, a blue flashing light reflected in the rearview mirror. Moments later, they heard the ominous trilling of the famous Winkworth bell located to one side of a plate that spelled: POLICE.'

CHAPTER THIRTY-FIVE
HAWKSMEAD CHRONICLE

Happy New Year to all our readers. It was back to work with a heavy head for many after the New Year celebrations of last week. Naturally, we are all wondering what 1966 holds for each of us, personally, for our families, and for our country. But, before we look ahead and make predictions most, of which, will turn out very differently to how we imagine, we feel it behoves us to summarise the shocking events that occurred at Inniscliffe School for Girls over the Christmas holiday. It is a tragic tale of deceit, death and murder that began a few years after the war.

Eva Reimann was born in 1939 to a Jewish family in Hungary, now under Soviet occupation. In 1944, she and her mother were transported to Ravensbrück Concentration Camp built by the Nazi regime to house women and children for experimentation. Simply typing those words fills us with a profound and renewed sense of deep shock.

Ravensbrück is a village north of Berlin. It is estimated that over one hundred and thirty-two thousand women passed through the camp during the war years, 20,000 of whom were Jewish. The rest were political prisoners from many countries, including Russia; some were Romany gypsies. It is too abhorrent to describe in depth the horrendous experiments conducted by German doctors on the women prisoners, including children. Suffice it to say, over fifty thousand women and children perished in the camp during the war years, mostly from starvation, but many dying from injuries inflicted by sadistic women guards and heartless doctors. Over two thousand were murdered in gas chambers.

There were a high number of children in the camp whose mothers were either Jewish or Romany. Most children died of malnutrition, others from cruel experiments, but a few survived. One survivor was Eva Reimann, sadly an orphan aged six. We do not know how she found her way to England, but we believe she was sponsored by a Jewish charity and lived with a family in Leeds. Aged thirteen, she was granted a partial scholarship at Inniscliffe School for Girls where she excelled academically. The one fly in the ointment was the arrival of Gretchen Müller, a Swiss-German doctor, who married local solicitor, Edmund Bircher, and who Eva Reimann recognised as Herta Oberheuser, a doctor who worked at the Ravensbrück camp and is a wanted war criminal.

Shortly before the arrival of the German doctor, Colonel Edward Craig took up a post at the school as maintenance engineer and gardener. In the last few days, we have learned that the genuine British war hero, Colonel Craig, died in a private clinic from injuries sustained in the war and that Friedrich Schellenberg, a former officer in the notorious SS, who had been working for the British authorities in West Berlin, assumed the mantle of Colonel Craig's name and pension, and passed himself off as the perfect Englishman. We understand that Friedrich Schellenberg and Herta Oberheuser were friends if not lovers during the war and thanks to Schellenberg, she managed to avoid capture by the Red Army when it liberated Ravensbrück in April 1945.

For over ten years it has been assumed by the authorities that Eva Reimann had run away from school, but new information has been revealed that the young Jewish girl, who suffered so much at the hands of Nazi monsters, was served up to the very same monsters, in a place considered safe, and was killed by them in 1954.

The heinous crime was uncovered by a schoolgirl attending Inniscliffe who also fell victim to the murderous hands of the two Germans, but was heroically saved by the school chaplain, The Reverend William Longden.

In order to effect their escape, the Nazi fugitives murdered lighthouse keeper, Reginald R. Sterck, but were apprehended en route to Harwich where they intended to board a ferry for Holland.

'Lily.'

She lowered the newspaper and recoiled. 'What do you want?'

'I came to say, auf wiedersehen.'

She looked up from an armchair in a side ward of two beds at the man she thought had once loved her. 'I didn't expect to see you again.'

'Colonel Craig told me you were dead, and he would kill Sylvia, too, if I didn't run. When I heard the news that Schellenberg and Oberheuser had been apprehended, I handed myself over to the police and told them what I knew.'

'So, it's back to Inniscliffe for you?'

He shook his head. 'No, I am returning to Germany.'

'Germany?'

'West Berlin. I have a job with the Bundesnachrichtendienst. It's the West German

Federal Intelligence Service.'

'And the Soviets? Am I still under threat?'

'Your brother's death drew the KGB's attention to the remaining child of a top diplomat. They saw your termination as an opportunity to put pressure on the British Government, and in turn the Americans. For you to be safe, your father must leave Moscow and resign from the Foreign Office.'

'What will happen to your mother and sister?'

'One day, I will get them out.'

'I wish you luck.'

He looked down at her and she felt herself drawn to his deep blue eyes. 'I will always love you,' he said.

'Sylvia deserves your love, not me.' She looked across at a massive bouquet of flowers.

'I owe her much, which is why I am leaving.'

There was an uncomfortable pause.

'Almost a private room,' he said, looking at the two beds, one still waiting for a patient.

She pushed herself to her feet and tightened her dressing gown cord. He reached for her hand, but she moved it too quickly.

'Lily. Whatever you do in this life, marry for love. Not out of obligation, expediency, or misguided gratitude.'

She stared out of the hospital window at the car park below. 'I am not a good prospect for a long marriage.'

'I don't understand.'

She turned and smiled. A wry smile. 'Dr Bircher. She killed Eva, and countless others before. I am the latest notch on her stethoscope.'

'What are you saying?'

'I'm dying. Slowly, not yet, but I will not make old

bones.'

'You were knocked out by chloroform. Not strychnine.'

'They've done tests, and it appears I breathed in so much chloroform it's affected my liver and kidneys.' She shrugged. 'Herta Oberheuser can claim another victim, but I am a lot luckier than Eva.'

'Does the Reverend know about your condition?'

She shook her head. 'Please don't tell him. None of us knows how long we have. Worrying is no way to live.'

'I mean your pregnancy.'

Their eyes locked. 'I lost the baby.'

CHAPTER THIRTY-SIX

It was barely light that February morning in Berlin. The freezing fog made it difficult for Colonel Craig, as he still thought of himself, to read the sign warning that a few steps further east and they would be leaving West Berlin for the Soviet Union. His hands were particularly cold, but as they were cuffed behind his back, he could not rub them together. He and Gretchen had been separated since they were apprehended, and he was desperate to give her a hug. He still thought of her as his fiancée and as Gretchen, rather than Herta.

He was surprised by how quickly the police had handed them over to the British Secret Service. He had tried to bargain for a pardon, pleading that his work for the Allies in the immediate post war years and as Rainer's controller forging documents for the British authorities, proved that he was a model citizen. The killing of the lighthouse keeper was not his doing, and he refused to admit that his treatment of the schoolgirl was attempted murder. It hadn't worked. He was to be traded for certain prisoners held by the Soviets. His hope was that his experience working for British Intelligence would be deemed useful by the KGB.

Gretchen was wanted by the Soviets for a different reason – punishment. Her crimes working as a doctor in Ravensbrück women's concentration camp, where thousands of Russian women had suffered torture and death, would not be forgiven and she faced the noose. There would be a show trial, but the verdict was not in doubt. He wanted to wrap his arms around her, to comfort her, but even talking was verboten; and escape, with or without handcuffs, was impossible. Each side of the white-painted, wooden guard house, where he and Gretchen waited, were two armoured vehicles and numerous, heavily-armed American soldiers. There were also four British handlers who he assumed would also be armed. Ahead, there were concrete barriers forcing vehicles to slow to walking pace in order to weave around.

The phone in the guard hut rang and he saw rather than heard the soldier answer. He hung up and nodded to the chief handler who gripped Colonel Craig's arm.

'Friedrich, time to go.'

He glanced across at Gretchen and saw tears rolling down her gaunt cheeks. They walked towards the barriers, facing a colourless city. At one point Gretchen wailed and sunk to her knees. Hands lifted her back onto her feet as she sobbed, begging the men not to trade her. He knew it was a forlorn plea. Of course, crying hadn't helped any of her victims in the women's camp.

They arrived at no man's land, and he looked through the mist and sudden drizzle towards a small group. Someone behind him signalled, and it was acknowledged. A key was inserted into the lock of his handcuffs, and he relished being able to rub his hands. As soon as Gretchen was free, she hugged his arm.

'Go,' a man behind ordered.

Colonel Craig turned to Gretchen. 'Komm, mein Liebling, lass uns eine gute Show abziehen.' *Come on, my darling, let's put on a good show.*

She sniffed as she lifted her head. They walked forward and saw six people, a mix of men and women, walking towards them. After about thirty yards, they met, paused and carried on. He could hear Gretchen weeping the closer they got to the Stasi officers who aimed their weapons at them, but Colonel Craig's mind was distracted. Amongst the small group starting a new life in the West, he recognised Rainer's mother and sister. He smiled. He had underestimated the young German.

There was no time to say goodbye. Gretchen was torn from his arm and dragged away. He looked at the officer in front of him. 'Guten Morgen. Bring mich zur Stasi-Zentrale.'

The Methodist Chapel in Crowford was full, not solely with Lily's school friends; her mother's sister, Jessica; and the groom's family, jammed together on aged wooden pews, but with many others who had heard the tragic story of Eva, uncovered by a courageous schoolgirl who was about to marry her heroic fiancé. Eager onlookers from neighbouring villages lined the chapel path from the lychgate to the tall oak doors, with many spilling into the enclosed graveyard.

The weather had been arctic during the first half of January, when Reverend William Longden had officiated at the funeral of Lily's twin brother, but a sudden change in pressure had drawn in warmer temperatures from the southwest. He stood at the front of the church by the altar table with its large brass cross and equally large brass candlesticks. Rising above all, were the church organ's impressive alloy pipes. His attire comprised, patent-leather shoes, striped-grey trousers, grey waistcoat, white shirt, winged collar with a grey-striped cravat, complemented by a black coat and tails.

Standing beside him, similarly attired, was his Best Man Malcolm, supported by a black beech walking stick with an ornate silver cap, the scar on his head, vivid, despite his best efforts with a comb. Each wore a calla lily boutonniere pinned to their lapels. Placed on the front wooden pew were two black-silk top hats, each draped with a pair of grey, calf-skin gloves.

The organist gently filled the church with Claire de Lune for Organ by Claude Debussy, a beautiful, soft, romantic melody.

'Thank you for being the most wonderful support, Malcolm. I know you love Lily, as much as I do. You are a true friend to us both.'

They shook hands.

'I am honoured to serve as your Best Man and am immensely grateful to you for helping me get through my black dog days.'

The organ music changed to Pachelbel Canon in D Major; an exquisite, tear-inducing melody that accompanied the most beautiful woman William had ever seen, escorted by her father, John, a man who had suffered the loss of his wife and son, but looked so proud as he walked his daughter down the church's side aisle. She was wearing her late-mother's bridal dress of ivory silk with a lace appliqué pleated bodice and a floor-length skirt with barely a train. Her youthful face could be clearly seen through a tulle lace veil, secured by a Victorian crystal tiara. On her feet, were ivory silk shoes, and in her hands was a white bouquet: a mix of sweet William, lily of the valley, hyacinth, and myrtle.

In front of The Reverend Manson, from the Methodist Chapel in Hawksmead, John gave his only daughter, his only child, to the arm of a hero he would honour for the rest of his life.

As the organ music gently faded, Lily turned and handed her bouquet to Sylvia, who was dressed in a simple three-quarter length sheath dress in faded powder pink with a short jacket over a brocade top.

Reverend Manson opened his arms in welcome. 'Dearly Beloved, we are gathered together here in the sight of God, and in the presence of these witnesses, to join together William and Lily in holy matrimony.'

Lily looked up into the face of the man who had saved her life and whose strength and love had enriched her soul. More than anything, he gave her hope.

CHAPTER THIRTY-SEVEN

HAWKSMEAD CHRONICLE

STOP PRESS

It is with joy in our hearts we have learned that The Reverend William Longden and his wife, Lily, are the proud parents of a baby girl. By our calculations she is almost two months premature but was still a healthy seven pounds and eight ounces at birth. We understand from their good friend, Malcolm Cadwallader, that William and Lily have recently moved to the Methodist Mission in Liberia, on the West Coast of Africa, where William will personally Christen his daughter, Eva. She is named after the Jewish girl whose remains were discovered in a cave by Mrs Longden but, sadly, could not be recovered. We pray that Baby Eva will enjoy a long and happy life. She could not have kinder or braver parents.

Sylvia put down the newspaper and wondered if Lily would ever tell Eva that Rainer was her biological father. She stood and looked out of her sitting room window. It was the start of the long summer holidays and there was much to do. Selling the school was now a priority as the murder of the lighthouse keeper, and the young Jewish girl, had caused a mass exodus of pupils and the school was no longer viable. In some respects, Sylvia was slightly disappointed to be losing her role as headmistress, but she had relished telling Old Ma Barry that her days terrorising young girls were over. According to the Estate Agency, there was interest in turning the school into a spa hotel or razing it to the ground and building a seaside resort, albeit one with no beach at high tide. Sylvia laughed at that idea. Clearly, potential developers had not experienced a winter standing at the cliff edge with a cutting wind direct from Siberia.

But it was July, and she was alone. Her new friend, Malcolm, was calling in later for tea. She thought he may have been interested in her romantically, but all he'd offered was the hand of friendship, for which she was content.

She picked up Bella's lead and her true best friend pricked her ears. 'Come on girl. The tide is out.' Bella barked excitedly.

She didn't bother to lock the main door to the school - thieves were welcome to relieve her of school desks and chairs. But, sleeping alone in the giant-sized building was a little unnerving, even with her beautiful collie taking Rainer's side of the bed.

She let Bella off the lead and watched her loyal friend bound across the sward to the now notorious cliff steps. Looking down the first flight always increased Sylvia's heart rate. Even in summer the steps were slippery, so she hung onto the pitted handrail.

The gate at the bottom was unlocked. She had recovered the key from under Lily's mattress and kept it in her pocket when walking on the beach, fearful of being on the wrong side of the locked gate at high tide. Bella scampered ahead along the tunnel onto the vast expanse of beach. At this time of the moon's cycle the tide was very low but would also be very high, when it came in.

On that beautiful July day, the sea looked benign, calm, friendly, but she knew how deceitful it was and that within hours waves would be pounding the shore.

Bella ran ahead, enjoying all the wonderful smells and chasing unwary birds. She loved her dog. Yes, she was easy on the eye and soft to stroke, but her keen intelligence was the real attraction.

For a moment she stood, awed by the sheer scale of the cliffs, the summer home to puffins and gannets, and their fledglings who survived marauding herring gulls. Out at sea was a fishing vessel, puffing smoke as it trawled for cod.

Bella barked.

It wasn't a fun, excited bark but one of alarm. Her dog was standing by the mouth of the large cave looking in, limbs tensed for flight.

She barked again. And again. Reversing up. Clearly seeing something that scared her.

Sylvia broke into a half-run on the wet sand and comforted Bella. 'All right, girl. What is it?'

Bella barked again and scampered across the beach, disappearing into the narrow passage. Sylvia was about to follow, but decided she had to see what had disturbed her dog. She stepped into the cave's interior, such a contrast to the bright light of the summer's day.

'Hello,' she said, a little nervously, her voice echoing as her eyes adjusted to the wet interior. 'Hello,' she said again, and took a step forward onto the compacted sand. Could she see an animal lurking in the dark recesses, or a person? There were no footprints, which gave her the courage to go further. The lightless void was oppressive, and the smell of seaweed that hung limply to the roof and sides, overwhelming. At the cave's furthest extremity, was the winkle-style spiral and nothing apart from limpet shells. She shivered, keen to feel the sun on her face again. Whatever had spooked Bella was gone. She turned and looked towards the bright light of the cave's mouth.

Silhouetted, was a teenage schoolgirl.

Thank you so much for reading my novel. I hope you enjoyed it. If you did and have a moment, please leave a review or a simple star rating on Amazon. It helps others discover my book and it encourages me to continue writing! Romola xx

ABOUT THE AUTHOR

Romola Farr first trod the boards on the West End stage aged sixteen and continued to work for the next eighteen years in theatre, TV and film - and as a photographic model. A trip to Hollywood led to the sale of her first screenplay and a successful change of direction as a screenwriter and playwright. Bridge To Eternity was her debut novel, and Breaking through the Shadows and Where the Water Flows are standalone sequels. Eva is Waiting is a standalone prequel.

Romola Farr is a nom de plume.

romolafarr@gmail.com

@RomolaFarr

BOOKS BY THIS AUTHOR

Bridge to Eternity

'Lose yourself in this wonderful story.' SUSIE FOSTER

'An outstanding debut novel and a hugely satisfying read.' ALLIE REYNOLDS

'A stunning debut by an author I will actively seek out in the future.' AUDREY DAVIS

'What separates this book from others are the subtle yet powerful emotions which trip from the first page through to the last. This novel left its mark on me long after I finished it.' LEE-ANNE TOP 1000 AMAZON REVIEWER

'Absolutely loved this debut novel. Fantastic characterisations, intriguing and clever plot which took twists and turns. I genuinely could not put it down.' Elizabeth Estaugh, Amazon.co.uk

'The different strands of the story in this book were beautifully woven together. I found it really exciting and couldn't wait to find out what happened.' Sarah McAlister, Amazon.co.uk

'I absolutely loved Bridge to Eternity so much, I read it within a day. I look forward to reading more from Farr as this was such a wonderful debut.' Jojo Welsh girl,

Amazon.co.uk

'The icy bleakness of the landscape is expertly reflected in the lives of many of the central characters. Deeply buried emotions are intermingled amongst present and past events. It is both atmospheric and unnerving in equal measure as characters struggle with their own personal demons. This is a really intriguing and powerful debut novel.' S J Mantle

'A brilliant read ...a real page-turner with finely-drawn characters that the reader cares for.' Sue from Wimbledon, Amazon.co.uk

'A gripping novel ...a thrilling read. I read it in two sittings.' KJA, Amazon.co.uk

Breaking Through the Shadows

'The author writes with skill and humour, drawing the reader into a world laced with darkness and light.' AUDREY DAVIS

'Absolutely gripping, I could not put this book down!' ELIZABETH ESTAUGH

'An absolute gem of a story.' SUSIE FOSTER

WHAT AN EXCITING READ!
'It's a page-turner for sure. The book follows Tina's story and she's a great character; really ballsy in spite of everything that life has thrown at her. The many strands of the story are skillfully interlocked and come to a very satisfying conclusion.' Sarah McAlister, Amazon.co.uk

ANOTHER EXCELLENT READ
'It was captivating from the start, I was hooked. There were so many twists and turns throughout that I had to force myself to put it down to get on with some work. It truly was an excellent read.' Jojo Welsh girl, Amazon.co.uk

A GRIPPING TALE

'Breaking Through The Shadows is a gripping stand-alone exciting story. A real page-turner, with well-defined characters. Televisual in nature, full of movement and pace. It kept me guessing right up to the thrilling denouement. More please Ms Farr!' Sue from Wimbledon, Amazon.co.uk

STUNNING SEQUEL to 'Bridge to Eternity'
'Absolutely loved this sequel! The dramatic events encountered by the characters, including Tina, Audrey and Malcolm, took unexpected twists and turns. Absolutely gripping, could not put this book down!' Elizabeth Estaugh, Amazon.co.uk

ANOTHER MUST-HAVE NOVEL from Romola Farr
'Superb thriller romance which hooked me right from the start! I loved Romola Farr's first novel, and the author has absolutely nailed it again with another page turner that I simply couldn't put down. The descriptions of people and places completely immerse one in the plot, and the roller coaster ride of suspense and romance, is such that the reader is captivated right to the final page.' H. Hopkins, Amazon.co.uk

Where the Water Flows

A STUNNING SMALL TOWN MUST READ
'A perfect, stunning, page turning beach or fireplace read with a great gang of characters that will sweep you away...' BOOKWORM86

BEAUTIFULLY WRITTEN
'It made me feel lots of different emotions.' EMMA FITZGERALD

ANOTHER STUNNING BOOK BY ROMOLA FARR
'This is a beautifully written story that is a rollercoaster of emotions. I was hooked from the start.' JOJO WELSH GIRL

COMPELLING
'Romola Farr is a talented writer, who takes her words

and makes them into something quite beautiful.' SARAH KINGSNORTH

'What an absolute stunner from the extremely talented Romola Farr.' KIRSTY WHITLOCK Book Blogger

'Unquestionably, one of those books that once you're a few chapters in you really don't want to put it down.' NIKI PRESTON Book Blogger

'I loved the writing style. The book is beautifully written and I look forward to reading the other books in the series.' VICKI ATKINS Book Blogger

'The story gives the reader a beautiful sense of warmth and hope.' LAURA (TheBookishHermit)

'By the time I had read a few chapters, it had drawn me to the point that I didn't want to put this book down for anything!' SHARON RIMMELZWAAN Book Blogger

'This is so well written ...the narrative pulled me in deeply.' LAURA MARIE PRINCE Book Blogger

'It's well done, with well-developed characters. I wound up caring about each and every one of them.' ELIZABETH CAREY Book Blogger

EVA IS WAITING

Printed in Great Britain
by Amazon